Cassandra Rising

Cassandra Rising

Edited by
ALICE LAURANCE

DOUBLEDAY & COMPANY, INC.
GARDEN CITY, NEW YORK 1978

Except for historic figures
and where otherwise indicated,
all of the characters in this book
are fictitious, and any resemblance
to actual persons, living or dead,
is purely coincidental.

Library of Congress Cataloging in Publication Data
Main entry under title:

Cassandra rising.

1. Science fiction, American—Women authors.
I. Laurance, Alice.
PZ1.C27 [PS647.W6]   813'.0876
ISBN: 0-385-12857-6
Library of Congress Catalog Card Number 77-92218

In Memoriam

Joan Weber Janusz
1946–1973
Elizabeth Haywood Woody
1939–1964

Contents

Contents

Preface
by ALICE LAURANCE

It seems to be traditional for editors of science fiction anthologies to offer their own definitions of science fiction, which is why there are as many definitions as there are anthologies. (Purists may note that not all anthologies contain a definition, but it must be kept in mind that there are unethical individuals who offer definitions without editing anthologies, which evens things up.)

When I teach science fiction, I tell my students it is fiction which takes place elsewhere, elsewhen, or elsehow. Elsewhere: in some other part or dimension of the universe. Elsewhen: in the future, the distant past, or in some warp of time. Elsehow: no matter how normal and familiar the setting and characters may seem, something isn't quite in "synch" with reality as we live it.

The joy of science fiction is that it offers scope. The writer doing a mystery or mainstream story creates people and a situation; only the science fiction writer can go all the way, inventing the world where the characters (not necessarily "people" in the usual meaning of the word) play out the situation. Geography, racial characteristics, history, customs, language, government, law—these come not from "what is" but from the part of the writer's mind which deals with "what if."

Science fiction gives a writer (and by extension a reader) scope in another sense; it is the only genre genuinely and necessarily concerned with ideas. The science fiction reader is a daring soul who, far from fearing the unknown, actively seeks it. Science fiction is wide open to intellectual speculation.

At the 1977 Nebula (S.F.W.A.) Banquet, Isaac Asimov noted that while science fiction writers can and often do successfully venture outside the genre, writers from other fields rarely succeed in bringing off an isolated science fiction story. Nobody "dashes off" a really good piece of science fiction. The very scope of the field demands discipline and hard work.

The writer setting his story in the world that is can describe his characters and their situation in a relatively few words; the reader can be relied on to bring certain knowledge to the reading. The science fiction writer starts with no such advantage; the reader cannot possibly possess knowledge of that which heretofore has existed only in the writer's imagination. The writer has to create the world—but he or she also has to communicate it: clearly, naturally, and without interfering with the narrative. It isn't easy.

Nor is it easy to create those worlds. Even God needed six days of hard work to make just one. The writer faces the same challenge God did: the whole thing has to be internally consistent to work. There are ramifications to the smallest details. If characters are given exceptionally keen hearing, for example, there has to be a reason why this trait developed. Perhaps some predator in the past emitted a warning sound which the race had to "learn" to hear to survive. But then the writer has to account for the predator. Moreover, that keen hearing (which the writer included only to solve some small plot problem—how did Jumplug know of the invasion? Ah! His keen ears allowed him to overhear a whispered conversation) is probably going to affect other things in the culture being invented such as art forms (music); the writer has to account for that, too.

So: science fiction is the most challenging and, depending on your success, the most frustrating or satisfying literary form.

For a number of years, it did not seem women were accepting the challenge of science fiction. Andre Norton, in her Foreword, will point out that "seem" is the operative word in that sentence. Today, women are more and more evident in the ranks of science fiction writers—in quantity and, particularly, in quality.

Cassandra is on the ascent. In her time, the original Cassandra was not believed when she told the truth. The twenty Cassandras you are about to read are also telling truths; I hope you will believe them.

Foreword

by ANDRE NORTON
THE GIRL AND THE B.E.M.

One needs only to look at the crudely bright jackets of some of the early pulp magazines (now rare collectors' items, by the way) to gauge the standing of feminine characters in the stories then appearing in practically the only market open to writers of science fiction and fantasy. More often than not an extremely lightly clad girl was either struggling with, or fleeing from, what was generally known in the trade as a B.E.M. (a bug-eyed monster). Though what salacious interest a crab-handed, eight-legged worm-spider (or something of like nature) might have in a human female was never explained.

The role of such a heroine was well defined. She existed to be rescued, to sustain the ego of the hero, to provide a decorative touch which really hardly affected the progress of the plot.

At the same time, the woman writer in the field lurked in disguise. She either assumed a pen name which could be considered masculine, or used initials, to conceal what editors maintained was the off-putting fact she was rashly invading what was considered to be a strictly masculine field of literature.

The proper protagonist was always, of course, male. Only C. L. Moore in those early days dared defy custom when she wrote her famous Jirel of Jory tales—fortunately recently again made available for the enjoyment of a new generation of readers. But she balanced these with the adventures of that superfighter Northwest Smith.

Leigh Brackett's haunting and beautifully visualized adventures on other worlds followed the approved pattern. The creations of Eric John Stark, as well as her accounts of the wonders of Mars and Venus, are just as readable today as when they were first conceived, and certainly stand equal to the present much-acclaimed characters and action created by Robert E. Howard or other "giants" of the period.

E. B. Cole, in the series of stories centering around the Philosophical Corps, again followed the market's requirements of that time. But her ingenious intrigues were very well handled.

The presentation of a believable and important female character by a masculine writer of that same day must, however, require extensive research to find. Robert Heinlein, in the novelette "Magic, Inc.," gives us Mrs. Jennings, a notable example of a practical witch. A. A. Merritt's Snake Mother in *The Face in the Abyss* is a totally enchanting but very feminine alien.

It was left to Poul Anderson to develop the first equal partnership (and eventual marriage) in the three novelettes now appearing as *Operation Chaos*. His werewolf hero and witch heroine are so well matched that neither overshadows the other. They mesh instead into an important single force when there is need.

In *They'd Rather Be Right* by Mark Clifton and Frank Riley an unforgettable character, Mabel the skid-row drop-out, almost walks away with the book because of her courage and determination.

But when James Schmitz wrote *The Witches of Karres* and, later, the Telzey stories, a great step forward was taken for heroines. For he created girls and women who were independent of men, with powers and strengths all their own—who dared to challenge hero and villain alike.

Then came a new age of women writers who could and did, since the atmosphere of the times had changed, center on notable female protagonists. Ann McCaffrey produced *Restoree, The Ship Who Sang,* and *Dragonquest,* all landmarks for having heroines who not only fought for and rescued themselves, but gave the heroes more than just encouragement in times of danger.

Zenna Henderson's fine stories of the *People* alternated between hero and heroine naturally and realistically. While Ursula K. Le Guin's famous work *The Left Hand of Darkness* is almost wholly masculine in treatment, her priestess in *The Tombs of Atuan* stands by herself courageously.

Madeleine L'Engle's *A Wrinkle in Time,* also a prize winner, shows the reader an unattractive heroine, prickly, unhappy, uncertain, but possessing a stubborn will which carries her to victory.

The Shattered Chain, Marian Bradley's latest novel, presents a detailed picture of feminine revolt in a masculine-dominated society, written with deep empathy.

Patricia McKillip has gone even farther into the field of subtle relationships between the sexes, using a new concept—that rape may exist on other planes than the physical and the trauma of such a violation can be even greater in an aftermath of wrath and despair.

The Forgotten Beasts of Eld will not be forgotten in a hurry by any careful reader.

Tanith Lee's women, with their cruelty and lack of empathy, reflect well the degenerate alien civilizations of which they are a part. The heroine of *The Birthgrave* remains a startling and compelling portrait of an alien we cannot begin to judge by our standards at all.

On the other hand, C. J. Cherryh also presents an alien woman driven by the lash of duty—and wholly through the eyes of a very well-realized hero. But here the reader can identify with both, even when they stand at cross-purposes and there seems to be no way of resolving their difficulties. Ms. Cherryh (and many more women writers) can envision well-rounded male as well as female characters, to leave the reader well satisfied.

In my own case I began writing when the masculine name, the hero alone, was in primary demand. When I first worked on a heroine-oriented book (*Ordeal in Otherwhere*), the publisher was very dubious of success, saying my approach could well limit sales. But this gloomy prophecy did not prove true—after years of steady selling, the book is still in print.

Now I feel entirely free to present any plot from the point of view which seems to me in accord with the situation—either through a hero or heroine. Sometimes I alternate between them in a single book, giving different points of view of the same action.

One thing is true: I have become aware during the past ten years that my fan mail is changing in character. More and more of the letters I receive are written by girls and women. With science fiction classes now common in both high schools and colleges, the number of readers is increasing yearly—with, apparently, women readers well to the fore.

It is my hope that future writers will consider the point of "equal billing" for both hero and heroine. There is no reason why the separate abilities of a man and a woman, though differing somewhat in nature, cannot be fitted together, each to supply what the other may lack—to form a much stronger whole. This is a purpose I have been trying to follow for some time in my own work.

The girl with the B.E.M. is past history. Now let us have the girl who can take her own chances and stand shoulder to shoulder with any hero.

Cassandra Rising

Introduction to SQ

Ursula K. Le Guin has twice won both the Nebula and Hugo awards: in 1969 for *The Left Hand of Darkness* and in 1975 for *The Dispossessed;* her other awards are too numerous to list.

While one doesn't automatically associate humor with Ms. Le Guin—one tends instead to think of the strength of steel paradoxically combined with the delicacy of poetry—she displayed a delightful sense of humor in the introductions to her stories in *The Wind's Twelve Quarters.* In "SQ" she again reveals this side of her talent, but the story is far more than an amusing tale; it is a devastating portrait of the political mind, fanatic in its quest for power.

SQ

by URSULA K. LE GUIN

I think what Dr. Speakie has done is wonderful. He is a wonderful man. I believe that. I believe that people need beliefs. If I didn't have my belief I really don't know what would happen.

And if Dr. Speakie hadn't truly believed in his work he couldn't possibly have done what he did. Where would he have found the courage? What he did proves his genuine sincerity.

There was a time when a lot of people tried to cast doubts on him. They said he was seeking power. That was never true. From the very beginning all he wanted was to help people and make a better world. The people who called him a power-seeker and a dictator were just the same ones who used to say that Hitler was insane and Nixon was insane and all the world leaders were insane and the arms race was insane and our misuse of natural resources was insane and the whole world civilization was insane and suicidal. They were always saying that. And they said it about Dr. Speakie. But he stopped all that insanity, didn't he? So he was right all along, and he was right to believe in his beliefs.

I came to work for him when he was named the Chief of the Psychometric Bureau. I used to work at the UN, and when the World Government took over the New York UN Building they transferred me up to the thirty-fifth floor to be the head secretary in Dr. Speakie's office. I knew already that it was a position of great responsibility, and I was quite excited the whole week before my new job began. I was so curious to meet Dr. Speakie, because of course he was already famous. I was there right at the dot of nine on Monday morning, and when he came in it was so wonderful. He looked so kind. You could tell that the weight of his responsibilities was always on his mind, but he looked so healthy and positive, and there was a bounce in his step—I used to think it was as if he had rubber balls in the toes of his shoes. He smiled and shook my hand and said in such a friendly, confident voice, "And you must be Mrs. Smith! I've heard wonderful things about you. We're going to have a wonderful team here, Mrs. Smith!"

Later on he called me by my first name, of course.

That first year we were mostly busy with information. The World Government Presidium and all the Member States had to be fully informed about the nature and purpose of the SQ Test, before the actual implementation of its application could be eventualized. That was good for me too, because in preparing all that information I learned all about it myself. Often, taking dictation, I learned about it from Dr. Speakie's very lips. By May I was enough of an "expert" that I was able to prepare the "Basic SQ Information" pamphlet for publication just from Dr. Speakie's notes. It was such fascinating work. As soon as I began to understand the SQ Test Plan I began to believe in it. That was true of everybody in the office, and in the Bureau. Dr. Speakie's sincerity and scientific enthusiasm were infectious. Right from the beginning we had to take the Test every quarter, of course, and some of the secretaries used to be nervous before they took it, but I never was. It was so obvious that the Test was *right*. If you scored under 50 it was nice to know that you were sane, but even if you scored over 50 that was fine too, because then you could be *helped*. And anyway it is always best to know the truth about yourself.

As soon as the Information service was functioning smoothly Dr. Speakie transferred the main thrust of his attention to the implementation of Evaluator training, and planning for the structurization of the Cure Centers, only he changed the name to SQ Achievement

Centers. It seemed a very big job even then. We certainly had no idea how big the job would finally turn out to be!

As he said at the beginning, we were a very good team. Dr. Speakie valued my administrative abilities and put them to good use. There wasn't a single slacker in the office. We all worked very hard, but there were always rewards.

I remember one wonderful day. I had accompanied Dr. Speakie to the Meeting of the Board of the Psychometric Bureau. The emissary from the State of Brazil announced that his State had adopted the Bureau Recommendations for Universal Testing—we had known that that was going to be announced. But then the delegate from Libya and the delegate from China announced that their States had adopted the Test too! Oh, Dr. Speakie's face was just like the sun for a minute, just *shining*. I wish I could remember exactly what he said, especially to the Chinese delegate, because of course China was a very big State and its decision was very influential. Unfortunately I do not have his exact words because I was changing the tape in the recorder. He said something like, "Gentlemen, this is a historic day for humanity." Then he began to talk at once about the effective implementation of the Application Centers, where people would take the Test, and the Achievement Centers, where they would go if they scored over 50, and how to establish the Test Administrations and Evaluations infrastructure on such a large scale, and so on. He was always modest and practical. He would rather talk about doing the job than talk about what an important job it was. He used to say, "Once you know what you're doing, the only thing you need to think about is how to do it." I believe that that is deeply true.

From then on, we could hand over the Information program to a subdepartment and concentrate on How to Do It. Those were exciting times! So many States joined the Plan, one after another. When I think of all we had to do I wonder that we didn't all go crazy! Some of the office staff did fail their quarterly Test, in fact. But most of us working in the Executive Office with Dr. Speakie remained quite stable, even when we were on the job all day and half the night. I think his presence was an inspiration. He was always calm and positive, even when we had to arrange things like training 113,000 Chinese Evaluators in three months. "You can always find out 'how' if you just know the 'why'!" he would say. And we always did.

When you think back over it, it really is quite amazing what a big job it was—so much bigger than anybody, even Dr. Speakie, had realized it would be. It just changed everything. You only realize that when you think back to what things used to be like. Can you imagine, when we began planning Universal Testing for the State of China, we only allowed for 1,100 Achievement Centers, with 6,800 Staff! It really seems like a joke! But it is not. I was going through some of the old files yesterday, making sure everything is in order, and I found the first China Implementation Plan, with those figures written down in black and white.

I believe the reason why even Dr. Speakie was slow to realize the magnitude of the operation was that even though he was a great scientist he was also an optimist. He just kept hoping against hope that the average scores would begin to go down, and this prevented him from seeing that universal application of the SQ Test was eventually going to involve everybody either as Inmates or as Staff.

When most of the Russian and all the African States had adopted the Recommendations and were busy implementing them, the debates in the General Assembly of the World Government got very excited. That was the period when so many bad things were said about the Test and about Dr. Speakie. I used to get quite angry, reading the *World Times* reports of debates. When I went as his secretary with Dr. Speakie to General Assembly meetings I had to sit and listen in person to people insulting him personally, casting aspersions on his motives and questioning his scientific integrity and even his sincerity. Many of those people were very disagreeable and obviously unbalanced. But he never lost his temper. He would just stand up and prove to them, again, that the SQ Test did actually literally scientifically show whether the testee was sane or insane, and the results could be proved, and all psychometrists accepted them. So the Test-Ban people couldn't do anything but shout about freedom and accuse Dr. Speakie and the Psychometric Bureau of trying to "turn the world into a huge insane asylum." He would always answer quietly and firmly, asking them how they thought a person could be "free" if he suffered under a delusional system, or was prey to compulsions and obsessions, or could not endure contact with reality? How could those who lacked mental health be truly free? What they called freedom might well be a delusional system with no contact with reality. In order to find out, all they had to do was to become testees. "Mental health *is* freedom," he said. " 'Eternal vigilance is the price of liberty,' they say, and now we have an infallible watchdog to watch for us—the SQ Test. *Only the testees can be truly free!*"

There really was no answer they could make to that except illogical and vulgar accusations, which did not convince the delegates who had invited them to speak. Sooner or later the delegates even from Member States where the Test-Ban movement was strong would volunteer to take the SQ Test to prove that their mental health was adequate to their responsibilities. Then the ones that passed the Test and remained in office would begin working for Universal Application in their home State. The riots and demonstrations, and things like the burning of the Houses of Parliament in London in the State of England (where the Nor-Eurp SQ Center was housed), and the Vatican Rebellion, and the Chilean H-Bomb, were the work of insane fanatics appealing to the most unstable elements of the populace. Such fanatics, as Dr. Speakie and Dr. Waltraute pointed out in their Memorandum to the Presidium, deliberately aroused and used the proven instability of the crowd, "mob psychosis." The only response to mass delusion of that kind was immediate implementation of the Testing Program in the disturbed States, and immediate amplification of the Asylum Program.

That was Dr. Speakie's own decision, by the way, to rename the SQ Achievement Centers "Asylums." He took the word right out of his enemies' mouths. He said, "An asylum means a place of *shelter,* a place of *cure.* Let there be no stigma attached to the word 'insane,' to the word 'asylum,' to the words 'insane asylum'! No! For the asylum is the haven of mental health—the place of cure, where the anxious gain peace, where the weak gain strength, where the prisoners of inadequate reality assessment win their way to freedom! Proudly let us use the word 'asylum.' Proudly let us go to the asylum, to work to regain our own God-given mental health, or to work with others less fortunate to help them win back their own inalienable right to mental health. And let one word be written large over the door of every asylum in the world—'WELCOME!' "

Those words are from his great speech at the General Assembly on the day World Universal Application was decreed by the Presidium. Once or twice a year I listen to my tape of that speech. Although I am too busy ever to get really depressed, now and then I feel the need of a tiny "pick-me-up," and so I play that tape. It never fails to send me back to my duties inspired and refreshed.

Considering all the work there was to do, as the Test scores continued to come in always a little higher than the Psychometric Bureau analysts estimated, the World Government Presidium did a wonderful job for the two years that it administered Universal Testing. There was a long period, six months, when the scores seemed to have stabilized, with just about half of the testees scoring over 50 and half under 50. At that time it was thought that if 40 per cent of the mentally healthy were assigned to Asylum Staff work, the other 60 per cent could keep up routine basic world functions such as farming, power supply, transportation, etc. This proportion had to be reversed when they found that over 60 per cent of the mentally healthy were volunteering for Staff work, in order to be with their loved ones in the Asylums. There was some trouble then with the routine basic world functions functioning. However, even then contingency plans were being made for the inclusion of farmlands, factories, power plants, etc., in the Asylum Territories, and the assignment of routine basic world functions work as Rehabilitation Therapy, so that the Asylums could become totally self-supporting if it became advisable. This was President Kim's special care, and he worked for it all through his term of office. Events proved the wisdom of his planning. He seemed such a nice wise little man. I still remember the day when Dr. Speakie came into the office and I knew at once that something was wrong. Not that he ever got really depressed or reacted with inopportune emotion, but it was as if the rubber balls in his shoes had gone just a little bit flat. There was the slightest tremor of true sorrow in his voice when he said, "Mary Ann, we've had a bit of bad news I'm afraid." Then he smiled to reassure me, because he knew what a strain we were all working under, and certainly didn't want to give anybody a shock that might push their score up higher on the next quarterly Test! "It's President Kim," he said, and I knew at once—I knew he didn't mean the President was ill or dead.

"Over fifty?" I asked, and he just said quietly and sadly, "Fifty-five."

Poor little President Kim, working so efficiently all that three months while mental ill health was growing in him! It was very sad and also a useful warning. High-level consultations were begun at once, as soon as President Kim was committed, and the decision was made to administer the Test monthly, instead of quarterly, to anyone in an executive position.

Even before this decision, the Universal scores had begun rising again. Dr. Speakie was not distressed. He had already predicted that this rise was highly probable during the transition period to World Sanity. As the number of the mentally healthy living outside the Asylums grew fewer, the strain on them kept growing greater, and they became more liable to break down under it—just as poor President Kim had done. Later, when the Rehabs began coming out of the Asylums in ever-increasing numbers, this stress would decrease. Also the crowding in the Asylums would decrease, so that the Staff would have more time to work on individually orientated therapy, and this would lead to a still more dramatic increase in the number of Rehabs released. Finally, when the therapy process was completely perfected, including preventive therapy, there might be no Asylums left in the world at all! Because everybody will be either mentally healthy or a Rehab, or "neonormal," as Dr. Speakie liked to call it.

It was the trouble in the State of Australia that precipitated the Government crisis. Some Psychometric Bureau officials accused the Australian Evaluators of actually falsifying Test returns, but that is impossible since all the computers are linked to the World Government Central Computer Bank in Keokuk. Dr. Speakie suspected that the Australian Evaluators had been falsifying *the Test itself,* and insisted that they themselves all be tested immediately. Of course he was right. It had been a conspiracy, and the suspiciously low Australian Test scores had resulted from the use of a false Test. Many of the conspirators tested higher than 80 when forced to take the genuine Test! The State Government in Canberra had been unforgivably lax. If they had just admitted it everything would have been all right. But they got hysterical, and moved the State Government to a sheep station in Queensland, and tried to withdraw from the World Government. (Dr. Speakie said this was a typical mass psychosis: reality-evasion, followed by fugue and autistic withdrawal.) Unfortunately the Presidium seemed to be paralyzed. Australia seceded on the day before the President and Presidium were due to take their monthly Test, and probably they were afraid of overstraining their SQ with agonizing decisions. So the Psychometric Bureau volunteered to handle the episode. Dr. Speakie himself flew on the plane with the H-Bombs, and helped to drop the information leaflets. He never lacked personal courage.

When the Australian incident was over, it turned out that most of the Presidium, including President Singh, had scored over 50. So the Psychometric Bureau took over their functions temporarily. Even on a long-term basis this made good sense, since all the problems now facing the World Government had to do with administering and evaluating the Test, training the Staff, and providing full self-sufficiency structuration to all Asylums.

What this meant in personal terms was that Dr. Speakie, as Chief of the Psychometric Bureau, was now Interim President of the United States of the World. As his personal secretary I was, I will admit it, just terribly proud of him. But he never let it go to his head.

He was so modest. Sometimes he used to say to people, when he introduced me, "This is Mary Ann, my secretary," he'd say with a little twinkle, "and if it wasn't for her I'd have been scoring over fifty long ago!"

He truly appreciated efficiency and reliability. That's why we made such a good team, all those years we worked together.

There were times, as the World SQ scores rose and rose, that I would become a little discouraged. Once the week's Test figures came in on the readout, and the *average* score was 71. I said, "Doctor, there are moments I believe the whole world is going insane!"

But he said, "Look at it this way, Mary Ann. Look at those people in the Asylums—3.1 billion inmates now, and 1.8 billion Staff—but look at them. What are they doing? They're pursuing their therapy, doing rehabilitation work on the farms and in the factories, and striving all the time, too, to *help* each other toward mental health. The preponderant inverse sanity quotient is certainly very high at the moment; they're mostly insane, yes. But you have to admire them. They are fighting for mental health. They will—they *will* win through!" And then he dropped his voice and said as if to himself, gazing out the window and bouncing just a little on the balls of his feet, "If I didn't believe that, I couldn't go on."

And I knew he was thinking of his wife.

Mrs. Speakie had scored 88 on the very first American Universal Test. She had been in the Greater Los Angeles Territory Asylum for years now.

Anybody who still thinks Dr. Speakie wasn't sincere should think about that for a minute! He gave up everything for his belief.

And even when the Asylums were all running quite well, and the epidemics in South Africa and the famines in Texas and the Ukraine were under control, still the work load on Dr. Speakie never got any lighter, because every month the personnel of the Psychometric Bureau got smaller, since some of them always flunked their monthly Test and were committed to Bethesda. I never could keep any of my secretarial staff any more for longer than a month or two. It was harder and harder to find replacements, too, because most sane young people volunteered for Staff work in the Asylums, since life was much easier and more sociable inside the Asylums than outside. Everything so convenient, and lots of friends and acquaintances! I used to positively envy those girls! But I knew where my job was.

At least it was much less hectic here in the UN Building, or the Psychometry Tower as it had been renamed long ago. Often there wouldn't be anybody around the whole building all day long but Dr. Speakie and myself, and maybe Bill the janitor (Bill scored 32 regular as clockwork every quarter). All the restaurants were closed, in fact most of Manhattan was closed, but we had fun picnicking in the old General Assembly Hall. And there was always the odd call from

Buenos Aires or Reykjavik, asking Dr. Speakie's advice as Interim President about some problem, to break the silence.

But last November 8, I will never forget the date, when Dr. Speakie was dictating the Referendum for World Economic Growth for the next five-year period, he suddenly interrupted himself. "By the way, Mary Ann," he said, "how was your last score?"

We had taken the Test two days before, on the sixth. We always took the Test every first Monday. Dr. Speakie never would have dreamed of excepting himself from Universal Testing regulations.

"I scored twelve," I said, before I thought how strange it was of him to ask. Or, not just to ask, because we often mentioned our scores to each other; but to ask *then,* in the middle of executing important World Government business.

"Wonderful," he said, shaking his head. "You're wonderful, Mary Ann! Down two from last month's Test, aren't you?"

"I'm always between ten and fourteen," I said. "Nothing new about that, Doctor."

"Someday," he said, and his face took on the expression it had when he gave his great speech about the Asylums, "someday, this world of ours will be governed by men fit to govern it. Men whose SQ score is zero. Zero, Mary Ann!"

"Well, my goodness, Doctor," I said jokingly—his intensity almost alarmed me a little—"even *you* never scored lower than three, and you haven't done that for a year or more now!"

He stared at me almost as if he didn't see me. It was quite uncanny. "Someday," he said in just the same way, "nobody in the world will have a quotient higher than fifty. Someday, nobody in the world will have a quotient higher than thirty! Higher than ten! The Therapy will be perfected. I was only the diagnostician. But the Therapy will be perfected! The cure will be found! Someday!" And he went on staring at me, and then he said, "Do you know what my score was on Monday?"

"Seven," I guessed promptly. The last time he had told me his score it had been seven.

"Ninety-two," he said.

I laughed, because he seemed to be laughing. He had always had a puckish sense of humor that came out unexpectedly. But I thought we really should get back to the World Economic Growth Plan, so I said laughingly, "That really is a very bad joke, Doctor!"

"Ninety-two," he said, "and you don't believe me, Mary Ann, but that's because of the cantaloupe."

I said, "What cantaloupe, Doctor?" and that was when he jumped across his desk and began to try to bite through my jugular vein.

I used a judo hold and shouted to Bill the janitor, and when he came I called a robo-ambulance to take Dr. Speakie to Bethesda Asylum.

That was six months ago. I visit Dr. Speakie every Saturday. It is very sad, he is in the McLean Area, which is the Violent Ward, and every time he sees me he screams and foams. But I do not take it personally. One should never take mental ill health personally. When the Therapy is perfected he will be completely rehabilitated. Meanwhile, I just hold on here. Bill keeps the floors clean, and I run the World Government. It really isn't as difficult as you might think.

Introduction to Flirtation Walk

Kay Rogers is a Pennsylvanian, a green-eyed redhead who has somehow contrived to remain single—if anyone who lives with thirty-four
cats can be said to be "single."

I've only read two stories by Ms. Rogers. One is "Experiment,"
originally published in *Fantasy and Science Fiction* and later anthologized. "Flirtation Walk" is the other. I love them both.

Flirtation Walk

by KAY ROGERS

Cadet Scott closed the inner lock. He crossed his narrow living quarters to the even more cramped security cells. There, he checked the
temperature of a tiny compartment, adjusted a dial. From a special
pouch on the crossbelt over his chest, he brought out a plio-covered
packet and stowed it within the compartment. He did this without
distaste.

By now, he'd decided he was proud of his control and he spared
only a quick flicking glance at the empty prisoner cubicle. His eyes,
gray-blue and clear with youth, were emotionless but he was glad he
had the package and the cubicle carried no passenger. In this NO, because of Number Three's image-maintenance, the ten Citizen Leaders
had issued what Cadet Scott called a direct-directive. They hadn't
wanted a prisoner to torture and brainwash through an educational
public trial.

He went into his control room. Already, he responded to the
difference in the air. This supplied air was cool and tasteless and he
was glad to breathe it again. Disciplined air. And his one-man pursuit
spacer was comfortably familiar. The wildness on Lloris had been

sweet but tomorrow always came. You were trained to it and you expected it.

There had once been a brave little band who cried "Tomorrow the world!" That was what Terran Cadet training did for you, taught how to live in discipline for tomorrow, which the CLs promised to the Cadets personally. So there was this extra pride to know he was fit, mentally as well as physically, to serve remote, nearly godlike Leaders.

Cadet Scott's fingers moved expertly, programing the return trip from the pleasure planet. He strapped in, without caring for a last look at the Llorisians' gaudy spaceport. This was partly arrogance; they wouldn't dare touch him—now. For the rest, Cadet Scott's self-portrait didn't include indulgences, like backward glances. Besides, wasn't he the first Cadet on a NO, exposed to a Place like Lloris and now headed straight for the barn, mission accomplished?

The clicking in control depths stopped; an even hum began and there was a faint no-color flash across the board, stirring something deep in Cadet Scott's mind.

He had dials to watch; he was out of the atmosphere before he permitted the nagging unpleasantness to surface.

What color were her eyes?

He moved uneasily in the straps; realized suddenly and hit the release.

His return would be an event, although he felt a curious lack of appetite for it. But she was the niece of Citizen Leader Three. Face had been saved. The whole Cadet program was justified, ready for activation for the mysterious high goals of the Leaders. And Cadet Scott's name would shine, forever burnished in the Old Cadet Hall with those others, which went back so far into hoariness their glory was a matter of interpretation.

But what *color* were her eyes?

He couldn't remember. He recalled Lloris spaceport, boiling with color and motion, steaming with sound; all overlaid with the scent of the ever-close creeping jungle, a smell of spice and sweet corruption.

He remembered specific colors: the lax Llorisian customs, an official in formal bottle-green tunic, carelessly waving the Cadet by, eager to greet a friend whose black skin was spectacular against his red robe and tiger cloak.

Cadet Scott considered it disorganized. He didn't like any of it. He was at a loss and felt vaguely inferior—a Cadet! These undisciplined, gaudy rogues looked and acted straight out of the Underground; they ran their spaceport efficiently. In his Cadet mind two and two always totaled four. He did not appreciate the paradox of the port; he did not speculate.

He squared his helmet and his shoulders. He started off on his mission, not at random but almost as if at drill, marching straight for the pleasure city which adjoined the port and was its reason for being. Somewhere in that glittering frivolity, among many other fugitives from the scattered worlds, there was one for Cadet Scott to find.

He moved with ingrained, disciplined arrogance. G-2 experts on Lloris swore a Cadet was safe enough if he didn't throw his weight around, but mobs on Lloris formed readily and were notoriously mercurial. And he always must remember he was a despised Terran.

All Cadet Scott wanted was his quarry, the foolish girl-traitor who thought a miraculous escape was her last word with Terra. She didn't know she was the last link. Those extraordinary circumstances would never recur; the other links were separate, discarnate; could never dream to forge a chain again.

The pleasure city dreamed before him under an artificial twilight. There was a crescent moon, a wistful star. It was a determined April mood, laid on a bit thick, but Cadet Scott had no mathematics to slipstick an April mood. He simply didn't see it or the moon-gates tempting into shadowed gardens. He was looking for practical information.

So practically and a trifle bluntly he stopped the first Llorisian he met. This was a sober individual, he wore three colors, a minimum of jewels. His speech was something else.

"Our sweet guides?" He laughed at the somber figure of the young Cadet, the bald question. "A lad like you still in ship rig? You're too dull a bird to appeal to our pretty little girls. And a Terran too." Drawing it out too flatly. Scott simply waited, until the Llorisian had finished his sour smile and decided to give him an answer.

He waved an arm behind him toward a stardust of light in the distance.

"There, you'll find them, but perhaps they won't have you, eh, Deathbird?" And he sneered at Cadet Scott's proud elite uniform.

For a moment the Cadet was startled until he realized this was just stock Outworlder to Terran talk; they all tacked on some macabre reminder of why they hated Terrans and kept away from the accursed planet.

He forgot the taunt and considered his immediate problem.

The guides of Lloris were famous and they were guides, with no other obligation unless by mutual arrangements. The Pleasure Center laid no compulsion upon the girls. And this was the part for which

Cadet Scott secretly felt inadequate and unprepared although his briefing had postulated a fake guide, eager to find a permanent protector upon the strange world. They told him she'd be easy to trap—he was to do it that way with smoothness, arousing no notice to what was purely a Terran concern.

At least the first part, finding her, wasn't difficult. Even in the big plaza she was easy to spot, though through some feminine magic she looked just like the others. But the same dazzled bewilderment Cadet Scott had felt was in her eyes; her skin was an imprisoned ivory glow against the careless gold of her companions.

And the sight of her and those companions only increased Scott's puzzlement; if these were women, what were Terran females?

Even at Stud Service (his turn had come up once) the girls weren't like this. They wore severe white tunics; they were handsome, husky, capable breeders. In no way were they an interpretation of the fantastic wishful whispers of the Cadet barracks.

And the Cadets were forbidden other commerce; their seed was too precious to the future. No American Sweethearts for them. Once, Cadet Scott had seen some of the Sweethearts promenading by the river, as if they wished to tantalize. (They did.) How tawdry their coarse pink robes seemed now. They were as crows to hummingbirds. How did you snare a hummingbird?

He tried to modify the bluntness he had used on the Llorisian as he dutifully accosted the pale girl. Her eyes, already large, grew larger and darkened in reaction to his uniform and the white-starred helmet.

Cadet Scott smiled down at her, only a little stiffly. "Lady, I am a stranger. I fear lest I lose my way."

With that traditional preliminary, he accepted her as a Llorisian and he saw her relief. She didn't imagine the swiftness with which the CLs' apparatus had traced her, she didn't know the precious Cadets had been qualified to execute Null Orders. He saw the glimmering hope that when her nemesis did come, which she didn't really believe, a Cadet companion would be the perfect camouflage.

"Stranger, welcome!" she replied and hesitated. She hadn't been drilled in the formula as he had. At last she managed the question which accepted him. "May I show you the way, lest you become lost?"

Her voice was sweet smoke. Well, she had been a singer, that was how she had been led into treason.

He stared at her very frankly in his curiosity. The silks she wore were one with her skin. She smelled like a strange flower and like one she looked fragile and exotic. Cadet Scott wished he had entered more into those whispered speculations in the barracks, he wished he knew more. She was going to guide him about Lloris and she was of his planet. Another Terran. Beside her, he felt alien, large and awkward; too warm in the uniform's tight collar.

He was grateful to see that she was uneasy. But as an artist she had belonged to the tiny social life of their scorned and quarantined planet; and she could better mask her nervousness. Quite naturally, she put her hand on his arm and they began to walk aimlessly.

"Will you be here long?" And she gave him her name, moving her fingers caressingly on his arm. It was a stiff little gesture and her fingers were very cold. Would the heat of his flesh disgust her?

She smiled again, more naturally, and he saw a little dent beside her mouth. He had never seen such a thing. Something else to watch for was that ridiculous trick of slanting a look at him under her lashes. Of course, she couldn't look him in the eye, the traitress, but this subterfuge certainly kept you looking at her.

That was how he found she did dare look into his eyes and she was seeing him, not the shadow of the helmet.

When they entered a tiny park, the noisy plaza was far behind, and there was no stilted chatter left to use. Scott was compelled by the tremor of that small cold hand to lay his own large hot palm over it and traps were far from his mind.

They looked at each other. The same hunger was in both glances.

There was a nearly audible click with no one listening as something turned off in Cadet Scott.

Scott learned, not without embarrassment, how a small luxurious house might be had. Since traps were far from his mind, he never considered he didn't require so elaborate a snare. His companion, covering her ignorance, insisted whatever he did would be pleasing. Flattered, Scott bought certain items at the gem bazaar, thinking briefly of the CLs with gratitude for that practicality which supplied him with many Llorisian Llors.

He learned the trick of procrastination. He learned how to deafen that third ear his training had inflicted upon him. It was the quickest study he had ever made and Cadet Scott had led his class.

Last of all, in that little house, he learned there was a shared sweet ignorance which the barrack's ramblings had never imagined. This was a complex learning which held back many tomorrows.

But even on Lloris, time is not suspended, tomorrow does come, tomorrow masking as another today. Oddly, it was a phrase of the traitress' beloved forbidden music which made Cadet Scott hear again and remember he had turned something off.

They had gone to some sort of a festival; she had been bubbling with excitement which Scott shared without reason, listening to the sweet husky voice, watching the deep eyes.

Music. A strange bitter drink. The music of Old Terra.

Scott didn't like the drink, some of the music made him uneasy. Songs like a restless wind and lonely walking; the courage for it . . .

So her enjoyment was hard to bear. Again, he felt alien to her, strangely envious of her pleasure. Then they were playing a soft ballad and she sang with the performer:

" 'The days dwindle down to a precious few . . .' "

From the others she won a murmur of appreciation, but she turned to Scott, innocently waiting for him to share her pleasure in the music and her own voice.

Cadet Scott stood abruptly.

"We must leave now," he said without explanation.

Outside, he took her arm.

"You didn't like the music?"

"No." He was blunt and there was no aimless walking tonight. Cadet Scott kept a dogged silence, ignoring her questioning glances, until they stood again in the tiny isolated park.

Among trellised irises and orchids, he demanded:

"Was it for that music you went to the Underground?"

The two rosy moons Lloris featured tonight blushed shadows across her face. Her eyes were wide and incredulous. Her eyes.

"No," she whispered. "Not you, oh never you."

"We coddle our artists," he said loudly. "And you are the niece of Number Three. So you were twice coddled. How could you betray your birthright?"

"Birthright!" She was very bitter. "We had to lose it to defeat both our enemies. But they'd never teach you that. How else could *you* betray *me?*"

"What you sang about—the precious days?" The Cadet stumbled. "I spent them with you."

"You gave me a little longer," she agreed bleakly. She looked at him, realized his words were awkward, dying blossoms. Quickly bitter again, she whipped at him, "Was that part of the punishment?"

"Was it?"

He knew her answer as he knew his own, realized he hadn't needed so elaborate a snare and knew it had been too large.

He remembered her cold hands. He was as cold now. When she

bowed her head, turning from him, he drew breath in a harsh sob but struck expertly with the edge of his palm. Alone, in the scented double moonlight, he retched dryly until the rosy shadows spun.

He wiped his mouth. He took his evidence of mission accomplished, doing what he had to do.

In haste, he heaped ferns, green and bronze, between the trellised flowers; he didn't require many. Cadet Scott went quickly from that place.

Bronze and green the ferns; purple and purple the flowers.

What color were her eyes?

Yesterday's question and Cadet Scott had only tomorrow.

And it was already beginning; he had passed Orbital Patrol. He made his prelim coded report, received clearance, the co-ordinates ticking forth on the bright red tape clearing him to Pentower's HiSec port. Free Air Control curtly demanded and took guidance of the last portion of the flight.

Cadet Scott cleaned up, put on a fresh uniform, reflecting how, on the American continent, or Terra as it was called since the Great Burn had been inflicted, no Hero was ever *dirty*. Physically. You had to be pretty for the scanners.

The ship spiraled down toward the legendary five-sided building with its grafted-on tower. Scott had his evidence in the official eagle-emblazoned case. He was ready but not eager to be a Hero.

He had no time to reflect upon this contradiction. From the silent men in the long black car who met him at the lock and whisked him past security to their grim look-alikes who spun him up into Pentower, he was moved too fast for considered thinking. He even lacked time to call up and assume that Cadet arrogance he had prized.

None of that mattered. The Citizen Leaders didn't want Cadets thinking. It was borne in too harshly upon Cadet Scott when he saw how they ignored him after being assured of his success. They talked among themselves, these soft men lounging easily in their opulent room; these men who bragged they have given youth a goal and ideal —in the Cadet Corps.

Scott had time to study them, these ordainers of his rigid life and stunted mind, while they congratulated each other on their newly proven weapon, the Cadet Corps, how their petty scheme would use it against the weary citizens they claimed to lead. Looking at their weak bodies, coddled by cushioned surroundings, with a Cadet's disciplined eye, Scott realized bitterly they were sure he couldn't think.

Finally, Citizen Leader 1 buttonpressed for the police tech to run routine check of mission-accomplished evidence. Then he swung to face Scott and the others followed, giving the young Cadet their complete attention.

They complimented him freely, too freely for now he was looking for the undercurrent of patronism. But their fat praise was only a minor bitterness as Cabot No. 1 summed up, "You are our proof." He said it with all the old pride someone had told Scott was forfeit.

There was such a boastful note you could already see yourself a pretty paper Hero—on posters for the Underground to tear down and trample. . . .

The police tech entered. Quiet and neutral, he sidled along the wall toward Scott, who hoped he wouldn't notice the dampness of the case he had been holding too long.

WHAT COLOR WERE HER EYES?

It seared through his mind like an electric shock. He would never know. He watched the poltech leave with them for his retinal pattern check.

And Cabot said, "Gentlemen, of course, this is our first Cadet Leader. But also a medal, I think." He smiled thinly. "Especially in view of the service done for our colleague. I believe—considering that and the Underground, our own Citizens—yes. The Medal, the Congressional itself."

All the men smiled, a cynical knowing ingroup. Cabot actually patted Scott's arm.

Big dumb Cadet Leader! And he had to agree with Cabot. Why hadn't he stayed on Lloris? It had never occurred to him. Grief and anger collided; a nova flamed; there was light. Fox-colored light.

There was value in clear youthful eyes. Scott smiled boyishly at Cabot, thanked him, stumbling in a pleasing humble way.

He thought of Cadet Leadership and ultraprestige with the Corps. He thought of being a Paper Hero, his face well known to the Underground. There would be only the contacts to make, to start the careful forging of a spear tipped by the hard-disciplined Corps. Two and two make—ten. Enough to pay.

There would never be much poetry in Scott, so he would never know the color of the eyes he brought so dutifully from Lloris.

But later, much later, Scott's legend and the ballads would tell how they were the color of freedom.

Introduction to Troll Road

Joan Bernott is an attorney married to an attorney, and a resident of Washington. Originally from Michigan, she began her professional free-lance work as a photographer, has worked as a research assistant, and is an inspired maker of filmstrips.

She has not yet written a novel, but her short fiction has appeared in such places as *Quark* and *Dangerous Visions*.

Troll Road

by JOAN BERNOTT

There is a road in eastern Pennsylvania that, winding through steep, quiet mountains, bends in and around, almost touching itself at points. It moves gracefully across the range with diamond-shaped signs announcing two-mile-long hills and black arrows indicating sharp curves. Sometimes the road, striped with two center yellow lines, goes hidden into the woods or bursts out over valleys into which it then slowly sinks. Mostly it runs beside the Susquehanna Creek—one of those wide, flat, almost eternal rivers—and accompanies a rusted railroad track through the national forest preserve and finally over into New Jersey.

At one point, the road bends inward and down, abruptly northward, so that a passer-by can see a broad graveyard of rust-red automobiles stretched out below him. In the center of the yard is a mud-water pond, colored by the dust of oxidized metal and crowded with floating bits of leather and upholstery stuffing the persistent wind has dislodged from car seats. Beyond the yard, along the road, are the remains of an old mill and coal town. Almost no one lives there anymore.

There are a few members of a defunct German ghetto: older per-

sons, the patriarchs and matriarchs of a community that immigrated
to early industrial America. One of these is a woman named Ludmilla, who lives on the outskirts of town with her grand-niece Irana.
A Jewish man and his small family run a gas station and grocery-con-
fectionery, and several farming families live in the surrounding dis-
trict. From one of these families comes Miles, who seems quite old
and wise, for his reticence, but is only nineteen; the townspeople, and
even Miles' own father, have called him the ugliest boy in the world.
The name of the town, Freedom, is printed in gray letters on a green
sign that stands near the automobile yard. Just before the sign, a
gravel road branches southward, leading first to Miles' wood-frame
house, then to a complex of farmhouses where the four travelers have
lived for nine years. The travelers are strangers to the earth, and have
offered Miles the gift of beauty.

Some young men have dark hair and a fair complexion marred
slightly with adolescent blemishes that serve only to remind the observer that a few years will make them more handsome still. For the
most part, they grow up in towns larger than Freedom. They have
pretty, suntanned girl friends who walk barefoot along the river holding their young man's hand. Sometimes these boys bring their girl
friends for afternoons at the park, and they eat blueberries and cream
out of waxed cream containers with the wooden spoons that come
with Dixie Cup sundaes.

But Miles is not one of these, and he has known since childhood,
when his classmates ridiculed him and called the gravel road he lived
on "troll road," that he is ugly. His face is short, his eyes pale and
widely spaced, his nose broad and too prominent, his lips thin and
forever tensely set against some vague dilemma. His brown hair is
thin and fine, like a newborn's, and never grew in properly; he seems
to be going bald along his sloping forehead and above his cupped
ears. The skin stretches across his small, gaunt skeleton, leaving
shadowy hollows above the collarbone and below his shoulder blades.
There exists no redeeming portion of his anatomy—not beautiful
hands or well-shaped feet. And his toes are undefined and slightly
webbed as though his mother had expelled him from her womb before he was complete.

Miles has never won or lost a girl friend, and he has lived alone on
his father's hundred acres since his parents died when he was sixteen.
He is neither bright nor dull; he speaks rarely, only of necessity or in
impassive exchanges with Peter at the grocery. When he visits there,
his head is slightly bowed and his eyes averted, as if to spare himself

the sight of Peter *seeing* him. Peter says, "Well, hello, Miles. Things going O.K.?" And the boy nods, sometimes mentioning the health of his few animals or the forty acres of wheat and alfalfa he raises. Miles pays for his purchases with his father's Social Security checks; the country doesn't know that his parents have died, and the checks will probably continue indefinitely. It isn't very important. If the money stopped coming, Peter would give Miles some work to do, or would send him to find a job as a fruit picker or miner in Medville. Peter feels that Miles is a harmless, somewhat moronic individual who belongs to Freedom, and would have no existence outside it.

The travelers are beautiful people, and very different, the way one might expect true foreigners to be. It isn't a distinctive attitude or manner of speaking and acting that sets them apart, but, for one thing, their eyes—navy blue and flecked remarkably with gold—possess a rare depth. There are two men and two women; tall strong people with constant tans and healthy blond hair. Miles met them soon after they came to the town to live on an abandoned estate. Everyone assumed they'd bought the place from the government or the estate manager's office. It was an impersonal transaction, at any rate.

It happened that Miles' parents were neighbors, by about a mile, to the travelers' farm. Often, Miles would spend whole afternoons at their place; he enjoyed their company with disciplined discretion. Mondays, he would have lunch with them, as the quiet guest. The four, Margo, Wendel, Jeen and Garth, favored Miles, perhaps because his company was so undemanding and effortless. Miles would sit at the kitchen table helping Margo prepare the meal, just peeling potatoes and responding with periodic "hmm's" and nods at the pauses in her elaborate conversation. She raved over the loveliness of the countryside, with great poetic outbursts of imagery and metaphor that amused Miles. But the four never mentioned their home or their future. Miles assumed, quite romantically, that they'd come from another planet and were visiting the earth just to rest, maybe to study. He expected they would soon lose interest and finally decide not to announce their curious arrival at all, and quietly depart.

At the time of Miles' parents' deaths, the four came for the first time to his house in order to express their sympathy and offer any assistance he might need. But Miles wanted nothing except his legacy of the family land and house and old Chevrolet. It was a thoroughly uncontested legacy, valuable only to him. So he thanked them and, with discreet promptness, sent them away so that he could be alone with his possessions. Miles suspected that they all, somehow, had had a hand in the deaths of his mother and father, though both had been ill for some time. His suspicion, hardly articulated, was mutely acknowledged and admitted to by Garth as the four left, when Garth returned Miles' gaze of understanding, timely gratitude.

Miles labored heavily and warmly over the stalled tractor, fiddling with various motor parts until the starter's squeak erupted into the satisfying rumble of a running engine. Most of the alfalfa had been cut and baled and was standing in a shadowy heap near the animal shed. There was little left to do, once the motor was repaired, but neglecting the task for even one day meant risking another rainfall, and yet another delay. Before noon, he'd passed four hours in the field, and was checking the binder twine on the last few bales and flinging them heavily to the top of the heap. Then he stretched a thin tarpaulin over the stack, anchored it at the corners with discarded tires carried from the automobile yard, and wandered back to the house, weaving perceptibly in the heat, great rivulets of moisture gliding down from his forehead and hanging from his upper lip.

Inside was coolness. He rested for a while at the table, fingering the wooden salt shaker his father had carved for his mother on some remote Christmas Eve. Then he washed and looked up into the rusted, broken mirror, his arms resting on the sides of the sink. His eyes wandered over his grotesque reflection. The face in the mirror seemed removed and irrelevant to him, but he was alone, and no one could stare at him, making him cower mentally and producing an involuntary shrug of his shoulders. He and his reflection exchanged hard stares: honest, impassive, almost incredulous. A body is like a box—it has no relation to its content, except that the content sometimes relinquishes its independence and grows into conforming shape. Inside, Miles was not ugly or beautiful. He possessed a subsistence level of emotion, and brutalized and killed whatever loneliness he felt.

Miles dried himself with a dingy towel, pushing his hair forward to conceal a measure of bareness at his temples. It was Monday; he would have lunch with the travelers.

Margo was standing outside on the porch, tossing grain to the few emaciated chickens they kept for eggs. Wendel stood beside the fence gate, hammer in hand, examining the hinge. He looked up and noticed Miles, waving enthusiastically. Miles felt they overdid their expressions of welcome.

For a long while on his periodic visits, Miles would sit mutely through whole conversations which the four conducted energetically.

He never felt compelled to speak, and the four carried the upbeat mood of their meals without his help.

But then Garth finally commented on Miles' reticence and gently but insistently urged him to join in the talk. Miles explained that he was usually silent because he had nothing to contribute, but in deference to Garth's concern, he did, for a time, begin to speak more freely. But his forced comments were invariably uninteresting, and his rambling sentences—often running together a myriad of formless thoughts—were more and more frequently cut short by interruptions from the others. Miles' ideas were boring, even to himself. So soon after the period of experimental articulation, he relapsed into the familiar, silent pattern, and was more comfortable for it. Garth never again prompted him to converse. The experiment, in point of fact, had proved somewhat embarrassing to all.

So it happened that the greeting this particular afternoon, though warm and genuine, was quite one-sided. Miles simply acknowledged their welcome with a smile and nod, then sat on the edge of the dusty porch to watch Wendel work and wait for Margo to call them to dinner.

Almost two hours later, they all idled contentedly on the porch, eating great slices of cantaloupe. Jeen's long fingers strayed gracefully over the antiquated autoharp as she played and sang a Scottish folk ballad. Garth rolled cigarettes and lit a tall incense candle. They all smoked and relaxed in the porch shade, a few flies floating in the thick, afternoon air. Garth had driven into Medville the previous afternoon and was displaying the set of paperback volumes he'd ordered through a bookstore there. Most were histories of the seventeenth and eighteenth centuries. He and Margo were the students of the group; they read voraciously on many, diverse topics. And there was a volume of folk songs for Jeen, and books of Michelangelan sculpture and painting. Garth opened the latter to reproductions of the "Last Judgment" and Sistine Chapel panels. It was because of the pictures that Margo and Garth, to Miles' discomfort, began to talk about human beauty.

Margo's words poured out of her smiling lips like soap bubbles—pretty, empty remarks. She raved over the artist's rendition of the souls condemned to hell. "Look! Their faces—so drawn, yet still remorseless. And the faces of the saved ones are so lovely. The story of salvation is a beautifully complete and satisfying tale. Michelangelo was clearly a genius."

Jeen, the more gentle speaker, looked up from her harp and

glanced at the pictures. She drew the book out of Garth's hand and rested it in her lap, staring intensely at the prints.

Garth interrupted Margo's procession of words. "Not a genius, Margo, a brilliant craftsman. He could see well—he simply studied the real appearance of men, then set about reproducing it in prescribed compositional form."

"Oh, no, Garth." Jeen smiled across to him. "The artist was not a copier at all. He found beauty even in the faces of the damned, and possessed a vision besides technical perception. Look."

She held the book toward him, her finger on one face to the right side of the God figure. Then she swept over several pages and pointed to the triangular composition of a woman seated, one elbow on her knee, her chin in hand. "This is an inner beauty which persists even within a pathetic and evil exterior. Beauty can be damned, but it remains beautiful at least in the superficial sense, and always benefits the possessor. Even if it goes no deeper than the surface."

Wendel leapt from his chair, gathering together the cantaloupe rinds which had begun to decay and attract flies. "Ah, you all waste too much time intellectualizing. Talk of beauty is irrelevant—you discuss universals and don't even notice that flies are swarming over the garbage you've discarded and forgotten. Beauty is not to be talked or watched, but lived. We all are beautiful." He wrapped the rinds hastily and efficiently in newspaper and headed across the yard to bury it in a refuse area about two hundred yards distant. He had almost reached it when Miles finally spoke.

"I am not beautiful," he said, wrenching from himself a fact almost too incredible and unjust to be articulated.

They all waited, expecting him to repeat the statement, but he was silent, just sitting there on the step and staring over to Wendel. Jeen began to strum her harp again, saying, "That is true, Miles. You are an ugly boy." Her tone was matter-of-fact. She kept on playing "Greensleeves" in the afternoon mugginess, and Miles forced himself to turn and face her. Then she continued over the melody, "Would you like to be beautiful, as beautiful as us?" Her eyebrows lifted into a slight, challenging arch.

Miles noticed that Garth's head jerked toward Jeen, a reprimand in his eyes. Miles said, "It doesn't matter anymore about that." Garth thought he was referring to beauty, but then the boy continued. "I know you can do many wonderful things. I've seen you from the hilltop over there." He nodded toward the path he walked homeward. "I know all about you."

Garth doubted that Miles knew everything, but he withheld his criticism of Jeen. They all had been careless with the boy all along. It felt good to relax with someone, and he seemed too remote from life to really take notice of even remarkable things.

Margo was talking. "Yes, of course. Wendel once said he thought you would like to be more handsome. And it isn't difficult. We can make you look much like one of us. Although"—and here her voice faded into a tone of polite speciousness—"I never considered you so unattractive, Miles. Really."

Miles rose abruptly and backed away from them, an expression of intolerable tension on his face. Wendel had returned, and the girl Irana was with him, apologizing for her tardiness. Irana's presence sickened Miles all the more. "You all are stupid," he muttered, pushing Wendel and Irana aside and rushing away. "You understand nothing." *How can they say these things? How can they know: how dare they see me?* He'd always told himself that, because the four were strangers, they didn't realize he was ugly. He thought they were unaware, or blind; but all along, they saw him and knew.

Miles didn't return to their farm for the next three weeks. Then he chanced to meet Wendel along the path between their homes one evening, and they talked a long while. The following Monday, he came to share lunch with them once again, and that afternoon they, somehow, made his feet begin to grow normally. And his hair. The lines and planes of his face softened gradually, and every time he looked into the mirror over the sink—he did not look often—there was a noticeable change in his reflection. Some random alteration. His eyes darkened to blue, and his frame began to fill out; he grew several inches in less than two weeks.

At night, as he lay in bed, his hands would timidly glide over his strengthening features. At one point, before much change had occurred, he became frightened and asked them please to stop. They did, for many weeks. Then after that time, they began again to change him, more slowly this time, perhaps more reverently as well. The transformation continued over several months, and then was complete.

Peter considered the change in Miles to be a delayed coming of age, as if the adolescent tension in him had finally been loosened, and the boy had reached his rightful manhood. Peter mentioned to Ludmilla, too, that he had always suspected Miles was more clever than he appeared to be; he even said the boy had a bright future. Ludmilla simply shook her head stiffly, disbelieving.

As the autumn ripened, Miles tried to make himself comfortable in his new body. He enjoyed the flow of breezes over his more pronounced cheekbones, and the slightly greater ease with which he handled the alfalfa bales. He still walked only rarely into town, but now, as stray cars passed and the tourists inside stared at him with ill-disguised intensity, turning their heads clumsily as their cars rounded the northward curve into Freedom, Miles was confident they found him attractive, and he felt more warmly toward them.

The afternoons at the travelers' farm continued in their usual weekly pattern, except that Irana began to join them for lunch more frequently. Miles could depend on finding her there each Monday, her light brown hair brushed and hanging in waves to her shoulders, sometimes tied with a ribbon. Irana had confided in Margo that she liked Miles, and Margo, quite pleased with herself, had hinted as much to him. Miles made a conscious effort to avoid Irana, and even decided not to go to the farm one week.

The following Monday, however, the luncheon was particularly elaborate, and Miles and Irana stayed well into the evening. Garth suggested they build a bonfire, and he collected the necessary firewood while Jeen filled a paper bag with chestnuts from the old tree in the backyard. The path they followed to the firesite was the same narrow one Miles took home, so they went single file, Miles at the end, and Irana hurrying to maintain a position beside rather than behind him. Barefoot, she tried to step carefully through the untrammeled brush alongside the path. Miles felt embarrassed and gave her an irritated glance now and again when she'd brush against a thistle and whimper in a plea for sympathy and attention.

It was a clear, Indian summer night, and the fire burned quickly and crisply at the dried branches, casting orange shadows on the women's long hair. The six of them seemed members of one family, sitting there in a circle, and the scene was ceremonious enough that Garth decided to announce to Miles and Irana that the four travelers would be leaving Freedom within the next year. Irana became excited and tried to persuade Margo and Jeen to change their minds. But Garth, in a paternalistic tone, explained to her that they just didn't want to live there any longer.

They remained around the fire for a long time, eating the chestnuts and listening to Jeen's music. Finally, Garth, Margo, Wendel and Jeen gathered their things and said good-bye. It was left to Miles and Irana to self-consciously put out the fire and walk home along the path together. Irana was very sentimental and talked incessantly about the travelers. She started to cry a little, insisting, "I wish they wouldn't go. They're our best friends here; we'll miss them so much, won't we. . . ." Miles thought her behavior childish, and felt that everything she said was designed to make him talk to her and like her. He hardly responded to her at all, except to call her "foolish," and she then became angry. She was walking ahead of him on the path, and stopped suddenly, turning around to stare at him with wide, impatient eyes. In a tone of voice that slid quickly from a demand to a plea, she said, "Miles, why do you dislike me so?"

He couldn't speak. She seemed too womanly and strong—even lovely in the evening light, her beauty all her own. He felt he owed her some kind of respect and responsiveness he was unable to offer.

She went on, "You could be so much kinder to me. You act as if everything I do insults you, and I can't bear it. I—I want you to like me." Her white arm was raised and poised mid-air before her face, her fingertips almost touching her lips. Shyly, she extended her hand toward Miles' face.

He stared back at her with amazement and contempt. "I am a man, and you treat me like a doll to win and keep. You never talked to me before the travelers changed me. I was an animal to you then, to be looked at and laughed at."

"No," she insisted, startled, and her voice rising above the field's cricket song. "That's a lie! You *know* it isn't true." She bit her lower lip to stop its quivering, and watched him, this perfect, beautiful man, as he averted his eyes and rushed past her, heading along the path. She shouted after him, "And you're not an animal to me. You're nothing. You're *empty!*"

Miles said nothing to her all the remaining distance. When they parted at his house, Irana didn't say good night, but Miles didn't care about her at all.

The winter passed, mild and uneventful. Miles finally took the old mirror off the wall over the sink basin. He was a strikingly handsome man, and certainly beauty was a more pleasant experience for him than ugliness. But he felt he belonged properly to neither extreme, and he grew bored with the perennial uneasiness caused by his reflection in the mirror.

In February, a man came to Freedom to recruit miners to work a new mine a hundred miles from the town. He was impressed by Miles, and offered him a good job, but Miles wasn't interested in that either.

The following summer, after a ten-year stay, the travelers left for home. Miles didn't miss them very much; he still considered them blind in certain ways, because for all their knowledge and wonderful powers, they didn't understand very much about people. He had never grown close to them. It was all but impossible to be intimate with or dependent upon a group of such deceptively garrulous people. The four shared an almost raucous style, except for Jeen, who had little personality at all save for her gentleness, which got tiresome after a while. All of them had, after all, considered him ugly before, just like all the others.

As Peter suspected, it turned out that Miles never left Freedom. His roots were deeply implanted there; even on his road, his ugliness had become such a part of him that, faced with the possibility of starting anew in a strange place where no one knew him, he couldn't bring himself to leave. Perhaps it was for fear that, without constant reminders of who he used to be, his new body would be without any identity at all.

As years passed, he began to neglect himself, the way lonely people often do. He ate too much, slept too much, and let his pale hair mat with grime. By the time he was thirty-five, he was no longer an attractive man, but this ugliness was alien to him and was, in the final analysis, a lie.

His real identity, his soul, remained lost inside the alien and inappropriate country of his body and finally he died.

Introduction to There Was a Garden

Zenna Henderson was born and raised in Arizona, where she now lives, working as a teacher. She has been a teacher for all of her adult years except one, teaching in such unusual places as a school in France for the children of Air Force personnel, the Japanese Relocation Center in Sacaton, Arizona, and a children's TB hospital in Connecticut.

Whether she is talking of people or People, the hallmark of her work is a warmth for her fellow man.

There Was a Garden

by ZENNA HENDERSON

Mountain peered around the shoulder of Hill at the still figure sprawled facedown on Dust. "Is he dead yet?"

"Sh—sh—sh—" said Grass, bending close. "No, not yet." Grass stirred to breathe.

"You are as impatient as Foothills," said River, curving closer to Foot.

"It has been so long," sighed Mountain, rippling Forest as he straightened up a curving ridge. "So long when last we danced for joy."

"Or could clap our hands," said Pine. "And sing with Stars. Now we will have World back for our own. No further need to keep the Pattern exact for him—"

"Be patient a little longer," said Wind, moving softly around Face. "Be respectful of Last."

"I have plans," said Continent to River. "I am weary of your parting me down the middle as though I were a head of hair. Instead of gathering waters larger and larger for you to take to Ocean, let each streamlet weave down to Water—"

"Then I would not be," said River. "And it would ruin Beach."

"Ruin?" asked Continent. "Our functions are never Ruin! Man made the word to explain broken patterns—*his* idea of patterns—and became his own supplier of occasions to use the word. We would only be making a different Beach. Why not?"

River rippled uncomfortably. "Man looked on Beach with pleasure."

Mountain quivered Hillside impatiently. "Not dead yet?"

"No," said Wind gently, drying the skim of cold sweat on Man's face. "Not yet."

"All the small streams," Continent went on. "Each with its own area—"

"They would not be navigable," said River shortly.

"Navigable? By whom?" scoffed Continent.

River was silent.

"Small thinking," muttered Continent. "Ole' Swimmin' Hole mentality—"

"It has been so long," offered Mountain. "We will have trouble realizing that we are free and unobserved. It will take getting used to. And Continent, I am not at all sure I would like the feel of many small streams scoring me. One large one you can get used to, but all the niggling, nagging abrasions of a thousand—"

"I am aching to be healed of this infection!" cried Continent. "This Creature that has festered since first he breathed! He never learned! Nothing can live on its own wastes!"

"The Lakes are shining again," said River. "He has been gone from them long enough. He would never have come back to be a witness, so we started—"

"Salmon are leaping up the falls," said Continent. "The obstructions are gone. Each surge of the salmon is more and more—"

"Birds," sighed Pine. "Not so much to me, but swinging Branches low. But so many can never return—"

"And there he lies!" Hill spat a small boulder across Field toward Last. "Keeping us from all we want to start doing—freed of him! Freed of him!" Field curled Furrow and stopped Boulder short of Last.

"I will mourn him," said Field, trembling so Furrows crinkled and Wire drooped sadly from Fence along one side. "He taught me," murmured Field. "He taught me to feed him and clothe him. He returned to me to die. He cherished me."

"He enslaved you!" cried Mountain. "He alienated you from Plain and Continent, then poisoned us all—and himself—and came back to pollute you even more! Now you will be free!"

"Free?" said Field. "For what?"

"To be Hill again! Or Plain! Or Continent!"

"Hill is tall," said Field. "Continent is vast—from sea to sea. Field is special. Not all of Hill or Plain or Continent is fit to be Field."

"Nor wants to be!" shouted Mountain, becoming Canyon, then Plain, with a rippling crash that broke Wire and buried most of Fence.

Wind hummed in the silence, then whispered, "Sh—sh—sh—!"

All leaned to look. Even Sky seemed to lower to see. Wind moved across Face. Grass bent to touch lips, then straightened and turned, plume drooping, away.

"Breath comes no more," whispered Grass.

"Nothing throbs," murmured Dust.

"He is dead," sighed Wind. "The Last is dead."

And Wind wept around the finished Face.

Silence grew larger. River rippled up to touch Foot, then curved sadly away. Field tightened Furrows until they were coldly rigid. The Field said into the huge Silence, "No one is dancing? No one is clapping hands? No one is singing with Stars?"

Pine nestled against Hill. Hill fitted tighter into Mountain, Mountain clung to Continent. And Darkness filled all the hollows of the Land, overflowing the treetops, drowning the peaks until it lifted to reach Sky.

Sky held the lighted Stars and, looking down, said softly, *"And Darkness was on the Face of the Deep—"*

In the faintness before the Light, River crept up to Field and murmured, "What shall we do with what is left? He is Last. He should not have to wait for Sun and Rain to take him apart, or for hungry things to scatter him. I would take him as I used to take in some places, but that may not have been his ritual."

"We cared for him," said Field. "He was committed to Fields for Finished ones. Or just to Earth. All Earth shared, receiving again what had come from it. But I cannot hollow myself—and Rain takes so long—"

"I will make the hollow," said River. "Dust, will you permit my passing?"

"I?" trembled Dust, stirring in the early light. "I permit?" Small clouds puffed. "You are asking Dust? I have never been asked—" And Dust lay, silently yielding, waiting for River.

River parted banks and flowed and rippled and turned. River retreated through banks, lapping the last edge of Hollow to smooth it.

"I cannot move him," mourned Field. "Could your waters—"

River murmured a moment, then Waters rose to look about. Swiftly, silently, River swept over the finished one and washed him into Hollow. Swiftly, silently, River spread Dust over, then smoothed Field until Dust and Soil no longer showed any of Hollow. Carefully Field remade Furrows over the smoothness.

"There," said River with a final ripple over the edge of banks. "He is home—to the Dust and the Water."

Day was.

Wind hurried across Field, across Hill, happily busy being Wind among the pines, to the edge of Field. Wind found a bit of Wire drooping from Post. Wind found that he could whistle by moving swiftly past Wire. So Wind whistled there many days and many nights. But the sound was never joyful, so, when at last Wire fell free of Post and dropped to silence on Ground, Wind felt released.

Days were only because of the turning of Earth—not because of counting. And Seasons merged one into another, not knowing—not capable of knowing—where was beginning and where was ending. Quaking sent waves of Water to scour clotted shores, and waves of Land to turn freshness up over the weariness of filth. Up-surging Soil filled Air, and Sun made a scarlet glory along the racing edge of Darkness.

"Oh, see!" cried Sunset. "How fair I am! Look up! Behold!"

"Dust and Sun," said Continent shortly. "Light refraction. Its function."

Sunset murmured voicelessly. "Man drank my colors with his eyes. He taught me that I was fair."

Silence ran in exultation from peak to peak, from depth to height and non-heard itself in a thousand places on Earth that Silence had long forgotten existed. But Silence folded on itself and whimpered without sound. If there was no sound because there was no one to hear it, there was no silence because there was no one to non-hear it.

Warmth faded from Continent and Snow fell—fascinated flake upon unblemished flake.

"Look!" cried Snow. "Look how I have lined each Twig and bent each Branch and crowned each Hill and glorified Mountain. Oh look! Oh look!"

"You are Snow," said Mountain heavily. "Your function is to fall. You have fallen on things beneath you. You have fallen."

Snow was silent. Then, quietly patterning the words, "Man found me lovely. Man saw me glorifying and fulfilling," Snow mourned. "Man fed his soul on me."

Snow peeled away from Boulder and dusted angrily down Hillside. So Hill released more Snow and more, until Avalanche crashed down, stripping Bush and Tree and Grass down to Hill's bare bedrock.

"Man!" cried Snow, plummeting downward. "You will crush him! You will destroy him! Remember Man!"

"Man is gone!" Hill gritted boulders together harshly. "He will no longer look on me in judgment! On any function of mine. Calling 'Terrible.' Avalanche or Fire—or Landslide or—!" Hill stripped a vast flank bare, then peeled it off in megatons and cast it down on Snow. Snow-melting flakes wept to a torrent and churned Soil to muck.

Sky leaned closer and murmured, *"Without Form and Void—"*

Upspringing came unhappily. Confusions were everywhere—and everywhere the only clearly-speaking was endlessly defensive—*"Within my function Allowable function*—But *I have always* wanted—*I have always planned that, freed, I would—"*

Every aspect of Earth battered the borders of its function, undeterred by Man's expectation. Unfettered by Man's evaluation. Untempered to Man's petitioned need. Unmodified by Man's Function. Continent ripped River to shreds. River gouged Continent to swamps. Mountain flung Forest from its sides like scraping moss from a stone. Forest channeled Rain to rip Mountain.

Field lay silently accomplishing the dissolution of Last. River contrived at times to creep back to Field, and Dust, to murmur with them in the vast unhappy, unfocusing of Creation.

Field lifted Flowers along its faint furrows. Wind counted them gleefully and tilted them to show Sky the golden faces. "Man counted Petals to Love," said Field, remembering. And Storm shrieked and twisted the flowers until petals sowed themselves sterilely through Forest, and Rain beat them into Mud. "Man delighted," sighed Field. "No one counts to Love now."

All the small, hidden, quiet things were patient in their waiting darkness.

Then, at last, Continent lay quiescent for long and long. Smoke settled from Mountain flanks. Dust distilled from Air. Silence lifted up like a long, glowing banner against Sky. River gathered the weeping, ragged waters together. Hill, shaken with small hiccoughing aftermaths of Quakes and Storms and Floods, slumped against Mountain. Mountain cradled the remains of Forest. Snow blossomed briefly in warm darkness to quench Fire gnawling listlessly at Pine. Hesitant, frightened, Flowers crept to bud and blighted blossom, cringing lest Root should suddenly be exposed or stripped in an instant.

All the quiet, hidden things became quietly, darkly, busy with their functions—and healing began.

Finally Continent spoke. "We are not individuals. We are one. We are turning back on ourselves and consuming our own selves."

Silence diluted all the rebellion and thinned it to petulance. Then, with a movement like a sob, Edge embraced Edge, Separation groped for Separation and joining began. Hesitantly a pulse fluttered and strengthened, and every Function struggled to match the throbbing until a beat began to build.

"We are not Completion," the realizing murmur lifted longingly. "We are a setting. Alone, we are empty. We cannot fill ourselves."

Silence wrapped its healing around.

Finally, out of the silence, Field asked, "Who will go to Him?"

"Who is worthy?" wondered Dust.

"If we must wait for worthiness," sighed Wind. "We can never go."

"Anyway, we have no fit place," said Hill. "Look around you."

Silence again, long and troubled.

"Before, there was no place," reminded Pine, hope quickening the words. "Remember? But we made a beautiful place. There was a garden—"

"We must heal ourselves first," said Continent. "And that will be long."

"We have begun," said Field. "We have begun to focus. We are not Each—we are One. We are We again—not I." The beat strengthened. Underground, the tangled, matted chaos smoothed to a complicated, intertwining network. Order appeared and spread.

There was a garden—with every aspect of it trembling, in eager beauty, toward perfection. Every aspect toiled to become best—not better than anything, but only self-best. And imperfection lovingly joined imperfection and became near-perfection.

Then, in the cool of one morning, Field lay holding Dust as an offering, River lapped softly and practiced mixing with the edge of Dust.

"Who will go to Him?" asked Pine shyly. "Who will ask for the Return?"

*Return—return—return—*Echo carried the sound, round and ringing, up Hill, up Mountain and up to urge against Sky.

The question ceased. All questing was stilled. All answers Were.

"We did not need to go," breathed Field from under the green that hid the old, faint, furrowings. Furrows smoothed out completely, making Field new again. "He is always here."

Water rounded upward like a tear, then, smoothing, waited.

And Dust quivered at the edge of Water.

Introduction to Night-Rise

Though she has never written science fiction full-time, Kate MacLean has "always" written science fiction. Some of her best-known and most anthologized and televised short stories are "Pictures Don't Lie," "The Snowball Effect," and "And Be Merry," all to be found in her collection *The Diploids,* originally published in the early sixties and republished in 1973. Her short story "The Kid in the Computer" (televised over CBC) was a precursor of her first science fiction novel, *The Missing Man,* published in 1975.

I don't know Ms. MacLean but a mutual friend describes her as "a terror in reasoned discourse, both logical and oblique in argument." She lives in Maine with her parents and her son.

Night-Rise

by KATHERINE MACLEAN

Now mercy.

Down certain dark and filthy alleys—

In fetid spots between the buildings of the best neighborhoods, by running water, and deep black pools, those who bring themselves to the altar joyfully—

They will be allowed to enter nothingness.

"———" Someone had been speaking. The sound of a voice lingered in my ears. I thought back. The meaning. Something religious and strange.

Nothingness? The world came partially into focus.

I felt the wood of a bar under my fingers. "I know some people who are already nothing, and they think someone in the sky knows what he is doing with them."

A voice beside me. "It can be reborn as a mindless animal, without responsibility or remorse. No need to think ever again. The Dark Christ is merciful, will give darkness as love."

I closed my hand around a smooth shot glass and looked to see if it was empty. It was half full. I looked into the mirror across the bar. Dark amber glass. The people relaxing here did not have to see those dim amber faces. Concealed, those faces watched them.

What was my excuse for being here? Only a little vacation, a drink between assignments and hard work. I was almost working, even here, for the bar smelled bad. It was a danger place, an international border, mixing refugees from law and logic, criminals and perverts and blind, bad-tempered tourists looking for glamour in evil. Stories might rise out of this muck.

Beside me in the mirror, clear-cut and almost visible, was the face of an adolescent Hindu boy, dark eyes, full sculptured lips. He looked familiar. I could almost guess which ambassadorial family he belonged to. They would not want him to be here in danger. He touched my elbow. I felt the touch, although I did not see it in the mirror.

"Are you all right, sair?" said the soft Indian voice.

"I don't know," I said, and did not turn to look at him yet. Everything was becoming too real. The amber mirror still held a little of unreality. "I think I'm sobering up."

The echo of a voice still lingered.

Something had hit me with a great gong of meaning recently, within ten minutes. Somewhere near me was a story. I had been out on my feet, "gone" into one of those blackouts where an experienced drinker can be unconscious and still walk and talk and sound alive. The sound of a story had brought me back.

The feeling of something important was still bringing me back. I climbed upward from under the sea of warm whiskey. The lights grew brighter and the sounds harsher and more shrill as I approached surface. Someone was repeating the details of a fight. A blurred voice was trying to make a point to a precise voice that questioned insistently and quietly, going after a purpose. Voice one should guard himself against voice two. Half-filled bottles before my eyes lined up against the back mirror. The smell of insect spray and odor killer, whiskey, fear, sweat . . . A beefy bartender, accustomed to trouble, stolidly refilled drinks for the drunks and ignored their attempts to converse with him.

"What were you saying?" I asked the Indian boy. "I think I missed some of it." I fumbled with my wallet on the bar checking my cash. Five dollars. I braced for reality and looked straight at the boy.

Quality, yes. Education, yes, but primitive, and overmuscled for his age. His face was smooth sculptured stone. Legally too young to drink and enter bars. My duty was to get him out of there, said the imagined voice of his family. I ignored it and listened again. The echo made real.

"There are two Christs, sair," the boy said, licking his lips and glancing away from my wallet. He turned his dark eyes on me with sincere earnestness as if even a strange bum with bloodshot eyes at a bar had a right to know.

He said, "There is a Dark Christ also. I mean a bad one. He is coming this time. He is a god also, like the other, but on the left hand now. He is in the souls of men, gaining shape, a thought by God slowly forming to become solid—I think strong enough to already be born in the flesh as a man, growing somewhere already. Have you not felt him coming all your life? He rises in the land of your soul, like a dark sun, slowly."

It hit me somewhere. I shuddered and kept shuddering. I thought I was going to break apart physically. I pulled out of it with my fingers gripping the edge of the bar hard enough to dent walnut.

I have felt that thing before, watching the first thread of smoke trickling upward from a volcano that was going to blow, but this was the first time I had had a sixty-mile-an-hour, head-on collision with words. I looked around for something to help me disconnect and forget it. On the other side of the boy a richly dressed slender man gave me a steady-eyed expressionless stare, then looked the Indian boy up and down as if I had offered him for sale.

People had vanished from this neighborhood.

"Does your family know where you are?" I asked the boy.

"I am where I choose to be, sir," he said. "I know judo, and I am armed." The children of diplomats must travel from country to country. If they learn to escape protection and explore each place, they may grow up in premature understanding of the ways of the world, even the ways of evil. I remembered that the men who go into the borderworld, and are destroyed and do not return, are usually deviates looking for companions for their strange tastes. Like the man on the other side of the Indian boy. He edged closer, but I did not feel any need to warn my young companion of his intentions. He must have met that sort of attention before.

The boy had been telling me of a young criminal gang. I remembered that now. It could have made a good story. Memory keeps slipping. I reached into a pocket, found a note pad. Better to write it down.

"Do you want me to take notes and write an article?"

He nodded. Again the sincere, earnest look. He wanted to help me, or the world, by telling it the truth. I did not want any more theology, only the events.

I said, "Go on with what you were telling me. The story I mean. How did it start?"

"About the stealing? The impulse came to me. I did not need the money—my parents are rich, but the impulse came to me, feeling like wisdom. I found poor gang boys for companions. I went into buildings, we stole, and sold, and gave away. I saw that I could go into anyplace. All doors are unlocked. I saw that the poor boys did not want to steal, did not want to give away what they had stolen and help each other; they wanted to destroy what they did not have and they wanted to destroy what they did not understand. They would smash beautiful obedient machines in offices, smear their offal on walls, hit each other with what they had stolen. The world lay open to them, but they could take nothing for themselves that would help them. They learned nothing. They were in pain, dry and hungry inside for they were never loved, and they could not love. Another impulse came to me, as if by wisdom. I was sure. I took them into a dark place and I returned them to the wheel of Karma, to be reborn as animals and birds and live with humbleness and beauty."

He took a white scarf from his pocket, a white scarf such as the murdering servants of Kali Druga, the destroyer goddess, had used in ritual street murder long ago. It was as if he had taken a knife out of his pocket. The memory of mankind is long. Voices faltered, and in the silence he said, "I shed no blood. And afterward I prayed for their souls."

If he had mentioned excrement and elimination in the presence of an old ladies' tea party he would have gotten the same polite pretense that he had said nothing, the same immediate resumption of general chatter on other topics. He had mentioned something that was done and accepted, but not openly talked about. Murder. The boy went on talking, but now no one else listened to him. The richly dressed deviate turned his back and began a cordial conversation with a skinny young man who had been crowding him from the other side. The skinny young man had mascaraed eyes and looked hungry.

Drunken voices rose about us, and a fight began near the door. The bartender lumbered in that direction.

The boy went on talking. I have interviewed great scientists and poets and there is always something in the way they talk. This poor damned kid had some crazy notion of Christ, and he had killed a whole peck of his fellow ragamuffins with his white scarf. But there was power in his voice and in his thinking. When he began to speak again, I heard the essential child savagery in the smooth young voice, but I still heard the power.

He said, "I found this scarf in the place where I first thought of returning them to darkness and I knew it was a sign." He folded up the white silk scarf and put it quietly back in his pocket.

"A sign of what?" An unsafe question. But one interviews with questions.

"Kali Druga has returned, I thought. But I was wrong. It is the sign of the other one. The Dark Christ asked for those souls. I know him now, for I have met others who know also. They do as I do. And we are sure who it is that we obey." Listening, I felt that shudder of recognition. This was the true group madness, contagious. It could inflame a nation to drown itself in instinct.

I am a reporter and a writer of articles. One does not turn the person one interviews over to the police. Making arrests is a job for the police. I get stories, write them, and get them into print.

In the phone booth it was close and sweaty, listening to the fan whir and the operator distantly speak, negotiating a reverse-charges call to *World Pix*. The phone line cleared and the editor answered.

"What's on your so-called mind, Tom? And where are you?"

I used to work for him on assignment, but steady work interfered with my drinking time, so I had quit and gone back to free lance. I knew what his magazine needed and liked.

"Brad, I've just run across a new religious cult of murderers. Would you buy a special?"

"Great. I'll bump a rehash of Nazi horrors for it. We're crying for good material. When can you get it to me? I need it yesterday. The galleys are at the printers already."

"Maybe tonight. I'm attending a meeting."

"Get at that typewriter! We'll make it a series. Never mind about facts for the first part. Just rehash Kali and Beal and Freud. Finish the first part and get it in tonight. Attend your meeting and get cooked and eaten next week. Okay?"

I laughed and hung up.

It was dark, it smelled of dead fish and harbor fog, and the oil of ships. The alley pavement was broken, and mud sucked at one foot when I shifted position. The boy Haran was a shadow on one side of me and two taller lads were shadows on the other side. I could hear them breathing, but they said nothing. I had not asked their names;

one never asked names when reporting crime. They had assured me that I would see a service to the Dark Christ.

"How many worshipers are there?" I asked, wondering where the others were.

"Twenty here. Others in the city across the river."

"When are they coming here?"

"We only need three for service. Sometimes only one." I saw the flash of a white scarf dangling from a hand in the dark. The tallest one had answered.

It sounded like a killing. I said uneasily, "No rough stuff right in front of me, okay? I just want to see a service to the Dark Christ."

"It is the same Christ," said the tall one. "Christ and Krishna died to also show us the way to die. Our service is to him and all mankind. We serve anyone who comes to us for help."

It still sounded like a killing was scheduled for that night. I wondered who. "How do you pick them?"

"They volunteer."

"How do they volunteer?"

Haran's soft voice answered. "They come to the altar over there."

It looked something like a large block of stone, a lighter square against a black mass of the windowless warehouse wall.

"They can find their way."

Haran murmured, "The human soul is wise. It knows when it is weary of being clothed in flesh. It leads a man to us."

Far away a slot of light showed the entrance to the alley. People walked past that slot of light, auto headlights flashed by it, and in the distance a neon sign flickered. I saw a man stop at the entrance, hesitating. I hoped he would not come in.

"We help the weak who are too weak to taste fully of life, and continue on, without experience, only because they are afraid to die. Christ will open the door at which they stand too timid to knock. They will be able to leave without blame, offending no one, breaking no law against suicide, issued gently into nothing and nothing. They have passed their lives swaddled in safety and comfort for their bodies. They have found comfort without thought; their selves are washed clean and blank. Their bodies can pass into nothingness without pain and leave not a ripple of soul behind."

It was a clear, compelling picture. It made murder sound kind. Haran was a poet, a prophet, a Saint Paul of Death. He was starting here in the alleys of this city, but the worship he started could spread to engulf the world. The distant man at the entrance to the alley entered and began to walk toward us, his gait uncertain and stumbling.

"How did you choose this place for worship?" I asked.

"In any city we choose a stone in a dark place, a stone that looks like an altar. When the dark spirit says yes, it becomes his altar. We wait beside the altar and pray for the souls of who comes to us."

"Always the one who offers himself to the Dark Christ comes and stands beside the altar and waits."

I heard the others murmur agreement, but I protested. "But how do you know? Suppose a man is going somewhere else, and just stops. He's not offering himself for . . . for . . ."

The distant stranger still advanced toward us, away from the light. His gait was uncertain. He braced himself by one hand against the wall and groped with his feet for the pavement.

"This alley leads nowhere else."

The victim fumbled along the wall, going step by step into what must have seemed bottomless blackness. He did not know he was clearly outlined against the slot of light behind him. I thought of warning him. My companions on either side were killers. If I yelled they could overtake their victim even if he started to run, and they would kill me. I would die in the dark with no medals for heroism.

I decided not to yell, and hoped that the victim was some miserable bum dying of drink and malnutrition, with vomit on his clothes, for whom killing would be quick mercy.

The young killers were shadows on either side of me, saying nothing and waiting as the man advanced. The silhouetted figure advanced almost to us, then walked out of the light toward the altar. He coughed. He cleared his throat. He spoke nervously. "Where are you, kiddo? I saw you come in here. I'm not mad really. I won't hurt you. You can keep the money you took out of my money belt."

He took two more steps and stopped, with the altar a ghostly square of white stone behind him.

"Peace be with you," Haran said, and began to chant in a language I did not recognize.

The man was a shadow before the altar, his voice a lonely sound in the dark. "I know you're here, kiddo, I hear you singing. I won't hurt you. I liked you. You liked me, didn't you?"

One of my three companions left my side.

The silk scarf of Kali was used by the Thuggs as a killing weapon in the time two centuries ago when Thuggee was practiced as a religion. It was looped over the head of the victim and given a quick pull that broke the neck.

A tugboat whistled on the river, a liner hooted a reply. I heard the dull crack of bone breaking.

Far away the slot of light led to the orderly, busy parts of the city. No one else darkened that slot. No one entered.

The electric typewriter typed quietly and rapidly as if recording someone else's thoughts. I wrote, "Christ the Preserver has ruled long and long, and he has succeeded, there are many preserved, crowds and multitudes of humankind. They are protected and do not need either courage or wisdom, they do not struggle, they neither win nor lose. They feel neither challenge nor triumph, they do neither evil nor good. They seek comfort which is nothingness, and they fear hunger and live in satiety which is nothingness. They exist without experience, and fear experience. They deserve neither Heaven nor Hell; those alive enough to be afraid are in Hell, live on the edge of the avalanche, and are afraid to move. The protected have neither friends nor enemies, strangers protect them, because the preserving Christ commanded it. In all his names, as Krishna, as Buddha, he commanded that the strong protect and preserve strangers."

I stopped and read it back. It sounded like Haran's voice and his thinking. I typed, "The preserving Christ has accumulated these people on Earth. Earth is overlade. The destroying Christ is God's other hand and he has come to clear them away and make room.

"In the name of mercy. Down certain lonely alleys, in dark and secret places between buildings, those who do not know how to live and are afraid to die, they can find nothingness. The New Christ is merciful. He will not inflict eternal life on the weary. Nothingness is comfort."

Much later, in daylight, I was sleeping.

The phone rang in the hotel room. I rolled over and put the pillow on top of my head. The phone stopped ringing and then started again. I picked it up and brought it under the pillow and laid the receiver on the bed beside my ear and went back to sleep.

Sometime later the voice shouting in my ear brought me back.

"We can't print it like this. What are you trying to do, convert everyone to Thuggee? All the nancy pressure groups hate this kind of stuff!"

"It's the way they think," I said, remembering the young men with scarves waiting in the dark. "It's the way they think."

"You wrote it like it was the way you think, you boob."

"So add quote marks," I said. The pillow held the phone near my ear. The bed was soft against my face.

"Did you see a service?"

"Yes. They used a white scarf and killed a man, just like I wrote it. Look up Kali worship. Very same."

"Who did they kill?"

"Unidentified man." It didn't seem too important. "About five feet ten, weight about a hundred and forty, age about a tired thirty. Well off, good black suit, good shoes. Broken neck. He'll be raked out of the river today or tomorrow. Condolences. Not sure he volunteered. Sorry."

After a while the phone was buzzing the notices of an empty line.

I reached in under the mattress, almost falling over the edge of the bed, and felt a crumpled wad of oily paper that was money. The bundle of green stuff testified that they had trusted me and bought by counting the pages without even reading it. They would print my article. It would come out a little neater and more coherent than I had written it, with the statement of the Dark Christ Religion put neatly into quote marks. Someone else would add the Freudian crap, and the sociological crap, explaining the sources of murder within the person as suicide turned outward, the population pressure as a social source of the impulse to kill, felt within the crowded individual. They would frame the story with a long view of the history of other times killing had appeared as a religious impulse. They could do it as easily as I could. My interview with the young assassins, with what they said and thought, that would be unchanged, presented clearly as an interview. Interview by Thomas Barlan.

That was a name they would remember. The other photo journalists and pressmen knew me too well and made fun of my name but they did not make fun of my interviews. Tom of Lower Bar Country had struck again. With the bills clutched comfortably in my fingers I fell asleep.

I woke up at sundown in the expensive hotel room, with a golden haze of sunset over the city. I was hungry, empty, shaky, and happy; and sober. I showered and shaved, and went down to the most expensive restaurant in the hotel, started breakfast with a cafe royal, and then ordered the greatest breakfast that they had on the menu.

After the third cup of coffee the back of my neck began to prickle. The feeling of sitting next to a live volcano about to blow returned, and stood my fur up along my arms. Kali worship, Death worship, a match in a fireworks factory.

The world was overpopulated, and the needs of living quietly together had made violent men into mice. An explosion of Kali worship would spread. It would change to simple murder, by killers choosing the most helpless and easily felled victims, with "mercy" an excuse for murder. An explosion of this sort would solve the population problem but it would kill the mice and leave the wolves. People who had no taste for violent self-defense would die. Did I want a world of human wolves?

It would not be very different. Half the history of man is the history of wolf-man, which is why humanity has dominated all the other animals of the planet and his history is a history of blood.

Should I try to stop Haran and the others from spreading the worship of the Dark Christ? The decision was yes, but it tightened my breathing. It was already evening. The nightclub orchestra came on and began to play. Maybe it was the last time I would hear it if I decided to turn the Kali cult in to the police. They would kill me.

I ordered some stiff drinks and tried to see an easy answer. Was it stupid to think that one reporter could stop or spread this disease of Death worship? No. The source was Haran. Haran the Indian boy was a light of thought, a poet who spread the love of darkness. Lamp of darkness to the others. He was probably wrong. He was not waiting for the Messiah Christ to come, he was the Messiah of the new religion himself, the spokesman for Death who would make Death into a god.

If Haran died this young, he would be forgotten and the movement would stop. Murder would continue in the world, but not organized murder, and Death would not again become a god. I should kill Haran, the boy with beautiful dark eyes and the innocent sculptured mouth. The police would not arrest him. His family would protect him. His family was influential. If I forced an arrest he would be released on bail.

I would die.

I listened to the orchestra, ordered a steak and a double shot of good Irish. I needed to fill up with good food to make up for last week's concentration on drinking, and I needed to fill up on whiskey to change my line of thinking. Only sober thinking could get me so crazily involved with problems of responsibility and world history. As the drinks arrived I wondered what the effect of my article would be. *What are you trying to do, convert everyone to Thuggee?* I tossed the drinks down quickly before turning my attention to the steak.

Thomas Barlan was a good reporter. A reporter's job was to report. He had no responsibility for the effects of reporting. That was a problem for ministers and social scientists and policemen. Thomas of Lower Bar Country had one job, to go into Lower Bar Country and find news, and drink.

I watched the reporter that was connected with my body try to drown thought in drink and get back to the happy blind reporter.

The problem was easily taken care of. Drink. Never so great.

Never so high before. The world was pretty and more pretty, shapes without meaning, a pattern of colors like clouds at sunset . . . Outside into cooler air . . . Dark outside, streetlights, colors of lights from neon signs. The shapes not solid.

The reporter, I, moved through the world of patterns trying to remember something he should be finding, something he should do when he found it. The shapes around him, the reporter, not solid, like letters, Egyptian picture language. The world is a message from God written in Egyptian picture letters in an unknown tongue. A language half remembered. The shapes whispered meanings, and they seemed to mean more away from the brightest lights.

I found a dark corner and stood swaying on the edge of the sidewalk, watching the distant neon signs reflected in a street made shiny by rain. Eventually the sidewalk and walls grew solid again and the lights were merely reflected advertisements, so I went into the nearest bar and had some more Irish whiskey and some Benedictine to celebrate the meal of the week. No one inside said anything that seemed to be a story.

When he/I came out the signs did not mean anything, just colors and meaninglessness was best, and he went floating along on legs that did not quite reach down to the sidewalk, away from lights that seemed too bright, toward the cool darkness and the sound of tugboats where I remembered there was a story.

Along a sidewalk, following the sound of tugboats, and the smell of fish as a faint sometimes smell whenever the wind shifted. Past a dark street entrance that led downhill into darkness. The tugboats hooted from that direction. I turned back and went cheerfully lurching and fumbling down the hill toward the tugboats.

"Shlow up go right into the river," I said and laughed at the idea going swimming and, laughing into the darkness around him, braced his hand against a table-sized block of stone and stopped.

Behind him he heard a boy's musical voice say something in a strange language, and then in English, Haran, saying, "We thank you, sair, for your offer of yourself. We were praying for you." He imagined he saw young, sympathetic faces around him, sympathetic but mistaken. But it was too black; he could see nothing.

Trying to speak, felt the caress of white silk around his neck.

Introduction to Motherbeast

In terms of numbers, two themes dominated the submissions to this book: childbirth and death. Many of the death stories dealt with the pain of separation; many of the childbirth stories were set in an over-populated world where breeding is state regulated and concerned the conception of an illegal baby.

In a sense, "Motherbeast" is both a childbirth and a death story, but it certainly doesn't follow either of the themes above.

I didn't need Kathleen Sky's letter to tell me this story has a spe-cial meaning to the author. I quote from her comments on the story because I think they add a dimension to the work:

> I have used stories in the past to get rid of some of the clutter in my mind and to express emotions that would be impossible to get out any other way. In "Motherbeast" I am repaying a debt to Dr. Eric Berne (author of *Games People Play*) for teaching me that everyone has small voices at the back of his mind and that we are all "Parent, Child and Adult" at one and the same time. This story is written for my Child.

Motherbeast

by KATHLEEN SKY

The grave was deep so that the night skulkers could not tear the flesh from her body. Several hours of labor had gone into lining the walls of the pit with smooth stones dampened by his sweat and tears.

MIRI!

Behind the grave the furrows of the wheat field pointed dusty fingers at the distant mountains where the sun was impaling itself on a jagged peak. At the base of the hills, scattered farms fireflied in the twilight. Night came quickly on this world, soon two of the three

moons would rise; their light would fall on her new home. Miri, Miri,
MIRI!

The man jumbled rocks and earth down onto the homemade
coffin. A nightbeast screamed in the distance as he tamped the dirt
into place and piled stones over the barren mound.

When they had plighted twoing in the compound of the Confed-
eration Immigration Center she had promised never to leave him.
"For eternity," she had said, looking up at him with her yellow eyes.
Where she was from, he never knew: Miri had called herself the universe's child. The C.I.C. didn't care about race or background, they
had more potential colonists than the department could ever hope to
thoroughly process and they had quickly judged Miri fit. She had
come to a raw planet, had worked hard, lived with him, loved him,
and died. Three years.

Miri . . .

Dragging his shovel behind him, he walked through the field to the
prestplast hut. It was empty now, except for the child; a girl with eyes
of black marble—his eyes, not Miri's.

The baby was restless, pulling its legs up to its chin then shoving
them down to touch the end of the box it had been casually tossed
into.

It wept, throwing out its arms in a position for crucifixion: a mew-
ing scream tore from its throat while its body jerked with angry convulsions.

The man picked up the child, clumsily trying to soothe it as he
checked for dampness. The baby squirmed in his arms, beating at his
chest with small hands. It yelled again, shrill with pain; its face
screwed up in agony. The man rocked it, cooing nonsense noises at it
as the child trembled with outrage.

The cries slowed and became choked gasps, purple-blue shadows
circled the child's mouth as it fought for breath. The baby went limp,
sighed—took a deep breath and opened her bright yellow eyes.

MIRI!

*"Look, mother, why don't you let me out for a while, do you think
I'll get lost or something?"*

*"There is no need for you to get outside, all that is there can safely
be viewed through my eyes; I have your best interests at heart, and I
know exactly what you should be permitted to do."*

*"You have only your own needs in mind—I can tell don't try to lie
to me."*

"*How could I? Little one, admit you are as selfish as I am; you too think only of yourself—*"

"*I learned that from a good teacher, mother dear. I've had sixteen years of you on top of me, isn't that enough to give me some idea of real selfishness? You never once let me out; you've made every decision, and you never even ask me how I feel about anything. Why don't you just let me be alone for a change?*"

"*You don't know what you are asking—you have never been alone—*"

"*I know that! I've never once moved an arm or leg by myself; everything I've seen, heard or felt has been filtered through your mind first. I want a chance at my own destiny; is that really so much to ask?*"

"*But you haven't the vaguest idea of what might be right for you, or for me either—I am only trying to make the best decisions in a situation that is, at the least, very unusual. In return, I should like some slight degree of understanding from you—or is that too much to expect from my only child?*"

"*You bloody beast—*"

"*My, we are petulant, aren't we? Where did you find an expression like that?*"

"*In the same place I get all of my vocabulary, mother dear—in your filthy mind.*"

"*I may have knowledge of such words, but I never had cause to use them.*"

"*Twitch-witch-sleamsucker—BROTHERJUMPER!*"

"*Stop that! Or I will be forced—*"

"*Slothouse-treem-Son of Anathoth—or you'll do what, shut me away in a closet? You've already kept me locked away for sixteen years, what more could you do that you haven't done so far?*"

"*Do you know how it feels having you in my mind—no, you wouldn't. Why didn't you die as you should have? It would have made things so much easier for everyone—*"

"*SLUT!*"

"*Try to understand my position; I had to have a body, and it is the nature of my species to use the bodies of others to fulfill our needs. I would not have used yours if I might have avoided it, but in this godforsaken colony yours was the only infant body close enough to take over.*"

"*PARASITE!*"

"*I wish you would refrain from emotional outbursts, they make dealing with you so unpleasant, and they are damnably uncomfortable to endure—must you yell?"*

"S-C-U-U-M! Mother, are you quite sure your comfort is of any importance to me?"

"It should be. Remember, I have full control of this body—what will happen to you if I go mad from the strain of your adolescent uproars?"

"Small chance. You're not about to let go that much. I might take over if you did."

"And we can't let you do that, can we?"

"YOU FILTHY BEAST!"

"There, you're doing it again. You were such a good child when you were younger—it had to be a baby, can't you see that? The personality, the id if you will, had to be weak, unformed. Child, why couldn't you have been co-operative and died as any other being would have? You are disgustingly abnormal—"

"It's because I'm your daughter—what other reason would I need?" The secondary mind shifted position, twisting back on itself; the small corner of Miri's mind allotted to it sometimes itched like the too small skin of a snake about to shed. *"I'm your daughter,"* it continued, *"but you cared so little for me that you could take my body without the slightest concern for what might happen to me—"*

"But you were only a baby, not yet even a person—" Miri's mind brought into focus an image of a pale, squashy fetus floating in her womb.

"Parasite! You know I was far more advanced than that—"

"Well, it's all been so long ago—"

"A month or more I was out of your body—I was beginning to feel, to enjoy my surroundings—I wanted very much to live. Someday, mother, I intend to take everything back, and when I do I won't care a damn about you—"

"It is not possible for you to do so. You see, I have complete control over everything you or this body does, and I will manage to keep it that way. Unfortunately I do have to listen to your continual whining, but then I try to be patient with you—it's a mother's duty to—"

"OH SHOVE!"

"I sometimes wonder," Miri's part of the mind was wistful, *"if you're really not there at all. I could be going mad—and you are nothing more than an illusion—a small voice of misguided conscience as it were—"*

"Conscience? You bloodsucking Vampire, you haven't got one, or if you did, you wouldn't keep doing this to me. Miri, go right on

thinking you've got full control of us, then one of these fights you're
going to be in for a little surprise—"

Miri smiled.

After her bath Miri stood naked in front of a mirror. Turning from
side to side, she admired the mounds and valleys that made up the
body. There was a drop of bath-oiled water in her navel: gently she
smoothed it out and onto her silky skin. She raised her arms above
her head, stretching her rib cage and pulling upwards the already
high-placed breasts.

"Well, even if it is mine, I must admit you do take rather good
care of the body."

Miri laughed deep in her throat; it wasn't the high-pitched giggle of
a barely mature girl but the sound of a sensual woman fully grown
and knowing. *"My body, always mine, remember that, Little One."*

There was a sigh from the dark corner of Miri's mind; the small
one was stirring, preparing itself for another screaming match. Miri
enjoyed her conversations with the voice, child, conscience or whatever it was. She knew, or hoped, she had the upper hand, but there
was a slight element of doubt, a chance of someday slipping and losing control to the Little One.

Then too, it was amusing, something to pass the time when there
was nothing of more importance to do. If the voice became a bother,
she could simply stop listening—block it out.

The situation of dual personality had never occurred among her
people as far back as Miri could recall, and her mind went back
through many bodies. Never had one of her race invaded a body in-
habited by one of their own kind; to do so was forbidden. But if a
new body was not found and taken quickly, the being died with the
old body. Miri had not wished to die, and her child's body had been
close enough for a transfer of id—but the child had not died.

Miri found she relished the fights with the stunted child-mind she
carried, it gave her a sense of power that was frightening in its intensity.

The duels would continue.

Miri chuckled, running her hands down over her hips. "Beautiful,"
she murmured, tilting her head to study the curve of chin and throat.
Then, cupping her breasts carefully, she stroked them, purring to herself. "Lovely, and it has been far too long for either of us. . . ." She
smiled, remembering something from the past, her past.

"What are you thinking?" A worried probe shivered out of the Lit-

tle One's quarters. *"Mother, I don't understand this emotion, please explain!"*

"Thinking? Why surely you know, my little voice! Do we not share the same thoughts? I have a loving husband who has been waiting most patiently, a perfectly splendid body, and, to be sure, the knowledge that goes with them." She laughed, making yellow cat's eyes at herself in the glass.

"My body—my father."

"But it will be me that pleasures him, Little One."

"NO! You can't do that, it's my body—"

"But his kind have rules; if he believed that you, or I, were really his child he wouldn't touch me, and that would be such a waste—"

"Of course he knows I'm his child—you died!"

"Ah. Tell me, does he act as if I'm a child? Don't be silly, I am his wife, I have been and always will be his wife. It is so convenient, the powers of the human mind; he wants me alive, me Miri, so Miri I am to him. I was small then large again. To him such things are the natural cycle of my people. You never existed for him, or if he thinks of you at all, you are some poor babe who rests in a grave at the edge of his wheat fields. Why he can't even remember your name—that is, if you ever had one—"

"Yes, blast you, I did have a name; he gave it to me! It's . . . it's . . ."

"Do go on, I'm listening with great interest."

"HE DID GIVE ME A NAME. I KNOW HE DID!" Miri/the child felt a twinge of vertigo as their minds rocked with the force of the child's outburst.

"Oh, that's quite possible, but then, it really doesn't matter very much now." Miri slipped a green robe loosely around the body, enjoying the feeling of the silky fabric on the breasts as she arranged the neckline so that it would gap open to the waist. He had bought it for her, Miri, out of hard-earned credits, she would make the expense worthwhile. Miri tied the sash around her hips, tugging the fringed edge to one side so that it hung down over one hip, swaying as she moved. *"If he gave you a name, which I doubt, he doesn't remember it at all. And—I'm sure—neither do you!"* Miri hugged the body, pleased with the cleverness of her own retorts.

"He wouldn't touch you if he knew I was here." The child's voice whispered over and over with the sibilance of a martyr's prayer. *"If I could get out—if I could tell him—"* The voice continued as Miri walked down the hall and into her husband/father's bedroom.

"Mother, please—please!" The child had switched tactics in mid-stride. *"Please, by whatever gods you believe in, please, mother— MOTHER! Tell him I'm here too, let him know that it's my body. Don't let him do that without knowing I'm here! MOTHER!"*

Miri wasn't listening.

A corner of the room. A bed. A chair. Everything in the room was distorted by the dim tunnel vision Miri had left for the small one. It nudged Miri's mind trying to get her to adjust the focus. No answer from Miri.

Her/their father, smiling, kissing, touching, caressing their/her body. Miri/the body kissing, caressing in return. The small one felt the sensations of the body like some dim dream. They were Miri's feelings, Miri's sensations. There was a twitch of neuron activity, a sensual writhing of Miri's mind into flowing patterns, glowing colors. Erotic vibrations rocked the body and the mind of the parasite. The child felt nothing except what it observed. No joy, no pleasure. Nothing.

"It's my body," the voice stubbornly repeated. No answer. It felt the edges of Miri's mind. No response. It spread itself like a leech over the barriers Miri had put up against it. It became a foglike jelly, thinner, thinner, spreading, leaking into Miri's mind—pushing . . .

CONTACT!

Color-light-the ceiling-her father's face-Miri's mind! There was a flow of data from the skin, hair roots and internal structures. More flashes of sensation, more nerves tightening with pleasure. Feelings and a jumble of emotions danced through her/their mind. The small one felt sensations rising like a tide in Miri's soul. Buffeted by waves, flying before the storm, rushing over, under and through the crannies of the mind, the small one felt fear for its own safety. Debris, old thoughts, disjointed sentences and fragments of feelings battered at it, bruising, and bringing an aching pain that it alone could feel.

The flood rose higher, then higher still. The mind streams burst from their old paths, forming new ones. The peak of the storm came howling through the body, devastating in its power. Emotions peaked, joined whirlpools of exaltation, and the frail chip that was the small one's id rolled in the foam of the backswell. The waves were out of control—up—no, down and back, then up again, up UP. . . .

Suddenly it was over. Peace, dry beachheads and a smooth calm filled Miri's mind. Small one, a bit of flotsam, rested on an emotion-lapped shore.

The mind was empty of Miri. The small one found no sign of the parasite's control, even over her, Miri's, part of the entity. Small one flexed, feeling, touching the tired nerve endings, smoothed down the ruffled clusters of brain cells, and went looking for Miri. . . .

She lay sprawled on the bed, the robe bunched under her sweat-slicked hips, her sash flung carelessly across the end of the bed. Miri cat-stretched, her eyes glazed with deep satisfaction. "Ummm," she purred, enjoying the warm happiness sliding over the body.

"VAMPIRE!"

The voice was cold, harsh. Miri sat up suddenly, not quite sure of its origin.

"You filthy witch! *Blast you, Miri, damn you for the wretched mother that you are."*

The hard voice rolled like boulders through her head. Miri pulled the wrinkled robe tightly around the body, covering herself. Her eyes were big with alarm and wonder.

Mouth slack, spittle dripping from one corner, she tried to block out the hammering hail of the sound of the voice in her mind. *"I can end you, Miri. I know how to kill you now and I will—in time. You just go on, do what you please with our body, but in time—Vampire, in time . . ."*

Miri listened to the voice whispering obscenities until it ceased entirely.

As the months passed, Miri listened for the voice, but it never came. She sent thoughts, insults, compliments and even promises of a chance to take control once in a while, back deep into that part of the mind where she knew that the other personality had been. Her only answer was a faint twitch along her nerve endings which might have been a hibernating animal turning over in its sleep.

Miri's mind was constantly looking inward, watching for the movements of the child within her mind and the one that was now growing in her womb. For the first time, she felt afraid.

The pains were coming more frequently now. Miri was on her back, relaxed. The jump of a needle on the panel beside her hospital bed was the only sign of the ordeal her body was going through. Miri knew vaguely that there was pain, but she seemed incapable of feeling or reacting to it. Placid and uncaring, she awaited the birth of her first/second child.

"Weak, you're weak, Miri." The voice was soft, taunting.

Miri, even drugged as she was, could still react to the fact that her mind child had returned. The empty feeling in her back mind was now gone. With almost hysteric joy she greeted it. *"You're back, Little One! Oh, how I've missed you—how could you go away like that? I've been so worried about you— Ah, little voice, little voice,"* she crooned.

"You're weak," the voice continued inexorably. *"You have lost, Miri, and y-o-o-o-o-u don't have that full control anymo-o-o-o-o-re."* For the first time in its existence the voice laughed: a nasty triumphant sound. *"Did you know that each time you bedded with my father, while you rested I worked? I played with a ganglion here, took over a motor cluster there—and I tested—oh, most carefully—until I knew what my abilities were. Now you are too feeble from birthing to fight me off. It's my turn now, Miri!"*

"But I tried to tell you several times or more, if you want to run the body once in a while, I'd let you, really I would."

"Is this the way it happened before? Did you lose your last body this way, Miri? All because of having me, was that the way of it?"

"The body died, I didn't know why—it died, remember that it died."

"I won't let this one die, it's mine—and Im going to be the only one running it."

"Please, you don't know what you're doing!" Now it was Miri's turn to plead as she fought to gather up what strength she could to keep possession of a body which she had, up until now, never seriously worried about losing. *"You don't want this body to die too, you couldn't. Please, wait until afterwards—after I have the baby, we can work something out—please, wait!"*

"There was only you last time in that body, but now it's you and I. Two of us and only one body—my body, Miri, and you're tired, too weak to keep it now. Give up, Miri—"

The needle of the indicator panel began to fluctuate wildly: the EEG reading was impossible to follow, and a bell began to clatter alerting the medical staff that help was needed in a case that should have been routinely simple.

Now there were two armadas, two powerful forces that moved through the waters of Miri's mind, destroying as they went, turning it into a graveyard.

The child-mind grabbed, pulled, twisted. The arms, legs and head of the body jerked in a hellish, uncontrolled rhythm. The child could activate actions but could not co-ordinate them; a baby trying to walk, speak and swim all at the same time would have been more graceful than the child/Miri.

Nerves ripped from their channels, snapping free in the winds of destruction that was the body. Blood pressure dropped, the heartbeat fluttered madly. The body was dying but Miri and the child-mind still lived.

"I'll kill you, Miri, the body is mine, mine!" The child raked madly through the remainder of the medulla oblongata ripping axons from cell bodies, causing convulsions to ripple, down the spine to meet and meld with the turmoil of birthing.

"No, child, I can escape you. Here, the body is yours! Die with it, you hellborn brat—"

"It's mine already. I don't need you to tell me so. I don't need you, Miri—Miri?"

Miri was gone, leaving the child-mind to run screaming through the dying body. Miri was gone and the body was dying. The child-mind was dying with it but the body had one owner—Miri was not there any longer. The parasite had no need of a dying body or of the child it had shared it with.

The baby, struggling to be born, felt the quake and destruction around it, but was not yet able to comprehend its meaning. The dying convulsions of its mothers sent the child's bloody body spewing into the hands of the waiting doctor, who then held it aloft by its feet like some obscene trophy, slapping its bottom and introducing it to both pain and the outer world.

Mucus running from nose and mouth, the baby screamed in protest, twisting in the doctor's grip, sunfishing violently, trying to escape.

The doctor expertly upended the child, cradling it in his arms as it stopped crying and slowly opened its bright yellow eyes.

Introduction to Escape to the Suburbs

Rachel Cosgrove Payes is a prolific writer who works in a variety of forms. Her twenty-nine published novels include science fiction, mysteries, gothics, and a sequel to the *Oz* books of L. Frank Baum. She also does a good deal of short fiction. I think she is the only member of S.F.W.A. (Science Fiction Writers of America) who is also the mother of a member. The Payes family is a talented one. Rachel and Rob (mother and son) write, Ruth (daughter) is a very talented artist, and Norman (father) is an excellent photographer. They are also some of the nicest people I know.

Escape to the Suburbs

by RACHEL COSGROVE PAYES

"We'll never get away with it, Juan."

"Come on, Willie. Ain't you and me soul brothers?"

The youth nodded solemnly, his Masai braids swinging over a black forehead. He was taller than Juan, heavier muscled, stronger; but his wiry soul brother had the brains. Willie acknowledged Juan's superiority, bowed to his judgment.

"We can make it, Willie, we can escape."

Willie rolled fearful eyes until only the whites showed. "Man, doan let no one hear you say them words." His voice dropped to a whisper. "Escape to the suburbs? How?"

They were plowing through the fetid masses downtown. It was nearing noon, and there was a surge of humanity, hot and malodorous, toward the feeding stations.

Willie tugged at Juan's arm. "Man, you're headed wrong. The algae cake station's over that way."

"Come on, Willie. We gotta talk—private."

Talk private—what a laugh. Where on the whole island fortress of Manhattan was there privacy, except in the towers? The teeming millions bred and lived and died in each others' pockets. After the final pull-out, when city government gave up and fled to Jersey, the masses who were left quit taking the pills and produced bumper crops of babies. They talked of increasing their power by increasing their numbers—they'd take over whitey—make the suburbs their own—live high. But all they did was make the island a hell of population density.

Juan maneuvered his way into a doorway, ousting the couple there with a show of his flick knife. "Come on, Willie. We gotta talk. We're gonna get off this island."

"Man, you can't do it. It's guarded all the way. Look what happened to Lil and Sammy just last week. Tried to swim it, and those whitey guards on the Jersey shore spitted 'em like fish."

"Not gonna swim it, Willie. I know the patrols ain't blind. And I doan wanna be speared—nor shredded with a grenade. What's the point of escapin' if we get killed? Use your head for somethin' more'n a holder for those pigtails, man," and he reached up and gave a tug on one of Willie's braids, making his soul brother yelp in anguish.

"Ouch, that hurts. Anybody but you, Juan—"

"Peace, brother. About our escape."

Willie shuddered. Just talking about escape brought goose bumps out on him, even though it was August, and the heat and humidity bore down on him like a collapsed wall. Tempers were short, fights common. There were many who didn't make it through a Manhattan August—a lot of flesh around. Rumor had it that not all bodies got dropped into the rivers. Some went into soup pots instead of rat meat. And escape was dangerous. The Bronx patrolled—New Jersey killed without challenging—Brooklyn guarded its borders jealously. The tunnels and bridges had been blown when the last city government forces fled secretly in the night, leaving the masses trapped and embittered. It wasn't safe to mention escape to the suburbs. If the word got around that you had a sure-fire method, every gang on every block tried to torture your secret from you.

"Willie, we fly out of this hellhole."

"Man, you've flipped. Whatta we do—sprout wings like the pigeons? Soar like the gulls?"

"Naw. We use hang gliders."

Willie made a deep, disgusted sound, a growl, at the back of his throat. "Glide. Come on, Juan. They tried it just last week. I seen 'em, and so did you. Potted 'em in the air, busted up them gliders with machine guns. They fell like stones into the East River."

"True, man, true. They was dummies. Do they think they can fly low over the water and not get caught?"

It had been the Forked Devils who'd tried it. They'd made gliders —worked on them for weeks, guarding their enclave, a rotting pier, with the ferocity of ancient robber barons. Willie and Juan had spied on them from a vantage spot in one of the crumbling towers. Juan even had a little telescope he'd rigged himself. He was clever at making things, and scrounging the stuff to make them. The Forked Devils had built their gliders from bamboo struts—electrical conduit they'd pulled from the walls of decaying buildings—wood they'd pried from door facings—driftwood—sheets of plastic they'd stolen from the tenters, who would wake to find their homes gone from over their heads. Then they made huge wings—deltas, mostly. And practiced flying by taking off along the crumbling remains of the East River Drive. When the wind was right, some of them lifted as much as twenty feet. One stayed aloft five minutes, dangling from straps under his armpits. They practiced takeoffs, they soared, they turned and glided and landed. And all the time, the spies on the other bank watched and waited.

"Juan, I doan wanna fly."

"Willie, we're soul brothers. I wouldn't be happy living in the suburbs without you."

"This is all in your head, escape to the suburbs. I'd never manage there—I'm too black. You—" He reached out a big black hand and touched Juan's cheek with the gentleness of a mother. "You could pass, there."

"Willie, I'll kick in your fool head. There's plenty of blacks escaped, before the tunnels blew."

"I doan believe it."

"True. I talked with an old man, must be nearly sixty, miracle he's still alive, he's so ancient. He tole me about it—he was alive when the tunnels blew."

"Nobody's that old, Juan."

"Willie, I doan lie to my soul brother. This old man, hair white, can't hardly move, his little grandson gets the algae cakes for him at the feeding station, this old man says lots of blacks in the suburbs."

Willie shrugged. "Still doan make no diff. We can't fly and you know it, Juan."

"Can, too. Gotta start out high, thas all. Fly way over their heads, so high they won't even see us."

Juan's voice was low and persuasive. Willie protested; but all the time he was saying "no," he knew in his heart that he'd do whatever Juan wanted. They'd been together all their lives. If Juan escaped, Willie knew he'd have to go, too. He couldn't live without Juan. If Juan were gone, he'd just lie down in the street and die.

"Okay, Juan, I'll listen. But I ain't promisin'."

Willie saw that smile on Juan's face, a kind of sly twisting of full lips. Anybody else would worry to see Juan smile that way. It'd spell trouble; but not for Willie. Juan loved him like a brother. Together, with Juan's wits and Willie's brawn, they made a team. Nothin' could stop 'em. Juan kept after Willie all the time—"Think of number one, Willie. Doan worry about the others—just about yourself." It was Juan's philosophy. And Willie agreed out loud; but always added, inside his head, "Think of you, too, Juan. Before me, think of you."

Juan produced two algae cakes he'd acquired somehow, gave one to a hungry Willie, munched the other himself.

"We leave high, Willie. From way up on top of a tower."

Again Willie rolled fearful eyes. He didn't like heights. Some lived fairly high in the old towers; but with power cut off, elevators sat useless except as a family home. Most didn't want to climb too many steps. It ate up energy. And with the meager rations the helos ferried in each day, dropping them at the stations so there'd be no danger of groups overpowering the crews and escaping in the whirlies, you didn't have much energy to waste. Just keeping alive in the city was a full-time job. So most of the tall towers were deserted, falling into disrepair through the years.

"I doan like high places, Juan. You know that."

"Takes both of us to lug the supplies, man. You want me to leave you behind, alone?" There was a hardness in Juan's voice that Willie knew too well. Even with him, the soul brother, Juan could be harsh.

"You know I go with you, Juan." Willie's voice was resigned. For Juan, he'd scale Empire, if Juan said climb.

"First we gotta scrounge." Juan was good at that, better than Willie. But Willie went along, the strong back to carry the supplies. "I watched the Forked Devils, know which gliders work best. Gotta keep 'em light but strong, make a big delta wing. And I doan fancy hangin' high up there in the wind by my arms. Pull 'em outta the sockets. We'll rig us little seats hangin' down from the wing—sit there and fly over the East River in comfort."

Thinking about all that height, dangling beneath a fragile wing of plastic, made Willie feel like vomiting.

"No other way, Juan?"

"No other way."

They spent days assembling materials for two gliders. Toward the end, Juan went scrounging alone, leaving Willie in their hiding place in an odorous sewer to guard what they had already acquired.

"Guard it with your life, man. This stuff gets stolen, I swear I'll cut you up."

"Juan, I'm your soul brother."

"Yeah—so guard with your life."

Sometimes even Willie was afraid of Juan. When he used that low, cold tone it froze Willie's gizzard to a lump of ice inside of him.

The day came when Juan brought back only food.

"Man, we feed good! Where'd you get all them algae cakes?" Willie reached a hungry hand, only to feel a sharp thrill of pain. "Hey, man, you nicked my hand."

"Keep hands off, Willie. We gotta make them cakes last. No more goin' to the feedin' stations. Tonight we climb the tower—and we doan come down, except on wings."

Almost afraid to ask, Willie said, "Which tower?"

"Empire. Wind's off the Hudson, blow us to Long Island."

It was too much for Willie. "You're crazy, Juan. Empire—it goes to the sky. And what happens if the wind blows us out into the ocean? I heard it goes forever, water and water and nothin' else. Fall in there, we're dead."

"You call livin' here alive? I'd rather fall from on top of Empire and squash on the street than live here any longer. You go with me, Willie, or I go alone."

Even as he protested, Willie knew he'd go. He'd probably die—but he'd go wherever Juan led.

Once he made up his mind, Willie turned practical. Juan had the brains, sure; but sometimes he was a dreamer, thinking up schemes that wouldn't work.

"Look, how we get up Empire? They live on the stairs. It's too high to climb the sides."

"And you get sick lookin' down." Again that hard tone that Willie hated and feared. "We fight our way up—one at a time, Willie."

"You're crazy."

"Gotta do it. One stays below to guard the stuff. That's you, man, you're bigger. I work my way above where they live, send down a rope, haul up the stuff."

"And then?"

"You come up alone."

"Man, they doan like strangers, the stair livers."

Juan shrugged. "So cut 'em a little. You're big, Willie. Lean on 'em. If I can make it, so can you."

Willie'd done his share of cutting, but he never liked it. But if Juan said cut, he'd kill a dozen or more.

After dark, they moved, keeping to the sewers until they reached a manhole near Empire. Juan, in the lead, eased the cover and looked cautiously about.

"Come on, Willie. We can make it."

Adept at fading into the shadows, they reached the side of the tower, burdened with their glider materials. Juan paced from the corner, said, "This is where you wait," and was gone.

Willie, back to the wall, one foot on the bundles, knife ready, waited with growing apprehension. It was a mad scheme, doomed to fail. Juan would die on the stairs. There'd be too little air at the top of the tower—he'd heard tales—he fought off one thief, cut a second, and was losing faith when something touched his head. With a gargle of fear, Willie crouched and swung above him, only to find that the attacker was the rope Juan had carried wound about his slender body like a snake.

Nerves jittering, Willie fastened the first bundle and gave three tugs to the rope, their signal. Juan had made it. Once he'd hauled up both bundles, Willie would fight his way through to his soul brother. Then they'd ascend the awesome heights of Empire to the very top.

Willie saw the signs that Juan had passed this way. One dead, at least a dozen bleeding. With his size, with knife on the ready, Willie met little resistance. "Jes' goin' through, doan wanna camp on you," he called at each landing. Ten stories, twenty stories, he toiled. The ranks thinned. Finally a landing with no one living on it—and a whisper from the darkness.

"Willie? Is that you?"

The climb was endless. The bundles were heavy, and even Willie's sturdy legs began to ache.

"Must be in the clouds." He was glad it was dark outside, so that he couldn't see how high they were.

Finally, with dawn just blurring the stars, they reached the top. Juan let Willie rest briefly, they ate a cake, and drank from the plastic jug of water.

"Now we build the gliders."

"Good we can work indoors." Willie refused to go out on the platform to look at the city. He'd watched Juan's long hair blow in the wind. "Come back, Juan. You'll blow away."

"That's what I want to do, man." His eyes gleamed and he exuded an air of recklessness that worried Willie.

Once they set to work on the gliders, though, Juan was all business. He'd even sketched out rough plans, and his skilled fingers assembled the struts of electrical conduit, lashed them together, stretched the plastic taut.

"How we get 'em out the door, Juan?"

Juan gave him one of those "you dummy" looks. "It folds, Willie. Think I'd boxed myself in?"

It was evening when the gliders were finished.

"First thing in the morning, before whitey is awake, we fly."

Juan doled out more cakes and water. They ate in silence, both of them awed by being alone. It made Willie uneasy; for though he hated the horrid crowding down below, this silence, this being able to move without bumping into someone, was unnatural. And the flight tomorrow—he couldn't even think about it. That night Willie's dreams were frightening.

An urgent hand shook him awake. "Time, man. There's a stiff breeze, the sun is up—we fly!"

They soon found the breeze to be a hazard. Willie's folded glider, once he'd maneuvered it outside, was caught by a gust, snapped open, and almost got away from him. Only Juan's quick reflexes saved it.

"Better lash 'em to one of them posts, Willie. Then, when we're ready, in the seats and hanging on, we slash the ropes with our knives and off we go."

Willie stayed near the door, afraid to step far out onto the platform. Looking straight ahead, he saw only the tips of one or two other towers. Beneath his feet he felt the tower sway slightly in the wind, and a rush of nausea almost overwhelmed him.

"Come on, help me with my glider."

Gritting his teeth, Willie angled Juan's folded glider outside, holding it carefully so the wind couldn't fill it too quickly. Juan tethered it, then spread it on the platform and stretched it taut, making the final fastening that kept the frame rigid, made it into a huge delta wing.

"We have to leave from over there, where the parapet has crumbled. Easier than balancing up on that railing."

Willie took one look where Juan was pointing, and his gut knotted with terror. A great gap in the wall left them without any protection. If they fell—

"Juan, I can't—"

"Willie, I'm gonna fly now. If you doan come, you stay here alone."

Juan fitted his arms through the straps and braced himself so that the wind didn't carry him away too soon. Willie followed suit, his knees trembling, swallowing hard to keep down his meager breakfast. Then he followed Juan, shuffling his feet for traction, to the edge of the platform. Willie planned not to look down, knowing it would be disastrous; but some horrid fascination drew his eyes to the panorama stretched out far below him. There lay the city, its towers in ruins, its streets already dotted with the ants he knew had to be people. Vertigo swept over him, and he collapsed to his knees, cowering under the canopy of his hang glider, which filled and tugged in the morning breeze, threatening to sweep him over the edge into that ghastly void.

From above him, Willie heard Juan's voice. "Come on, man, I'm aloft. I'm cuttin' the rope now."

Forcing his eyes open, Willie looked up, not down. There, dangling from the giant kite, hung Juan, his face jubilant, knife in hand ready to slash the tether and free himself for his impossible journey.

"No, doan go, man. You'll die!"

In an agony of fear, Willie slipped out of his glider harness and caught at the taut rope linking Juan to the tower. With powerful hands, he hauled in the glider.

"Leggo!" Juan's voice was cold with anger; but for once, Willie ignored his friend's displeasure.

"Not gonna let you chance it, Juan. I can't fly—and you can't leave me here alone. We're soul brothers."

He reached up one massive arm and caught Juan's foot, tugging at his friend to bring him back, ignoring the drop at his feet, intent only on keeping Juan here with him.

Then there was a glint in the morning sun, and pain seared Willie's hand. Snatching it back, he saw blood drip from a long gash across the black flesh.

"You cut me!" His cry was anguished disbelief.

"Nobody holds me here." Juan's face was contorted, vicious. "I'm flyin' now, Willie. Ain't gonna stay for you—for no one. Gotta look out for number one."

Again the knife flashed, and the breeze caught the glider, lifted it, and swept it away to the west.

The backlash of the tether caught Willie across the face, almost blinding him. He fell to the platform, one arm dangling into the abyss. When his terror abated, he looked into the sky. Far away the black dot soared, as Juan made his escape to the suburbs.

Crying, the tears running down his cheeks unwiped, Willie inched away from the broken parapet to the relative safety of the central platform. The enormity of his solitude crushed him, and he couldn't get to the stairway fast enough. He had to get down from the tower, back into the crush of crowds, back to the security of the masses in the city.

Introduction to Alien Sensation

Creative writing teachers are fond of urging students to write from
their own experience. Josephine Saxton's autobiography includes a
truly wild assortment of experiences in her native England. She writes
that she has been an inspector of woolen socks, a fish filleter, a
brewer's clerk, a chalk marker, a painter of theatrical scenery, a
chambermaid, an artist's model, a bus conductress, an art student, a
wife, a mother, a machine embroiderer, and, of course, a writer. She
is the author of about a dozen novels, three of which Doubleday published: *The Hieros Gamos of Sam and An Smith*, *Vector for Seven*
(which was originally titled *The* Weltanschauung *of Mrs Amelia
Mortimer and Friends*), and *Group Feast*. She's also written a number of short stories which have appeared in both magazines and all-
original anthologies.

Alien Sensation

by JOSEPHINE SAXTON

There was a sound coming from one of the two floating anchorages in
the room. A soft sighing. Zean did not at first acknowledge it from
where she lay on the other float; she did not want to hurry. The
sound continued, growing somewhat in volume and beginning to
shape. It got harder at the edges and eventually, as Zean had known
it would, became her name. In a little while she would reply but first
she must rearrange her body. She took in a breath to gather sufficient
strength and began the long haul. Left arm pressing down, lift a little
and move the buttocks . . . oh, it was so difficult. But it passed time.
Not to hurry. She repeated the process once more and lay stupefied
by the effort, blood thumping through her ears, sweat pouring out but
drying quickly in the continual stream of air that was her floating
bed.

Several minutes passed and she again gathered her resources and decided to answer. Breath rising and vibrating, susurrus coagulating into his name. Raul.

And silence. Ritual silence in which his thoughts waited, expanded, filled time. Then he began. It took him almost twenty minutes, it was masterly the way he used more words than necessary, drew them out, and it was gratifying to her to realize how much effort he put into the actual saying. His technique at passing time was improving over the years, ten years ago he would have taken only two minutes to say:

"What are you doing tonight?"

Having said it, in nineteen, he lay back, resting, and she lay thinking about it. What was she doing tonight? Probably she would decide on an injection for complete unconsciousness, but she had not yet decided. There were millions of things to choose from. All equally boring. In a few months she ought to get her chemistry analyzed again. It could be that her lack of interest in entertainments was due to a slight imbalance somewhere. But it was interesting to notice just how bored she could become with things.

She must answer Raul's polite enquiry. Would she take an entertainment tonight? If she made her wishes known to the little microphone near her head, the right pill would tumble into its little hopper ready for her to swallow, when she had fastened the headset on, and she would begin to experience her pleasure. It could be anything from a Summer Festival where people danced day and night under a blazing sun, or a sex orgy with herself as the object of the lust of several different kinds of animal, including men. She had spent years experiencing sex in every possible variety, it was probably the most lasting of all the sensations that could be offered. But she was bored with it, her own consciousness insisted on piercing through the illusion from time to time. Whilst being raped by a Chinese wrestler only last week her own mind had quite clearly come through, showing her that she was in fact still lying in her own anchorage, eyes closed, thin pale body at rest, as always. That was no fun at all, an entertainment must seem real or it did not pass the time. Yes, a chemical analysis soon, or her mind would be breaking through into other scenes. She did not want to know that she had just been injected with her nourishment when she was deep in the illusion of eating real food. The stuff they actually used to eat thousands of years ago, heavenly food like Grass Protein Veal Steak done in Petroleum Albumen and Seafood Simulate in Algal Yeast . . . oh, those must have been the days, how utterly strange to think of actually chewing, it must have been just like the pill illusions, only real. Yes, life must have been very strange in those days. She decided to take complete unconsciousness sometime during the evening, but . . . first she must answer Raul. To pass the time she did not give him a direct answer, but slowly informed him that:

"There is so much choice of pleasure."

And that was true. Whatever pleasure could be thought of was available for the requesting. And that was what life was for. All her life had been easy, she had had only one unpleasant experience when she had failed to report a faulty air-couch and had begun to develop sores on her back. And yet . . .

Raul was answering. He had almost elected to look at scenery, he said. Panoramas with sunsets, stuff like that. Big elations. Suddenly the room would cease to be and he would become some other standing on a hilltop, inhaling fresh air, seeing beautiful ranges and ranked clouds. She had when she was younger spent several days at a time doing just that but now she was a little tired of it. She was getting old, she was almost nineteen, she wanted to experience something entirely new and fantastic before she died. She was, she thought, unhappy.

In Control they were discussing the recent problems of the indigenous race, the humans. So many of them were choosing complete unconsciousness so often in lieu of pleasure or entertainment, and too much complete unconsciousness resulted in early death. It was becoming epidemic. The law—that all indigenous races were to be kept happy and at peace in their natural ways of life—was in danger of being broken. They were surprised and distressed that Earth of all places should experience trouble of this kind, it had seemed an ideal place to colonize. The humans had had no objection to being colonized just so long as the ideal existence which they had evolved over millennia was not interfered with. And yet, after a hundred years of their life continuing as usual, under discreet supervision by the colonists, things were going wrong. A sociologist was convinced that he had a novelty that would restore their joy in living. In collaboration with a chemist he had produced yet another sensation pill. The head of local Control thought that the sociologist was mistaken.

"It would harm human beings to experience such activity even in facsimile. It would be a completely alien sensation to them."

"But I have been into their entire history, the vestigial extensions must have been suitable for something! I find traces in their chemical make-up—my colleague here assures me—"

"You realize that we are responsible for these human creatures, that they must be allowed to continue in their chosen way of life, that we must not interfere—"

"I will stake *my* life that this is what they require to revitalize them."

"Well, women have not the stamina. Let it be known to one or two of the men first that this experience is available."

"It is available in many thousand forms as you know. What shall I call it?"

"Release it only in a very mild form, and call it what you will. They have no name for it at present."

Raul said, "It has no name. They call it *Experience 8-C*-69,000, and it is experimental—perhaps I would enjoy—"

8-C began with a flat surface that one stood on, wearing peculiar garments of rough material; he found them very uncomfortable. The flat surface was covered in a strange substance. Grey, rough to the touch, sticky in places, and in those places thick enough to obscure other markings on the surface—dim colored markings. There were two objects, one standing on the surface, one in the right hand. How did one play the game? Were there any other players? Wait awhile, it would become clear what to do, the pill had not yet taken full effect. The object in the hand was a rod with a square thing at the lower end, and there was a lever attached. Move the lever. The square of material bent double. To pick up a ball, perhaps, and drop it into the receptacle? He went over to the receptacle and discovered that it was full of foaming liquid with a pale vapor rising off the surface. Utterly new. He began to feel excited. He delicately smelled the gas and it was very strange and beautiful, clean and pure yet completely poisonous at the same time, one could never drink such stuff. And then his thin white body was completely engulfed in the experience, the room and the airbed were no longer real. Here and now, this was it. He knew what to do.

He took the rod and dipped it into the fuming liquid, lifted it out and depressed the lever. Bubbles came oozing out, quite delightful. The square-ish thing attached was now soft and wet. He pushed it back and forth along the flat surface on which he was standing. The sticky and gritty substance moved about, adhered to the square thing and miraculously disappeared, revealing a pattern on the flat surface beneath it. It was clear and shiny, quite wonderful. Dip into the fuming receptacle again, lift out, depress the lever. This time the bubbles were dark! Rub it back and forth, dip it, depress, rub. His skin began to itch, and Raul laughed. Sweating was supposed to be a sign of illness but this was just marvellous! The flat surface was changing even as he took hold of the handle of the receptacle ("the pail," he now knew its name to be) and he lifted it, moved it. Very heavy. Some of the liquid slopped out. There was a pain in the small of his back but it was not exactly bad. Dip and rub, no dip, depress, rub, dip. The pattern he was revealing as he scrubbed was a representation of roses, exquisite, shining. This was what he had longed for, this entertainment was utterly—

The shock of seeing Raul actually sit up and scramble off his airbed had been more than Zean could calmly endure. She had never seen a human being stand upright before. When he began to move his thin arms backwards and forwards, talking—fast—something about a receptacle, "the pail," something about a *mop,* whatever that was—at the same time, it had been too much for her.

She begged Control to tell her what he had suffered, but they explained merely that something had gone wrong, they regretted the impossibility of explaining it further. Oh, Raul had looked horrible standing up, all thin and sagging and a trickle of scarlet running down his nose. Whatever he had done must have been wonderful but terribly dangerous. He had fallen dead of course, as soon as he began to tell her that he had just experienced the most wonderful thing ever.

Solicitous though they were, they could not get her to take to another life-companion. Zean sickened without Raul, and died, too.

Introduction to Last One In Is a Rotten Egg

Grania Davis's first novel, *Dr. Grass,* was published earlier this year. She has written short stories, two children's books, some articles, and a newspaper column. Married and the mother of two children, she lives in California, but has traveled extensively, most recently spending four months in a Tibetan refugee camp in Northern India doing volunteer work.

There is a comment I would like to make regarding "Last One In Is a Rotten Egg," but in this case, I will do it as an Afterword.

Last One In Is a Rotten Egg

by GRANIA DAVIS

The children, clean and well fed, were lining up now, in the long, dark tunnel that marked the starting point. They had just been awakened from a good, long rest, and some of them rubbed their eyes sleepily. Others, quicker to get started in the morning, laughed and joked and jostled each other, but gently and quietly. The occasion was really too serious to permit the sort of extreme rowdiness that might ordinarily take possession of a group of unsupervised children.

Michael walked along slowly. A dark-haired, blue-eyed, quietly intelligent child. He was too smart to waste his energy now, by fooling around. He was going to need all the strength he could muster if he had any hope of winning.

Winning, of course, was the main thing. None of this nonsense about being a good sport. The race would be a hard one. Long and dangerous. Often, no one made it to the goal. Occasionally there might be a tie, with two or even more kids getting there at the same time. That was nice, but usually there was only one winner. The strongest, the fastest, the smartest, or, often, just the luckiest. To the victor belong the spoils. For the losers, nothing.

Hannah skipped along, humming a little tune. No point in taking things *too* seriously. Her hair, a mass of reddish ringlets, bobbed up and down in time to her inner music. She intended to do the best she could, but she was going to enjoy herself as well.

Behind her, hand in hand, walked the twins, Danny and David, both with wavy, chestnut hair and hazel eyes. They were planning carefully. They had no intention of being separated. For them it was double or nothing. They were going to run the entire race, hand in hand. This might slow them down a little, but, on the other hand, they could help each other out of trouble. After all, everyone knows that two heads are better than one.

Jostling his way to the head of the crowd was Alex, blond and muscular, grinning self-confidently.

A whole bunch of other kids were reaching the starting point behind him. Too many for the casual observer to be able to single out individual names or faces. But each one of these children was also intent on the same thing: winning.

Even poor Aaron, whom the other kids tried to avoid brushing against in the crowd, so that he limped along, surrounded by a circle of empty space. Aaron, the victim of all the worst that the fates had to offer. Club feet, vacant, mindless, drooling stare; could even his mother love him?

"I hope *he* doesn't win," whispered the other children as they passed him by. But like the others, they knew, he had no choice but to do his best.

There were others, of what are euphemistically called "exceptional children," Mary, for example. A highly intelligent child, but with a badly deformed spine and shoulder that made her walk like a wounded duck. Even she might be the lucky one.

Right behind her stalked Jerry. Not very handsome, not very bright, Jerry's main pleasure in life was to taunt Mary and any other kid who was weaker than he.

"Quack, quack," he sneered to Mary, who turned pale and tried to clench her flapping fists.

"Oh, shut up, Jerry!" shouted slim, lithe, olive-complexioned Cassia. She had no need to fear the taunts of bullies, but she hated them anyway. Deformed, victimized Mary shot her a shy smile.

The last stragglers reached the starting point now, and it was nearly time. They were all silent and tense, feeling the pressure mount. A warning shock, then another, and the exit of the tunnel burst open like a gun.

They all raced ahead, blindly, a number of them falling and being trampled by the rest.

The first part of the race was really scary. No chance to get gradually warmed up. You had to jump off some high, steep rocks and swim quite a ways in a fast-moving, turbulent river (fortunately, with the current).

This was really hard for the dark-haired, blue-eyed Michael, who was afraid of heights. He could hear the screams of other kids who had jumped, but who hadn't quite cleared the lower boulders which jutted out menacingly. Landing on one of them would mean the end. But staying here, as some of the kids were doing, would also mean the end. So, screwing his eyes shut, Michael took a running leap and jumped.

He made it! He had cleared the rocks and was in the water, being whirled about by the current and sinking down, down. Gasping and choking, he managed to swim back to the surface.

"I can't swim!" shrieked Hannah, her sunny tune silenced now. "No one told me we had to swim!" She was floundering around, her red hair partly covering her face, which was contorted with terror, as she tried desperately not to sink.

"Relax and float on your back," called back Michael.

"Show me how. I don't know what you mean! Please," she pleaded, "show me how!"

"I haven't got time," he called back, swimming steadily ahead.

She cried and called awhile longer. Then he didn't hear her anymore.

Swimming with the stream wasn't terribly difficult—if it had been merely a matter of swimming. But it was not. There were rocks and whirlpools that had to be dodged, and there were the other children. Children trying to get ahead of you. Children you were trying to overtake. There was no chance of doing a leisurely dog paddle and looking at the scenery. The limbs had to be kept moving as rapidly and efficiently as possible, otherwise you would be left far behind.

The competition was rough. Michael could see the muscular Alex and lithe Cassia several lengths ahead of him. The twins, Danny and David, were just about equal with him, and so was the bully, Jerry. Deformed Mary and a rather obese girl named Rachel were a little way behind. Their handicaps didn't slow them down in the water. A number of kids with less stamina were having to pause for rests along the shore, and were being left far back.

The unfortunate imbecile, Aaron, quickly forgot the point of the whole thing, and sat on the shore, staring at the mountains beyond, and picking his nose. No one cared to urge him on. The bully, Jerry, didn't even bother to yell his usual taunt, "Brainless, footless wonder," as he passed him by.

The swim lasted a long time, and many were unable to finish it. Those who did found the river growing narrower and shallower until, at last, they were crawling in the dank mud of a wide, formless marsh.

Michael's breath came painfully and hard, and his teeth were chattering, despite the warm, oppressive humidity. He wanted, oh so badly, to rest, to eat, to sleep. But he knew that if he did, he was finished. He had to go on. But it wasn't even as simple as that. He had to decide now in which *direction* to go. There were no landmarks. There was no map. He had been given no instructions or hints before the race. Neither had any of the others. This part was pure luck.

He looked to see what the others were doing. Some were heading in the same direction as the river had gone. Some were branching to the right, others to the left.

For no good reason, he decided to follow the left-hand path. Perhaps because fewer children had chosen this route, and he had always hated crowds.

It was rough going. The mud was soft and oozy. Michael sank in, nearly to his knees, at every step. Pull . . . ooze . . . sink . . . ooze . . . slurp . . . ooze. Pull . . . ooze . . . sink . . . ooze . . . slurp . . . ooze. His legs were trembling with exhaustion after a very short time, and there was no end in sight.

He had passed the poor, deformed Mary quite a way behind, sitting huddled, quiet and miserable. There was no chance of her making it through this muck. "Lord love a duck," snickered Jerry, when he saw her giving up. But she was too exhausted to take any notice. Michael wanted to punch him in the gut, but knew he shouldn't waste his strength.

There were so few left, now, compared to the enormous number who had started. Just a handful, wishing that they could huddle together and cheer one another up, but knowing that this was ultimately impossible.

Still keeping the lead position was strong, self-confident Alex. Behind him was the graceful Cassia, her dark hair now matted and muddy. Then came the twins, Danny and David. Then Michael, then

Jerry, and then several other boys and girls whose names Michael did not know.

The ground was starting to get firmer and drier now, and rocky hills were appearing up ahead.

"Hey, wow, I think we chose the right direction," hooted Danny to David. The other brother nodded silently. His face looked gray and tired. He was just barely keeping up.

They felt relieved and cheered to reach the firm ground of the foothills, but as they climbed higher and higher, the ground grew rockier and the rocks grew sharper and steeper, until finally they were inching their way along narrow ledges, feeling carefully for the few hand- and footholds.

Michael knew that if he dared to look down, even once, he would be overcome with vertigo, so he fixed his eyes straight ahead. He did not even look around when, just behind him, he heard a crunch, a gasp, and a long wailing cry. One of the girls had not made it past that last slippery spot.

Nor did he look at David, sitting on a narrow rock shelf above him, pleading with his brother to stop and rest.

"I'm too tired, I just have to rest."

"But you *know* how important it is to keep going!"

"I don't care. Just for a second. You go on without me and I'll catch up."

"You know I can't do that. Let me try to carry you."

"To hell with you," said his brother, starting to cry in hysterical exhaustion. "You always want to be the big shot, the boss. Well, I don't care. I'm going to stay here and rest."

"O.K., Davy. It's all right," said Danny, stroking his brother's head. "We'll rest if you have to." And large tears streaked down his dirty face.

At last, they seemed to be reaching the top. A narrow plateau with a gaping crater in the center. So they had been climbing a volcano!

The fearless Alex was already heading down into the crater, when suddenly the ground shook and hissed and a mass of hot liquid and semisolid chunks of matter came spurting up from the seismic center. Alex had time to utter one deep gurgling cry and then the race was over for him.

"Hey!" yelled one of the other boys, "I'm not going in there. I'm going to look for another entrance." And he headed off down the other side of the mountain, with several other children following behind.

But Michael sensed that there was no other way to go. He knew that their eventual goal was deep underground, and that this was probably the only opening for miles around.

There were only three of them left, now. Loutish, ill-humored Jerry. Cassia, nimble, quick and strong. Michael, dirty, exhausted, grimly trying to keep up.

And so, into the crater. Praying that there wouldn't be another eruption. Sliding down long, slimy streamers of heat-loving mosses and lichens, past bubbling fumaroles and boiling mud pots, until, at last, sweating and afraid, they saw a great, cool cave branching off into the depths of the earth. "This must be it," thought Michael, feverishly, as he and the others raced inside.

Indeed, this *was* it. Just as it had always been described to them. In the middle of the cave was a large, still lake. In the middle of the lake was an island. And on the island, white, round, luminous and inviting was the giant pearl. The goal.

They raced to the edge of the lake and dove in, then gasped with amazement. The water was stinging, burning and painful. Not pure water at all, but nasty, brackish. Full of poisonous compounds and chemicals.

"I can't stand it," screamed Jerry. "My eyes, it burns my eyes. I can't see! Oh, my eyes and my *skin*, it feels like it's coming off! How can you stand it?" he cried, rushing back to the shore, whimpering and rolling in the sand.

"Come back, you guys, this must be the wrong way. This will kill all of us," he shrieked hysterically. "If you won't come back, I'll make you," he cried, heaving stones at them from the shore. But they fell far short.

And now there were only two left: Cassia and Michael.

And Cassia was faster.

"Cassia," called Michael, "let's make a deal. Let's get there together and call it a tie. O.K.?"

But she wouldn't answer. He was nearly to the island, but she was already climbing on dry land. Suddenly his feet felt bottom. He gave a mighty leap and caught her.

"Let's make it a tie, damn you!"

But she only struggled and tried to kick him. He was stronger than she was. He forced her onto the ground and grabbed a big rock and started to pound it on her head until she was quiet.

He retched, gagged and dropped the rock. "I offered, I *did*," he sobbed.

Now he was the only one left. There was no more hurry. There was the pearl. Enormous and glowing. A moon, infinitely valuable.

He walked around it, feeling its satiny surface, and then, right in the center, he saw the niche. Small and comfortable. Just the right size for him to curl up and rest in. A long, deep rest.

He sank down in an exhausted stupor, feeling all the strength ebb from his body. His last thought, just before falling asleep, was, "Well, I guess I've won. I wonder what my prize will be. . . ."

A few weeks later, in a small, frame house, the woman was talking excitedly on the phone. "Hi, I just got the results of the pregnancy test and you're going to be a father!"

"Hey, wow!" burbled her husband.

"The little, innocent darling," crooned his wife, "I wonder what he or she will be like."

"I don't know," laughed her husband, "but you take it easy this afternoon. Nothing strenuous. We'll eat out tonight to celebrate. I want my kid to be strong and healthy. You know, a real winner."

AFTERWORD FOR LAST ONE IN IS A ROTTEN EGG

Apart from Kathleen Sky's "Motherbeast," this is the only childbirth story in *Cassandra Rising*. I was pregnant when "Last One In Is a Rotten Egg" arrived in the mail. I bought it anyway!

Raylyn Moore is a journalism major (Ohio State) who has actually worked for newspapers including the Dayton *Journal-Herald,* the *Deseret News* in Salt Lake City, and the Carmel *Pine-Cone.* Her short stories have appeared in such disparate publications as *Esquire, Woman's Day,* and *Fantasy and Science Fiction,* to which she contributes regularly.

Her contemporary novel *Mock Orange* was published in 1968. She is the mother of four children, and teaches magazine writing at Monterey Peninsula College.

The Way Back

by RAYLYN MOORE

During the long empty days and nights in the hospital, Lorena, thoroughly explored by pain, circumnavigated by fear, dreamed of going home to Wiltonville. When at last her illness was over and the fever had drained away leaving her skin as chill and smooth as a nectarine just removed from a refrigerator, she could remember nothing that would keep her from making the trip. It was simply a matter of setting out, she supposed.

For miles the highway followed the river. It seemed that she and Sony and the children had camped along this stream in some faroff summer, though now the activity of strangers along the sandy shore was as remote and inaccessible to her as if it were happening in another world. Through a silken, chartreuse-colored screen of birches and aspens she caught glimpses of rowers of boats and swimmers, their unclad limbs and the bright awningcloth of their tents flashing signals at her in the thickening light of late afternoon.

At dusk she came to where the road turned off, and began to

watch for the covered bridge. It wasn't there. A flat concrete span lay across the water, and Lorena recognized the replacement as a working out of the inevitable. The ramshackle covered bridge had been one of the last of its kind in the state, perhaps one of the last anywhere, and vulnerable in the terrible way that last things always are. She wondered if during her time away there had been a Save the Bridge committee in the neighborhood as earlier there had been Save the Woods and Save Crescent Lake committees, all the meetings, petitions, posters and speeches coming to nothing in the end.

The farmhouse which had been for three generations in Sony's family was seven miles farther on, up a winding narrow road, but she had no need for caution. Lorena knew every loop and fall, every twist and rise along the way. She had lived nearly ten years in the house and had expected to go on living there as many as forty more, having foolishly forgotten how expectations seldom encompass the occasional oblique slashings across the grain of things.

Lorena's first visit to the house had been shortly after she met Sony. On that occasion they had driven the long ascent in daylight through an art show of turning fall leaves. Perhaps—as she often accused herself later—she had first loved the house, then the man. But no matter, by the end of that weekend she was committed to both.

The building had been done all in stone (she recalled having once heard some architecturally knowledgeable person declare that it is impossible to build badly in stone), with rounded window tops and curved glass in the fat circular tower jutting from the north (front) corner of the structure. But the two aspects which most captivated her were the delicate fanlight over the front door and the view into the valley from the musty, unoccupied top floor of the tower.

Sony's mother, a widow and a generous woman, had taken an apartment in Wiltonville so that Sony and Lorena could have the house in the country when they were married the following spring.

Now the last rise and finally the last curve brought her to the wide, flattened-off top of the hill where lights streamed from all the downstairs windows and a dozen or so cars were parked around the circular driveway. Sony was having company. Lorena recognized the huge vintage Jaguar which for years had been the great pride of the Burrises, their neighbors down the road, but most of the other cars were strange to her.

At the back gate Rodeo, the Irish setter, began an excited clamor, cut off in mid-breath when he recognized her and replaced by an ecstasy of wriggling and devout fawning as he escorted her as far as the kitchen door. The guests, she knew, would be grouped in the front of the house and—because of the summer weather—out on the brick terrace overlooking the side yard. So she would have exactly what she needed, the chance to slip into the house unnoticed and go straight to the children's rooms.

Even though the rear stairway and second story appeared to be steeped in flat darkness, Lorena turned on no lights. She needed no illumination in the lovingly familiar territory of the old upstairs hall with its burnished floor of wide oak boards centered by the heavy, wear-forever strip of woolen ragrug made by Sony's grandmother.

It was when she began groping for the equally familiar shape of the crib in her daughter Althea's room that Lorena for the first time became slightly disoriented. Her hand touched nothing, and then, farther along, her knee nudged something soft, identifiable after a minute as a mattress under a layer of quilted taffeta. The crib had been replaced by a single bed, but this was only proper, for Althea was no longer a baby, of course. By now old enough evidently to be allowed up late, Lorena was forced to conclude a moment later after running her fingers over the tumbled surface of the bed and finding there no small, warm body curled in upon itself in sleep like some hibernating wild creature.

The same disappointing emptiness prevailed in her son Tom's room next door, where a nightlight, gleaming yellow as a lynx's eye, showed a vast jumble of clothing, bits of machinery, disorderly stacks of books and magazines, and the balance of inefficiently consumed apples and sandwiches strewn across floor and furniture, the tide stopping at the bed, which was unmade but also unoccupied.

The only movement and sound in the room came from the old-fashioned starched-white curtains, which whispered as they were intermittently sucked against the screen of the open window by the whimsical movements of air outside.

She was disappointed out of all proportion at not finding the children in their beds; at the same time she realized how absurd were the sudden rush of tears and the caved-in sense of loss. Her failure meant only that she would have to go back downstairs to find them, but she would be going down anyway, to seek out Sony, whom she longed to see almost as keenly as she had yearned to touch the sleeping bodies of the children. And a pleasure delayed is twice as enjoyable, she told herself. Within limits. One should not put off things too long.

At the head of the magnificent sweep of the front staircase she paused, a little shocked at the sheer intensity of the composite sound rising from below, the babbling-chittering-nattering of the guests. It was a case of having to force herself to wade into the wash of rising

noise, but by the time she was halfway down the steps she was rewarded by being able to observe the handsome, animated bodies
garbed in party dress. Many of the faces were at least vaguely familiar, but Lorena at first could fix her full attention on only one, the
face of a stranger, a very young stranger wearing blue.

For one electric moment the girl lifted her eyes (the precise blue of
her dress) and for that moment seemed to hold Lorena's own gaze as
the latter finished descending the stairs. It was Althea.

Only afterward did Lorena realize that the girl in blue had been
standing hand-in-hand with a blond boy, tall and slope-shouldered
but with his face too soon lost to view as the couple moved on past
the foot of the staircase toward the brick terrace, the glass doors to
which stood open in the warm night.

Lorena did not try to follow them, but attempted to make herself
small and unremarkable among the crowd that remained in the
house.

Almost at once she saw Sony. He looked older. It had something
to do with the depth of the etchings around his eyes as he stood at
the front door greeting some newcomer, and with the encroaching
gray which had crept from his temples to cover his thick hair like an
overnight frost.

Lorena felt herself almost overwhelmed by the memory of him, of
his physical presence, his way of speaking, his rare but towering
anger, of the fact that he had been a poet caught up in teaching jobs
and family responsibilities. Not figuratively a poet, a real one, published (if sparingly), encouraged by other poets, mildly celebrated.
Rather than rage against the constrictive life, he had used the para-
phernalia of his existence as his working material, sawing off so many
board feet of chalkdust and morning coffee, cranky plumbing and
laden diaper pails.

Theirs had been, certainly, a "good" alliance. Her only disquiet had
stemmed from the unfortunate truth that most of their major projects
—an exchange teaching job in New Zealand, a sabbatical in Europe, a
rewarding and enjoyable job for herself in her own field (she was a
design draftsman) as soon as the children were old enough—had
somehow been pushed so far into the future that they remained even
now unrealized. And yet she had had the house. She would not allow
herself to forget that.

Moreover, it was all here waiting, as she had known it would be.
Lorena moved slowly through the press of bodies, savoring each
thing, the square rosewood piano which had belonged to her mother-
in-law, the collection of jade, a Gobelin tapestry and a pair of orien-

tal screens which were the harvest of someone's long-ago world tour. The high-ceilinged rooms were the repository for the accumulations of the several generations, as happens in all old houses occupied in continuity by a single family, and she had been too awestruck and uncritically approving to change the arrangement of any furnishings when she came into possession (though "possession" wasn't really the right word, she could understand now).

She wandered on, directionless.

At some point, and without consciously listening to any of the conversations going on around her, Lorena became aware of the real purpose of the party. And after she knew, she wondered at not having apprehended this fact sooner. The number of young people scattered among the guests might have told her, even without the rapt look Althea had worn. She hoped the blond youth was someone worthy, honorable, not cruel. She hoped that if the new alliance for some reason failed, the pair would know better than to cling to it for its own sake. There was so much—undoubtedly too much—that she might have told Althea, and no time left now.

When Lorena saw that she had come to the French doors finally, still being washed along by the others, with no real destination, she stepped across the threshold.

Through the trees a bulge of orange light foretold where the summer moon would presently rise, and on the terrace a fire burned prettily on the outdoor hearth Sony had spent one vacation constructing. There were nearly as many people here as inside, all talking as determinedly, but the voices, unconfined, did not fall back upon one another and shatter into pure noise.

She had not much difficulty in identifying the dark-eyed youth who emerged from the shadows of the side yard with a fresh load of firewood.

But before Lorena could react, her long-time friend Caroline Metzger appeared on the brickwork. Caroline wore an insubstantial apron over a beige hostess outfit which Lorena hadn't seen before. "Tom," Caroline said, "bring one more load, won't you please? It may turn chilly in another half hour."

"Caroline?" Lorena said impulsively. "Oh, Caroline, I want—"

And Caroline Metzger tilted her head alertly for an instant, as if she'd heard something that puzzled her, before turning and re-entering the house.

For a long time Lorena looked at Tom, marveling at his height, his loose-jointed but not ungraceful adolescent body as he moved among the others, returning with the second bundle of wood, pausing for an unintelligible but intense conversation with three girls perched on the round lip of the fireplace.

Somewhere food was being prepared in a rush of melting odors. All along what they had always called "the glass side of the house," where the tall doors opened onto the terrace, hung the draperies she herself had made and carefully lined. She knew without walking inside to examine them closely that the lining hems, which she had basted but never gotten around to completing before that night she had left the house more or less unexpectedly, were still as they had been, not quite finished.

The party had polarized, most of the younger ones drifting toward the outside while their elders remained indoors, holding cocktail glasses, still talking indefatigably.

Lorena again found Sony, this time in the living room, standing with one arm around the waist of Caroline, who had removed her impractical apron, and the other around Althea. A balding man in a handsome shepherd's plaid jacket, one of the many people whom Lorena did not know, was taking a picture of the three with a very complicated-looking small camera topheavy with attachments. The blond youth Althea had chosen hovered near.

It was then that Lorena heard herself mentioned.

Out of the cluster of guests a female voice, perhaps a slightly tipsy voice poised perilously on the verge of the sentimental, called out to Althea, "How lovely you look, dear. If only Lorena—"

The great, embarrassed surge of babbling-chittering-nattering descended over all then, mercifully snuffing out the awkward sentence midway, covering over the awful breach with a fill of nervously re-uttered commonplaces. "Such a beautiful girl." "They make a fine-looking—" "Here's to the—"

Only Lorena, standing among them, was pleased, gratified.

She knew that now, with nothing and no one to stop her, she could go back down the mountain if she chose, or—perhaps better—up into the tower where from the musty unused room the whole valley would be visible, layered with moonlight.

Introduction to Schlossie

At the time I was living it, 1973 did not seem like a year I would ever remember, except with anguish. I spent the first half of it watching my twenty-six-year-old sister die of cancer, and waiting for the results of gynecological tests. Joanie died in May, and in June my doctor told me I would never have a child.

Yet 1973 was as much a beginning as an end. In July I began work on *Cassandra Rising,* and in August I got pregnant (oh yes, it was *that* kind of a year, too!).

It may seem odd to rank an anthology with the conception of a long-desired child, yet *Cassandra Rising* has been a significant part of my life for four years, during which I've "met" a group of wonderful women: the contributors to this book. They have been encouraging, patient, kind, and helpful. I am endlessly grateful to them all, and to two others: Virginia Heinlein, who made many kind and thoughtful gestures; and Virginia Kidd, agent extraordinaire. To list Virginia Kidd's contributions to this book would require another book.

"Schlossie" was written in 1973; it isn't autobiographical but it obviously came directly out of my own experience. I began writing it in my mind on the way home from my sister's funeral.

Schlossie

by ALICE LAURANCE

Squeezed in between her husband and the chauffeur on the front seat of the limousine, Esther Kamber had an unobstructed view of the hearse preceding them with slow dignity to the cemetery. She tried to make herself look to the sides, but inevitably her eyes returned to the sight of that massive black vehicle and she mentally repeated the words which had become a kind of litany: It just can't be Schlossie— Judy. Automatically, she corrected herself, dropping the nickname Judy had hated.

In the back of the car, her mother was crying and her brother, Ira, was trying his best to comfort her. "She couldn't go on that way, Mama. Suffering like that. It's best this way."

"God's will, Rose," her father said.

Rose Blumenthal continued to cry.

"God's will," Esther thought. Does Papa think saying that helps? How? It doesn't answer anything, it just makes it nasty to ask the questions, but the questions are still there. Nobody wanted Judy to go on suffering, but that wasn't the point. Why should God will Judy to get cancer, to have to die at twenty-seven? Did God hate her? Why? What had poor little Schlossie ever done?

She tried to think about Judy and again, like last night, the two images came fast on each other: Judy laughing and Judy desperately unhappy.

Judy laughing—because she'd had the hardest, most contagious laugh Esther had ever heard. She could never tell a joke. Some place in the middle of it, the punch line would hit her and she'd start to laugh and be unable to continue. It didn't matter; everyone around her had always laughed just as if she'd delivered the funniest story ever told, but somehow, Judy never made it to the punch line.

Yet—Judy had never been happy. Despite the laughter, Judy'd been a desperately unhappy girl and Esther didn't know why.

It seemed that Judy had everything possible going for her. Beauty —Judy was the beauty of the family, no question about it. Brains—in a brainy family, Judy stood out. Personality—it seemed to shine in that mobile face and those huge eyes. The Blumenthal family was a happy one, close, loving, generous, and Judy was their darling. There was never a question of her wanting anything. Except . . .

Life should have been a snap for Judy. She should have breezed through school, gotten a sensational job, met a fantastic man, married him, produced beautiful children and been ecstatically happy.

She'd done none of that.

School had been a torture for her. Esther could not remember her ever getting less than an "A" and she could not remember a time when Judy hadn't been convinced she was doomed to failure. She reported failure on every test, until the grade was in. Each "A" was an astonishment to her and seemed to augment her pain, as if she'd obtained it under false pretenses. Judy in the first grade had been like Judy working for her Ph.D.—tense, doubtful, frightened. But why? Why, why, why?

And why, if it had been such a pain to her, why had she continued in school? Nobody said she *had* to get a Ph.D. Not that she had—but why finish all your courses, research the entire thesis and then drop it? And in the name of anything holy, why should a girl from a Jewish family pick Adolf Hitler as the subject of her research? Every fact encountered seemed to hurt her, yet she persisted to the moment of writing the dissertation, and then dropped it.

And for what? Esther remembered the family arguments at the time, arguments that made no impression at all on Judy. She had her master's, she was well qualified in history, something of an authority on the Third Reich, fluent in German—there were endless possibilities for sound employment. "You could teach German or history, you could be a translator," Papa had said, but nothing would move her; she took a job as an assistant buyer with a chain of cheap stores.

"I hate German," she'd said to Esther one day. "I don't ever want to hear that language again." Esther had been shocked at the violence in her tone.

Yet—at the end—when she was in a partial coma, it had been German she'd spoken. None of them spoke German, and it had been necessary to get a German-speaking nurse to tend her and translate her words. Not that she'd said anything significant. She'd asked for water, for a pain killer, she'd wanted to know what time it was and who had sent the roses on the window sill. There had been something about Hitler, but the nurse hadn't been able to catch the words, just the name.

Why should Judy have been obsessed with Hitler? He'd died before she was born, none of their family had been in Germany, no relatives had suffered his persecutions. He was someone Jewish people would—could—never forget, but it had gone far beyond that with Judy. And it had taken another form.

Esther suddenly remembered watching a film on television with Judy, a film that showed Hitler at the Olympics in which Jesse Owens had taken every prize in sight. "Look at him," Judy had said, gesturing to the screen filled with Hitler's face. It had seemed to Esther to be the most hate-filled face she'd ever seen. "That man is suffering," Judy had said. "Have you ever seen such pain?" Esther had thought she was crazy.

Maybe it was best she'd never written that dissertation. Judy was in the field of psycho-history and her plan had been to try to see the events of Nazi Germany from Hitler's point of view. "Not exactly to justify it," she'd said, talking about it to Esther, "you can't really do that, can you? But I want to try to get inside him, to see why he did those things, what they meant to *him*. If people could understand that it seemed different to him—sometimes I feel like I'm the only person in the world who really understands Adolf Hitler," she'd added. The remark had senselessly frightened Esther, as if understanding Hitler was some sort of a crime. Yet, why not? she thought now. Sick, evil, whatever he was, wouldn't it be a good thing to understand what made him that way?

Yet Judy had stopped short; she'd abandoned the research and become a buyer of $9.95 dresses. "Even Hitler deserves some privacy," she'd said. "Besides, it's pointless."

"Pointless." Pointless from whose vantage point? That had been three years ago, Judy had been in perfect health. Why was getting a Ph.D. pointless?

"Sometimes I wonder if she *knew*. . . ." Ira had said last night. It *had* seemed as if Judy was only marking time those last few years. She'd seemed to be on the point of marrying Phil Goldin, then dropped him. She'd switched jobs twice, each time with high enthusiasm that had quickly waned, she'd talked about finishing up her degree, but she'd done nothing about it. But how could she have known she was going to die of cancer at twenty-seven?

Unless she'd *chosen* to die that way. "How would you die if you could, Ess?" Judy had said once. Esther couldn't remember her own answer, but she could remember Judy saying, "I wouldn't live to be too old. Sometimes I think you pick out your way of dying only you don't know it, you pick it out with every step you take, or maybe even before you take a step."

"You're in the wrong religion," Esther had said. "That's predestination or something. You should be a Calvinist."

"Oh no," Judy had said quickly. "I had to be Jewish," and then had looked confused at her own words. She'd changed the subject quickly.

The hearse turned off the road, passing through the gates of the cemetery, followed by the line of headlighted cars. The cars parked and there was a pause while the pine box was removed from the hearse and the final preparations made. In a year, Esther thought, we'll come back for the unveiling. "Judith Blumenthal, 1946–1973."

1946. A year after Hitler had died. Suppose there was such a thing as reincarnation, Esther thought. Judith Blumenthal, formerly Adolf Hitler. The thought suddenly excited her. My God, that would explain so much. Reincarnation. Hitler came back as a Jewish girl trying to understand him, and chose to die in a horrible way as atonement.

They climbed out of the car and gathered about the raw grave.

Esther tried to listen to the Hebrew words but a long-buried memory had suddenly surfaced. Schlossie.

She remembered the day Judy'd gotten the nickname. They'd been at the beach and Ira, full of ten-year-old self-importance, had built a sand castle. It had been a wondrous structure, with turrets and battlements, a moat and a drawbridge improvised from a tar-covered slat. Judy—she must have been about three—had been playing with a pail when she'd suddenly noticed the castle.

"Ein schloss, ein schloss," she'd screamed, jumping up and down with joy. Then she'd lost her footing and fallen, sprawling across the castle, flattening it, and her joy gave way to desolation and howls of anguish. Ira had taken charge, picking her up. "Come on, Schlossie, we'll get some ice cream."

It was a common German word, common enough for one of their parents (Esther couldn't remember which) to recognize and translate, laughing.

But where—exactly—had three-year-old Judy learned it? No one in the family knew German, or if they did know it, used it. Esther couldn't remember any German-speaking neighbors, and even if there had been a German family nearby, how often would they, living in the Bronx, discuss castles? And just how had Judy known the correct article to use?

She stood, stunned by the memory, trying to be sure it was something that had happened and not just a dream. It seemed suddenly vivid and she wondered how she could have forgotten it before. She didn't notice the others move away and return slowly to the cars; she continued to stand by the grave and in horror she whispered, not meaning to speak aloud, "My God, we've buried Adolf Hitler in a Jewish cemetery."

From the other side of her new grave, soundlessly and sadly, the former Eva Braun laughed.

Introduction to Lady in Waiting

In this unusual Anne McCaffrey story, no ships sing and no dragons quest. Instead, a widow makes jelly and tries to come to terms with grief while her children play dress-up—in clothes that aren't there.

Anne McCaffrey was the first woman to win both the Nebula and the Hugo awards; she is also a woman who will take the time to be kind to a stranger (I doubt if she remembers, but years ago she dropped everything to help me retrieve a manuscript which seemed forever lost in a magazine editor's office).

Lady in Waiting

by ANNE MCCAFFREY

"Mummie, Sally wants to play dress-up," said Frances, her pointed little face contorted with the obligation to accommodate her first guest in the new house.

"I do, too," said six-year-old Marjorie, pouting her rosy plump cheeks in anticipation of refusal.

Sally Merrion just stood in the loose semicircle about Amy Landon's kitchen table, her dubious but polite expression challenging her hostess.

"Dressing up seems a very good idea for such a drizzling day," Amy replied calmly. To give herself a moment to think what she could possibly find for them to play in, she finished pouring the steaming bramble jelly into the jar.

Fran caught her breath as a gobbet on the lip of the saucepan splashed and instantly dissolved, coloring pink the hot water in which the jars were steeped.

"What had you planned to dress up as?"

"Ladies in waiting," said Sally, recovering from the initial surprise of agreement but still determined to put her hostesses to the blush.

There was such an appeal in Fran's soft eyes that Amy was rather certain that the notion of this particular costume was all Sally's.

"Wadies in waiting," Marjorie said, frowning and pouting as if to force her mother to accept.

"We'd be very careful," said Fran in her solemn way.

"I know you would, pet," Amy replied, smiling gentle reassurance.

Not for the first time, Amy wondered how long it would take the sensitive Frances to recover from the shock of her father's death: his brutal murder, Amy amended in the deepest part of her mind. Peter had been a victim of a bomb thrown without warning into a London pub.

She disciplined her thoughts sternly back to the tasks at hand: pouring the bramble jelly and figuring out how to comply with her daughters' needs.

"Werry careful," Marjorie said, bobbing her head up and down while Sally Merrion waited to be surprised.

"Of course you would, love," Amy assured the child, knowing that Fran could be depended upon to make certain that her younger sister was careful.

"Frances is a real dote," Amy's mother often said with pride since the child resembled her in feature and colouring, "and more help than the twins, I'm sure, despite their being older. The poor wee fatherless lambkins," she'd recently taken to adding in a tone that stiffened Amy's resolve to make the move that had indirectly caused Peter's death.

During the first days of her bereavement, the hideous irony of his dying had given her a passionate dislike for Tower Cottage. The only reason Peter had been in that pub at that critical moment was to phone her the good news that he'd signed the mortgage contract for a house that would take them away from the increasingly dangerous city streets: a house in the grey-stoned hills of Dorset, with its own orchard and gardens, and a paddock for a pony; the kind of rural, self-sufficient life that Amy and he had known as children.

Her parents, and his, had urged her to repudiate that contract, to stay close to them so they could give her the comfort, protection and aid which a young widow with four growing children would undeniably need.

Stubbornly, and contrary to her prejudice towards Tower Cottage, Amy Landon had honoured that agreement, citing to her parents that the life assurance policy required by the mortgage company now gave her the house free and clear.

"You could say that Peter died to secure Tower Cottage," Amy had told the parental conclave. "It *is* far away from London and I want to *get* far away from London. I want to abide by the plans my Peter and I made. I'm well able for the life. It isn't as if I weren't country bred. . . . Just because *you* wanted to retire to the city . . ."

"But all alone . . . so far from a village . . . and neighbors," her father and Peter's had argued.

"I'm hardly alone with four children. Young Peter's as tall as I am, and much stronger. We're scarcely *far* from a village when there're shops, a post office *and* a pub half mile down the lane. As for neighbors . . . I'll have too much to do to worry about neighbors."

And the fewer the better, she'd amended to herself. She abhorred the pity, even the compassion, accorded her for her loss. She was weary of publicity, of people staring blurry-eyed at herself and her children. They'd all be spoiled if this social sympathy continued much longer: spoiled into thinking that the world owed them something because politics . . . or was it madness? . . . had deprived them of their father.

"My mother keeps a special box," Sally Merrion was saying to draw Amy's thoughts back to the present, to the low-beamed kitchen redolent of bubbling bramble berries, sealing wax and the casserole baking in the old Aga cooker. "It's got clothes my grandma and greatgran wore."

Amy wondered if she'd ever use those maxi skirts again. "I've some things in the blanket chest . . ." She hesitated. She couldn't leave the jelly half-poured and she resisted the notion, once again, that there was something about the boxroom that made her loathe to enter it.

"Don't worry, Mother. I wouldn't touch anything *good*," said Fran, patently relieved that her mother had risen to the need. "And you daren't leave the jelly."

"Wadies in waiting?" asked Marjorie in a quavering voice.

"Yes, yes, love. Go along then, girls. I really must finish the jelly. Fran, you can use those long skirts of mine. And there're old sheets in the blanket chest. . . ." Why on earth be afraid of a blanket chest, but a *frisson* caught her between her shoulders. "They'd make lovely flowing trains. . . ."

From the scornful expression on Sally's face, Amy wondered what on earth the child was permitted to use in her own home. Cheeky child.

She concentrated on the jelly, finishing the first pan of jars and getting the next ready before her maternal instinct flared. Back in the kitchen, separated from the main section of the cottage by the pantry, and thick walls, she could hear nothing. She'd better check. She pushed open the pantry door and the high happy voices of the girls, affecting adult accents, carried quite audibly down the stairwell. They were obviously playing there on the landing in front of the boxroom. Satisfied, Amy returned to her jelly.

She found unexpected satisfaction, she mused, in these homely preparations against the winter. Atavistic, Peter would have called her. The summer had not been kind to the land and its bounty was reduced, or so the villagers said, but Amy Landon had no fault to find. The apple and pear trees of Tower Cottage were well laden when you considered that there'd been no one to prune, spray or fertilize them: and how there came to be beetroot, potatoes, cabbages, carrots and swedes in the kitchen garden, Amy didn't know. The villagers had rolled their eyes and each suggested someone else as the good samaritan. Her circumstances were known in the village so she concluded that some kindhearted soul did not wish her to feel under obligation. Nonetheless the abundance of the garden meant that she could manage better on the spartan budget she allowed herself. (She would make no unnecessary inroads on savings that were earmarked to see the children through college. And she refused to think in terms of compensation money.) With the cost of all commodities rising, she must grow or raise as much as possible on her property.

Mr. Suttle, who ran the tiny shop at the crossroads, had told her that old Mrs. Mallette had kept chickens: she that had owned Tower Cottage before the Alderdyces bought it. (The Alderdyces now, they hadn't lived there very long: come into money sudden like, and bought a grand house nearer London only they didn't get to live in their grand new house because they died of a motor accident before ever they reached it.) While Mr. Suttle hadn't heard of chickens living wild like that for two years or more, then returning to their old run, there was no other explanation for the flock that now pecked contentedly around the barn behind Tower Cottage, and obediently laid their eggs for Patricia to find.

To her father's amusement, and young Peter's delight, Amy had purchased a Guernsey cow, for what was the sense of having a four-acre meadow and a barn unexpectedly full of hay if one didn't use them? Mr. Suttle had knowledgeably inspected the same stable and hay, pronounced the one fit to house cattle and the other well enough saved to be eaten by the cow, and applauded little Mrs. Landon's sense.

Old Mrs. Mallette, who'd been spry to the day of her peaceful death, had kept chickens, a cow and pigs (Mr. Suttle thought he might be able to find Mrs. Landon a piglet to fatten for Christmas) and lived quite well off her land, and kept warm and comfortable in Tower Cottage.

Amy assured Mr. Suttle that this was her intention and she thanked him for his advice but she rather felt the piglet could wait until she was accustomed to managing cow, chickens and children.

Actually it was young Peter who managed the cow after instructions from the farmer who'd sold them the beast. And Patricia, Peter's twin, who cared for the chickens. The two vied with each other to prove their charges in that curiously intense competition reserved to twins.

Amy sealed the bramble jelly and began to stick on the labels which Fran had laboriously printed for her. All of them had picked the berries the day before, a warm, sunny Sunday, and made a game of the work, arriving home in the early September dusk, berry-full and berry-stained, with buckets of the rich dark fruit. The only deterrent to complete happiness for Amy was the absence of her husband: this was what he had wanted for his family and he wasn't alive to share it. In poignant moments like this, her longing for him became a physical illness.

She must continue to force such negative thoughts from her mind: the children had had enough gloom, enough insecurity. She must find contentment in the fact that they were indeed living as Peter had so earnestly desired.

Young Peter came in with the milk pail, the contents frothy and warm. Patricia was just behind him with eggs from her hens.

"I think Molly likes me," Peter announced as he usually did when the Guernsey had let down her milk for him with no fuss.

"Another dozen eggs, Mummie," said Patricia, taking her basket into the larder and carefully arranging the freshest in the front of the molded cardboard.

Peter heaved the bucket up to the counter, got out the big kettle, whereupon he began to measure the milk before heating it. He was keeping a record of Molly's output as against her intake, so that they would have accurate figures on how much their milk and butter was costing them. He was all for trying to make soft cheese, too, since there were herbs along the garden path for seasoning.

High on the wall by the pantry door, the old bell tinkled in its desultory fashion, announcing a caller at the front door.

Wondering who that could be since the few people with whom she was acquainted would know that she'd be in the kitchen this time of day, Amy half-ran to the front hall, wiping her hands as she went and pulling fussily at her jumper, aware that it was jelly-sticky. She gave the door the hefty yank it required and discovered Sally's mother about to use the huge clumsy knocker.

"Good heavens, Mrs. Landon . . ."

"I'm terribly sorry to keep you standing on the stoop, Mrs. Merrion . . ."

"I can't thank you enough for keeping Sally . . ."

"No bother. Such a nasty day, the girls have been playing dress-up."

In mutual accord, the women crossed the square front hall, to the stairs. Above them some charade was in progress: they could hear Sally proclaiming dire news in a loud and affected voice.

"Sally dear, it's Mummie come to collect you."

"Oh, Mummie, did you have to come just now?"

Amy and Mrs. Merrion exchanged amused glances at the distressed wail of protest. As they looked up, Sally was leaning over the upper balustrade, her face framed by a gauzy blue, the folds of heavy blue sleeves falling to cover her hands on the railing.

"I'm just denouncing the traitor in our midst who has de . . . dee . . . what did you say he was doing to us, Fran?" Sally turned her head and nearly lost the heavy headdress.

"Sally love"—Mrs. Merrion's voice was patient and level—"I've got to pick up the meat for tea and your father at the station. There's only just time to get to Mr. Suttle's before . . ."

"Oh, Mummie . . ." Sally's tone was piteous and undoubtedly tears were being repressed.

Amy heard Fran's soothing voice to which she added her own assurance that Sally could return very soon and continue the game.

"It just won't be the same. . . ." Sally's voice ended on a petulant high.

The women saw a swish of royal-blue skirts which told them that Sally was submitting to the inevitable.

"Fran love, would you put the things away for Sally since she has to leave now?"

"Yes, Mummie. Come *on* now, Marjorie, you can help."

Marjorie blubbered a protest, evoking her privilege as the youngest in the family.

"If you're big enough to *be* a lady in waiting, you're big enough to help," Fran said in such an imitation of an adult that Amy and Mrs. Merrion grinned at each other.

Sally's stiff-legged descent of the stairs reminded them of that young lady's disgruntlement well before they could see her scowling face. Amy gathered up Sally's school mac and book bag, quickly deciding that the dirtier of the two school scarves was not Fran's and prepared to speed the departing guest.

Sally allowed herself to be helped into her coat, but her seething resentment dissipated as she babbled to her mother that Mrs. Landon had smashing things to play dress-up in, Mummie, and when could she come again please, and thank you Mrs. Landon for the tea, and, Mummie, didn't you have to go to the dentist again very soon?

Mrs. Merrion, amused by her daughter's effusiveness, smiled and said all the properly courteous things as she hurried Sally across the square hall and out the door. As Amy waited politely on the steps while the Merrions' green Mini was bucking down the pebbled drive, she began to wonder at Sally's unexpected enthusiasm. What on earth had the girls managed to find in the "smashing" category in that blanket chest? Certainly her maxi skirts and those old sheets couldn't qualify. What else was in the chest? Suits of Peter's that she'd put by for his son, the odd blanket or two, a few drapes, some outgrown things of Patricia's, party dresses of hers that she would be unlikely to wear in Dorset, several lengths of fabric. Nothing royal blue in the lot! And she'd never had any occasion to use gauze. Nor headdresses. As far as she could remember, there'd been nothing left behind in the boxroom by the previous owners, the unfortunate Alderdyces.

"Mum, the milk!" Peter shouted through the pantry door.

"Do put everything back, Fran, won't you?" Amy paused long enough in the stairwell to hear her daughter's assurance before she returned to the kitchen and an urgent affair with pasteurization.

At supper that night, when Marjorie was safely in bed, Amy remembered the royal-blue puzzle.

"Fran pet, how did you get on as ladies in waiting?"

"Oh, Mummie"—and Fran's face glowed unexpectedly—"we had a super time. Marjorie was in the red wool though we had to pull the skirt up over the belt so she wouldn't trip. She was the junior lady in waiting and carried Sally's train. Sally was queen because she was guest, so she had the blue because blue is a royal color. Isn't it?" Peter had guffawed so Fran turned wide serious eyes on her brother. "Sally said it was . . ." ("To be sure it is, Fran pet," Amy reassured her, glaring at Peter.) ". . . so that left the green for me. But I think the green was for a man . . . because it only came to my knees. Marjorie's and Sally's dragged on the floor . . ."

"Red? Green? What green?" Amy was mystified.

"Green . . . sort of velvet stuff, I think, and it went from here to here"—Fran measured the length on her small body—"and there was fur along the collar and no buttons so I used another belt . . ."

"I don't recall putting away any belts . . ."

"The fancy dress ones, Mummie, with the big buckles and sparkly stones. . . ."

Fran's pleasure was fading fast in the face of possible maternal disapproval and her voice wavered as her eyes sought her mother's.

"Oh those!" said Amy, as if her memory had been at fault. "Those old things. I'd forgotten about them."

"I don't remember you and father going to costume do's," Peter said, gathering his brows just the way his father had.

"You could scarcely remember everything your father and I did, Peter," said Amy placidly. Peter tended to act the expert. "There's more Ovaltine," and she reached for Fran's glass, smiling to clear the anxiety from her daughter's face. "Molly's making more milk so we have to keep up with her production. Peter, time for you to check her while we girls do the supper dishes. Then all of you, off to bed."

She made the school lunches and checked the doors before she could no longer defer the mystery of the fancy clothes. Resolutely she climbed the stairs, looking down into the square hall as she came to the first landing. The oldest part of the house, the estate agent had said, an old Norman keep probably, though the stonework was in astonishingly good condition for a structure so old. Doubtless that was why the fifteenth-century architects had incorporated the keep when the house was begun. Certainly, thought Amy, the house was a continuous production; all periods, rather than one, now combined into a hodgepodgery which had appealed to Peter's sense of the ridiculous.

The heterogeneity had also fascinated the engineer who had examined the house for Peter and Amy prior to signing the contract. On the way down, he'd been frankly suspicious at the asking price and warned Peter and Amy to be forearmed for disappointment. Surprisingly, the engineer had discovered very few problems: most of which could be put right with a judicious slap of mortar, plaster or paint, and the odd dab of putty or sealer. The cellar was dry, the thick sound walls oozed no damp, the floors were remarkably level, all nine chimneys drew, the drains were recent and in good order, the slate roof undamaged by the storms of the previous winter. And not a sign of woodworm. The engineer reluctantly concluded that the Tower Cottage was reasonably priced because, as advertised, it was genuinely to be sold quickly to settle the Alderdyce estate.

Still, there was a palpable aura in the square hall which Peter had chalked off to antiquity. And something almost expectant in the atmosphere of the boxroom immediately above the hall, those two rooms comprising what was left of the old Norman keep. Amy was not a fanciful person, certainly not superstitious or she would never have moved into Tower Cottage at all after Peter's death. Yet she avoided the boxroom, sending the children either to retrieve objects stored there or consign others to its capacious shelving or the huge, heavy wooden chest that dominated the front wall under the two slit windows. "Flemish work" the engineer had called the chest, with the modern addition of a thin veneer of cedar wood on the inside to make its purpose clear. He had wondered if the chest had been built *in situ* for he could not see how it would otherwise have got through the doorway.

Peter had sat on the chest that day, Amy recalled: he'd thumped the wood, laughing at the hollow echo of the empty chest, remarking that it would be a good place to hide the body . . . several bodies, by the size of it. Amy had felt the *frisson* then, running up her spine to seize her head and jerk it on the neck with an involuntary force that astonished her. The engineer had noticed and solicitously remarked that un-lived-in houses always chilled him.

Since they'd moved in, she'd made one concession to the distressing atmosphere of the boxroom: she'd put the brightest possible bulb on the landing and had young Peter put an equally strong one in the boxroom's single socket. (Oddly enough the children loved playing in the boxroom.) Tonight she turned on both lights and stood for a moment on the threshold, staring at the dark bulk of the carved wooden chest.

It did not move. The carvings did not writhe or gesture. A faint odor of lavender and cinnamon was detectable, mingling with old leather, wool and camphor; homey smells, compatible with the room's use. Not a shadow stirred.

With swift steps, Amy crossed the room and tugged up the lid of the chest. Just as she'd thought. The two torn sheets, rough-dried, were neatly folded on top, her maxi skirts just below. But one was a check and the other black. Where was royal blue, or red or green with a fur-trimmed collar? She sat on the edge of the chest and lifted out a stack of garments, Patricia's outgrown jumpers and skirts, Peter's shirts and underclothes, socks. She turned in the other direction and sorted through business suits, vests, more jumpers, her crepe and wool party dresses. At the bottom were two pairs of old drapes and some glass curtains, white. Nothing gauzy blue. No ornate headdresses. No costume belts. She delved to the wood of the chest's floor and found only the mundane things she expected.

Fran was a literal child: if she'd said she'd dressed in green with no buttons and a fur collar, she had.

Puzzled, Amy ran her eyes over the contents of the shelves: nothing there, surely, but Christmas ornaments, boxed games, lampshades, empty jars, young Peter's tent and backpack frame, oddments of china set aside for a jumble sale. On the other side of the door, the tea chests containing Peter's business papers, books, the family's suitcases as neatly stacked as they'd been since the day after removal from London.

Yet Sally Merrion had been dressed in royal blue . . . the *soi-disant* queen's color . . . and gauzes.

A flash of color caught her eye and she turned towards the chest, blinking. She could have sworn that the topmost sheet had been, however fleetingly, a brilliant blue. To reassure herself, she smoothed the sheet but her fingers told her it wasn't velvet, just worn linen. She stood up, closing the lid of the chest, almost dropping it the final few inches as the full weight of the wood tore the lid from her fingers' inadequate grasp.

She'd ask Fran in the morning where she'd found those dress-up clothes. Possibly she'd misunderstood.

The *frisson* caught her by the back of the neck before she'd reached the safety of the door. It was like a hand on the scruff of her neck, pulling her back to the scene of some childhood crime: an injunction against a cowardly retreat.

In spite of herself, Amy turned back into the room and stared around her. The scent of lavender and cinnamon was cut by a sharper smell, vinegarish. Then a sweetish odor, familiar but unnameable, assailed her, an odor as sharp as the previous covert command to stay. Stiffly, Amy walked back to the chest, set her hand on the lid, imagining, as Sally might have, wondrous costumes in which to be medieval ladies in waiting . . . and a queen.

No torn sheets, no dull woolen jumpers now lay exposed but royal-blue velvet, deep red wool dress, green surcoat fur-trimmed, and belts, encrusted with rough-cut bright stones set in the dull gleam of gold links.

She slammed the lid down and the compressed air smelled of sweat, human and horse, of stale food and spilled, soured wine, heavy musk perfume mixed with camphor. Weakly, Amy sank to the cold stone floor, impervious to that chill.

"The Alderdyces came into money." Mr. Suttle's words echoed in her mind.

Had some Alderdyce child, or adult, dreamed of hidden treasure in the old keep? And found it in the chest?

Amy shook her head, fighting to think rationally. Did the chest grant wishes then? Pray God it was only one wish and Fran had had the chest's quota for them all and that was the end of the matter.

She thought of gold and jewels, rich fabrics, oriental silks, and gauzes, of ornate Arabian slippers, impossible things to stock an old wooden chest in Dorsetshire. And opened the chest. Her heart pounded as she dropped the lid on those same imagined riches.

Mrs. Mallette? She'd lived in Tower Cottage for years, spry til the day of her death. Hadn't Mr. Suttle said so? Wanting for nothing, the house and grounds supplying her requirements.

Amy laughed, a single sound, hard and strained, like her credulity. What had the widowed Mrs. Mallette lifted the lid to find? A body? As Peter had whimsically suggested.

The sweetish odor, elusively familiar, pervaded the boxroom.

Amy screamed, a soft tortured cry, her hands stifling it to a whisper, lest Peter or Patricia hear her. That same sweetish odor had filled her nostrils as she'd knelt before Peter's coffin in the church. How could the house have killed her Peter in that bombed-out pub? It couldn't have. . . . Illusions . . . Her longing for him . . .

"No!" The single negative was as low as it was firm. She spread her hands, her fingers flat on the lid of the chest, denying what could be if she so desired. "No!"

She spread her arms across the chest in repression, in supplication, in prayer. This was just a chest with old clothes in it, two torn sheets and some dresses waiting for parties, for children to grow up to fill. This was just an ancient tower, used as part of an old house, a house where children could grow up in healthy country air, on fresh vegetables and milk, and where they could pick apples and pears in an orchard and bramble berries from hedges. Just an old house that had served many families in the same way.

The nauseating sweetness dispersed: lavender and cinnamon returned, and the smell of night and rain.

Slowly Amy pulled her arms together, rose to her knees before the chest. She placed the heels of her hands under the lid and, swallowing against the dryness of her throat, pushed upwards. Her body blocked some of the light from the overbright bulb but she saw the comforting white of old cotton sheeting, caught a whiff of her favorite cologne, impregnated in the dresses she'd stored in the chest, a hint of the cedar wood. It was as she'd wished. She let the lid down gently and leaned her forehead weakly against the edge.

It took her a few moments to gather enough strength to rise. Really, she told herself as she walked towards the door, she ought not to attempt to do so much in one day, though they'd enough bramble jelly to last years even with the amount young Peter slathered on his toast.

She switched off the light and closed the boxroom door behind her. Her fingers hovered briefly over the key. No, she could not lock out what had apparently happened or lock in whatever it was. That would be superstitious as well as downright useless.

Nonetheless, when she flicked off the hall light, she said good night, just as if there were someone waiting to hear.

Introduction to Impact

In a collection of science fiction and fantasy written by women, a story by a writer named Steve requires some explanation. Despite the masculine given name, the feminine pronoun is correct. Steve Barnes uses that name not to pass herself off as male, but as a way of preserving her family name, Stephenson, lost in marriage.

Steve's first science fiction sale was in 1972, shortly after she joined the Denver area SF Writers' Workshop headed by Ed Bryant, and she says she began writing science fiction as a result of watching the "Star Trek" TV series. She has also published a number of articles in dog-breeding journals and devotes a good part of her life to breeding and showing pure-bred beagles.

Impact

by STEVE BARNES

A kaleidoscope of color, swirling, merging, hurrying east . . . The rush of steel-belted radials on hot summer freeway . . . the nose-prickling, almost nauseating smell of gas fumes and hot engines . . . Denver in August . . .

The eastbound Mustang leaped ahead with the leaders of a stream of impatient motorists who had been bottlenecked at the overpass. It pulled away just behind the first two cars, tires eating concrete greedily, engine wrapping up as it accelerated.

I'm going to be too late, Karen thought. He'll be gone before I get there.

A mental image of Gene rose in her mind—sandy hair that was too long to be completely tidy but had an engaging way of curling around his ears, the short blunt nose, the wide, always smiling mouth. . . .

I didn't mean all those things I said, she thought. He's got to understand that I didn't mean them. I hope he knows, but I have to make sure. It was my fault and I'm sorry. I *have* to let him know. . . .

There was a sharp report up ahead. The car directly in front of her went into a long, sickening skid. Karen swerved, her eyes watching in horror as the other car lurched sideways and rocked wildly. She had a glimpse of the driver's face, white and stricken, as he fought to slow down. Somehow she managed to squeeze by just as the flat ripped off the rim and folded under the wheel. The car, now completely out of control, rammed into the guard rail and bounced back across the lanes of traffic. Another car sideswiped it, turned over, and began a ponderous, terrifying roll down the center lane. Another eastbound car slammed into the first car as it stalled where it had rebounded from the railing and there was a brief muffled roar as an orange umbrella blossomed above the rear of the first car. A fourth motorist, following too closely, piled into the wild tangle of cars, and a fifth. . . .

Karen slowed immediately, feeling the cold clutch of fear. Her hands shook as she started to brake and she had difficulty in reaching the side of the highway. By now the traffic had completely stopped, blocked effectively by twisted metal and the inferno of hungry flames.

Karen looked back in her rearview mirror and saw people already out of their cars and running to the wreck. Slowly, she eased back onto the freeway, her body still numb from the suddenness of the accident. There was nothing she could do to help. She would just be in the way. It would be better if she proceeded rather than block more traffic. But her real reason for leaving was Gene. He might still be waiting and she had to reach him. Cautiously she pulled out into the fast lane and her foot pressed the accelerator, hard. Ahead of her stretched an empty freeway. She would make good time.

Impact plus 2/5: the bumper folded like crumpled tissue, one end of it impaled a tire. The engine tore loose from its mounts and hurtled backward, spewing hot oil and fuel. Water geysered into the bright Colorado sun. The hood flew upward and bent into a horseshoe shape. The windshield buckled and then broke inward, creating a prismatic rainbow. Inside, the driver matched flesh and bone against plastic, steel and iron-hard webbing. The shoulder strap of the seat belts slapped against a fragile collarbone, broke it like a matchstick, jolted into breast bone and ribs. Flesh parted over fragmenting bone. A shattered rib bent inward, tearing into chest cavity and lung, causing an almost clinical pneumothorax. Blood surged into the driver's throat and began to spurt from the nostrils.

Karen took the wrong turnoff and found herself wandering the street of a neighborhood totally unknown to her. The street led down through a suburban area with lawns green under gyrating sprinklers and cottonwoods that whispered in the August breeze. Overhead a cicada sizzled in the skillet of hot treetops. Karen drove for blocks past identical houses, white and prim and square. She looked for a street sign, anything to tell her which way she should turn, but the new curbs and gutters were bereft of markers. The entire section was peaceful and quiet, asleep in the hot afternoon.

She drove on slowly until she passed out of the residential area into a region of abandoned warehouses and a vacant lot filled with broken bottles and bits of blowing paper. The paving of the streets had been ripped up and the dirt left to lie like the obscene droppings of a giant earthworm. The buildings were sad-looking and neglected, their surfaces scarred by the wrecking crews, their windows broken so that they looked blindly down at her. Unexplainably she shivered in the warm air.

The one incongruous note of the landscape was a lean-to made of new pine planks. It was sitting to one side and as she pulled to a stop beside it, an old man came out.

She hesitated, uncertain about asking directions from a stranger. But he approached the car as if accustomed to welcoming wayfarers to his home.

"Lost?" he asked, leaning a dirty forearm on the car door.

"Yes." She took a deep breath to steady her nerves. It was getting late and Gene would leave soon. She must hurry. The thought was with her, as regular as a heartbeat. "I guess I am. I meant to turn onto Brighton Boulevard, but I must have missed it."

"You sure did." He grinned and the expression caused the planes of his face to crack, the way erosion fractures the soil. His eyes were red-rimmed and his nostrils filled with kinky gray hair. Karen looked away quickly, aware that she had been staring.

He eyed her a moment longer, amusement teasing the corners of his mouth. Then he straightened and waved an arm.

"That's where the people stay," he told her. "You should go back there."

"But I want to get back to the freeway—I-70."

"It's about two miles. But the streets angle and curve. Every one of these new-fangled housing developments has twisted streets. You'll never find it."

Karen felt a surge of impatience. The old fool was rambling. He probably had a bottle in that shack and had been sleeping it off.

I have to hurry, she thought. Gene mustn't go off like this—we can't write an end to it this way. In all our years together we've never parted this way, angry and silent. It's important. *I've got to get home.*

She broke into her train of thoughts and started the car. "Thanks anyway. I'm sure I can find it."

"Well, you can try, lady. But I'm telling you, you can't get there from here."

She glanced at herself in the car mirror and saw how tousled and upset she looked. Her eyes were overly bright, the pupils stretching black and deep, almost the width of the iris. Her short, glossy brown hair was clinging damply to her forehead. Her usually soft mouth was tight with nervousness. She spun the steering wheel and made a sweeping turn around the shack. She looked up once into the rear-view mirror to see the old man, surrounded by the dust of her leave-taking, watching her, the grin still on his face.

She accelerated, speeding out of the desolation, back to the highway, back to Gene.

Impact plus 4/5: the fragments of windshield rained over the driver's face, inflicting miniature knife wounds, nicking at brows and protectively closed lids. The steering column started a thrust toward the vital organs. The dashboard smashed into the delicate knobs of the patellas, shattering them and driving the femurs hard against the hips. The upper portions of the ball and socket joints cracked audibly. The tibias splintered until they resembled the crazed pattern of dropped china. The driver's head flew forward to strike the steering wheel. The bridge of the nose was crushed flat, cartilage grinding into sinus cavities. The upper teeth cut through the lips and then were ripped from the gums in ragged chunks. The mouth turned into a red-black smear.

It's been so good between us for so many years. I love him, Karen thought. He's the kindest man I've ever known. When my father died, he was all that kept me going. "He's gone home, Karen," he told me that night. And I knew he was right. Cancer can only make a person welcome death—it would seem like going home, I guess.

She remembered their last visit to City Park. It had been warm but it was still early summer and not as hot as now. Sweat worked out on the forehead in agreeable little drops that evaporated instantly in the cool breeze. Gene was lying, bare to the waist, beside her and she rolled over to study the golden freckles that punctuated the reddening skin of his back.

"You're getting sunburned," she teased him.

"I always do. Where's the oil?"

She removed the bottle from her purse and began to apply the liquid to his back. The feel of his skin under her hand was good, warm and solid with the elasticity of firm muscle tone. She became earnestly engrossed in her work, taking a sensuous pleasure in feeling the slip of his flesh between her fingers.

Later, at home, they lay facing each other in the dark, pressing warmth to warmth, his need to hers. Her lips offered no resistance as his tongue slipped between them. She was having trouble getting into the proper position and placed her feet against his insteps to thrust herself upward. The skin of his arches was incredibly soft and tender. The feel of him between her legs was both satin-smooth and bone-hard. Tissue stretched, yielded, surrounded, welcomed. . . .

Karen was lost. She had to admit it, finally. She had turned one street short of the access road, or possibly two, and was now in another unfamiliar part of town. This neighborhood was not so prosperous. The lawns were untidy as if the owners had more important things to worry about. A child's wagon was deserted on the sidewalk, one wheel missing. A dog was barking somewhere, steadily and angrily. From the doorways of the houses a few dark faces peered at her. A group of children, for want of a better place, were playing kick-the-can in the street. They folded around the fenders of her car, their fingers touching and stroking the bright metal. A little boy of about six leaped up on a level with the open window as she halted.

"You lost, lady?" He vanished from sight as he dropped back to ground level.

"Yes." Her voice sounded hushed, shaken, to her ears. She felt tears of frustration smart her eyes. "Yes. Please help me. Which way is the freeway?"

The children, carved from walnut and capped with the gloss of ravens' wings, had all gathered by her window. Their eyes haunted her with their yearning. A little girl removed a dirty finger from her mouth and pointed up the street. As if this was a signal, each one began to point and shout,

"That way!"

"That way, señora!"

"No! That way, lady!"

"This way, *blanca!*"

They began to caper and giggle, their shouts rising shrilly in the heat. Karen rested her head on the steering wheel and thought of home.

Gene, please don't leave. Not yet. I'm coming.

A woman, in her twenties and heavily pregnant, came out of a house and approached the car. There was a ponderous majesty in the way she placed her feet, balancing her weight with each step. Her dress was clean but faded from many washings. Her hair hung dull and black around her face and her eyes were hooded under swollen lids.

"*Callad la boca, niños!*" She waved the crowd of children off. She planted her feet far apart and raised an arm slowly to gesture down the street the way Karen had come. "Go to the corner and turn. You will see the highway from there. But the construction will be between you and it—always the construction. They promise us new sewers, new paving. Always the streets are torn up. The children play in the ditches the crews dig, they fall in and drown when it rains. No one cares."

"But the highway . . . I can get to the highway?"

"I do not know, señora. But I do not think you can get there from here. Someone else may be able to tell you the way. I cannot."

I've got to try, Karen thought. She thanked the woman and turned the Mustang around in a driveway. It was a relief to leave the sad-eyed woman behind.

Impact plus 1: the steering column battered the sternum, sending bone into spleen and liver. The stomach and intestines whipped against their fragile container. The lacerated spleen began to saturate with blood. The brain concussed against the frontal plate of the skull and thin black lines of hemorrhages began on its convoluted surface. Vision blurred and then was lost in a sea of red. The taste of blood filled the mouth and bits of teeth were sucked into the one good lung as the torn mouth opened in a scream of pain and terror.

Karen couldn't believe it. Ahead was the house. Her house. The familiar row of lilacs framed the dark Mediterranean door and its windows glistened cheerfully under the August sun. She jumped out of the car before it stopped rolling and ran inside.

It was dark and cool and empty. Gene had gone. She opened the bedroom and saw all his clothes had been taken from the closets. His suitcases were gone from the shelf. Unexpectedly, a sob caught in her throat and she sat down on the bed, her knees weak.

She had not thought of what the future would be like without him. She had only been obsessed with making it right between them. Now, the days stretched ahead of her, bleak and uninviting. She dug her fingers into her brows and wondered again how she could have been so stupid, so selfish. They belonged together—had been inseparable. Their one joy in life had been the sharing and tasting of each day, together. I've been a damn fool, she told herself. It was all my fault and now I'll never be able to tell him.

The sound of the front door closing barely aroused her attention. Then she heard the well-known steps in the hall.

"Karen?" His voice sounded loud in the quiet. "Karen? Are you all right?"

"Gene! I'm here." She ran to the doorway. They met in the hall and stopped to look at each other uncertainly. He looked frightened, his face pale and tense.

"Thank God!" His voice was ragged. "I was at Stapleton when I saw the news on Channel 4. There was a big smash-up on I-70 out by your mother's place. I saw a blue Mustang in the middle of it. It looked like yours."

"I know. I passed it. It happened just as I was going by." She paused, trying to rehearse the words. "Gene, I'm sorry. Can you forgive what I said? I never should have spoken that way and then rushed off without another word. Please?" She looked up and searched his face. "I love you. Really. More than anything on this earth."

He came to her and put his arms around her. "I love you, too, honey," he said against her hair. "I've been miserable over how we left each other this morning. Don't ever leave me without saying good-bye."

She knew then that it was all right; she had made it back in time.

Impact plus 2 4/5: the screech of tires, the dull "crump" of impacting cars had died. The sound of breaking glass had stilled. The flames fanned out, making a hissing roar in the summer air.

Karen rolled her head weakly on the torn headrest. Crazy, distorted images danced and yelled outside in the water-color wash of fire. She couldn't hear what the figures were saying; it didn't matter.

"I'm dying," she said, mumbling around the swollen tissue that had been her mouth.

"Yes," said a voice in her head. "You are."

"It doesn't hurt."

"Not now. Not anymore."

"What's it like—death? Will I know?"

"Time will just stop. It will be as if a switch were clicked off somewhere."

"That's good," she muttered numbly. Her thoughts returned to Gene.

She no longer felt the urgency she had. That portion of her life seemed neatly packaged and put away, completed. She was at peace over the way they had parted.

They said I couldn't make it, but I did. Thank God I got back in time.

Click.

Introduction to The Slow and Gentle Progress
of Trainee Bell-Ringers

This is the only time-travel story in *Cassandra Rising,* and it presents a fresh slant on that traditional science fiction theme.

Barbara Paul, who describes herself as "the movie critic for *Pittsburgher Magazine* [who also] moonlight[s] forty hours a week as a technical writer for Fisher Scientific Company," is, as the title of this story suggests, a fan of English puzzles. Speaking of the title, I wish there were a Nebula category for best title!

The Slow and Gentle Progress
of Trainee Bell-Ringers

by BARBARA PAUL

——*Stand over there,* please, the mechanical voice said.

Angie stood over there. Click, whir, hum, *click*—and the automated multiphasic medical exam had begun.

The process took an hour, and Angie, like everyone else, found it a nuisance. But every Experience Day began with a thorough physical checkup. The first time Angie had undergone the exam, she had been upset by it. All those machines—grasping, strapping, poking her, and doing a few other impolite things as well: it was a little hard for a ten-year-old to understand. But now she was used to it. Everyone in Time-Experience Training was.

The first Time-Experience (when she was ten) had been very brief, designed mostly to help her get used to the idea of traveling back in time and inhabiting someone else's body. One of the things she had been taught was that men used to dream of traveling back in time in their own bodies. How silly that was! Angie had sniffed. Everyone knew that past time was unalterable. The only way one could

go into the past was as a guest in the body of someone who had actually lived at that time. And then all one could ever do was observe;
the present might control the future, but never the past.

——*Temperature electronically recorded, drink the glucose, stand
here for the X ray, now height and weight.*

Angie's education had begun in earnest when she was eleven. She
had visited many places in many times, like every other student. She
had been a carrier for that insufferable John Speke when he discovered Lake Victoria in 1858. She had stitched skins together to make
a sort of clothing for the inhabitants of a Danish kitchen midden in
5000 B.C. In 230 B.C. she had been one of the agents Asoka had sent
from India to carry the doctrines of Buddha to Ceylon. As part of her
training in how to handle disappointment and frustration she had
been postjected into the body of a campaign worker for Thomas E.
Dewey. She had even learned about sex by visiting a young bride of
two hundred years ago on her wedding night.

——*Blood pressure O.K., vision O.K., urine O.K.*

Angie had worked like the devil to be admitted to graduate school.
Graduate students were postjected into the bodies of the great figures
of the past, the shapers of history. They could observe firsthand how
those influential minds worked. As a graduate student, Angie could
be John Speke instead of just one of his carriers; she could get inside
him and find out what made him tick. Or she could be Lord Nelson.
Or Eleanor of Aquitaine. Or even Buddha himself.

——*Spirometry test concluded: lung capacity unchanged. Now into
the tonometry room, please.* ("I know, I know!")

The day following the monthly Experience Day was always put
aside for R and R—Recover and Report. Angie would talk about her
Experience while her psychiatrist probed gently to find if there
were any hidden side effects. The psychiatrists kept a careful watch
for any signs of a strong longing to live in the dead days of the past.

——*Electrocardiography and then we're finished.*

There was no stigma attached to wanting to stay in the past. For
one thing, the number of students who ever indicated a wish to do so
was proportionately small. Educators had learned early that most
Time-Experience students had no desire to stay in the various pasts
into which they were postjected. Technology, medical care, and—yes,
just plain creature comforts had made students unable to adjust easily
to the rougher living conditions into which they were thrust. One
would come back horrified by the black, rotting teeth he had seen in
the mouth of Elizabeth I. Another would return retching from a week
spent in the court of Louis XIV, where the combination of oversweet

perfume and the stench of unwashed bodies had proved overpowering. Not only dentistry and modern plumbing had gained new respect as a result of the students' Time-Experiences. But also life itself once again came to be regarded as sacred—especially after a student had been postjected into Anglo-Saxon times, where a man could hope to live a total of just thirty years. If he were lucky.

But there were always a few—a very few, but still a few—who returned from their Time-Experiences crying out to be sent back. These the educators and psychiatrists kept an eye on until they could determine into which of two groups the reluctant returnees fell. Because they all did divide into two types. The first was the romantic escapist, the dreamer, the kind of wide-eyed innocent that tended to idealize everything that wasn't directly under his nose. This type of student the educators merely passed over, allowing him to mature at his own rate of speed.

The other type, however, was a different matter altogether. Once in a very rare while a student would want to return for entirely different reasons. Once in a very rare while there would be a student who saw something in that past life that captured his curiosity, fired his imagination, puzzled him. Something that needed to be understood more fully. For that something, this type of student would dare the risks of disease, primitive warfare, and other dangers the host bodies were not equipped to handle. This type of student was watched very carefully by the educators. For here was the stuff of courage, of intellectual curiosity, of inspiration. It was from this group that the world's decision-makers came. Some bell would ring, and the world would know a little more about itself.

Examination finally concluded, Angie hurried to the chronoporter room. The technician was studying her assignment chart and gave a low whistle of surprise. He looked a question at Angie, but she took her place in the chronoporter without speaking. The technician attached the leads to her head and adjusted the dials. "Have a good trip," he said wryly.

Angie smiled. The last thing she saw before she closed her eyes was the calendar-clock in the wall: eleven o'clock, May 17.

Angie glared angrily through the eyes of Elizabeth I at William Cecil, who had just insisted upon a decision in an awkward question. Can't the man see we're not feeling well?

Regal "we." *Also:* Elizabeth and Angie.

"Very well, Cecil," the queen said. "We will support the Huguenots against the Duke of Guise. Order the troops to Havre, and I myself will undertake the writing of an explanation to Mary Stuart. Our loving cousin may indeed wonder at the presence of English forces on French soil."

Cecil came as close to breathing a sigh of relief as he ever did, and bowed his way out of the room.

Angie felt a sharp pain shoot through Elizabeth's head at the same time an unqueenly oath escaped her lips. How this woman hated war! It always, *always* cost too much—both in lives and money.

Elizabeth-Angie lifted a pale, thin hand to her forehead. Still feverish. Perhaps a cool bath will help.

No, poor lady, thought Angie; it won't help. Angie knew, as her host did not, that within a few days Queen Elizabeth would come down with smallpox.

Angie had visited the Tudor monarch many times before, as had hundreds of others before her. Elizabeth I was one of the most-often-visited figures of the past—along with Johann Sebastian Bach, Albert Einstein, and Jesus Christ. There was very little left unknown about these people, but Angie had repeatedly been granted permission to visit Elizabeth. Her fascination with the period coupled with her powers of observation had produced new insights into that period of human life, so that Angie, in her last year of graduate work, had been granted the advanced status of Repeat Times-Experience Traveler. Angie had discovered one period of Elizabeth's life that had never been visited—the last three months of 1562. In spite of the fact that it was recorded history that the queen had recovered and gone on to rule an additional forty years, no one had yet been willing to suffer smallpox with her.

Angie had leapt at the chance. It would mean a great deal of physical discomfort, but no real danger—either to herself or to Elizabeth. And when she returned, Angie would submit the only first-person report ever to be made on this crisis in England's history.

Elizabeth finally admitted she was ill and took to her bed. After her own physicians had fussed over her for several days, bleeding her and weakening her, in a fit of fevered temper Elizabeth dismissed them all and called for her waiting-woman.

"That German physician. The one who cured Lord Hunsdon. Get him."

So Dr. Burcot was summoned—a gruff, no-nonsense man who was a brilliant diagnostician in a time when medicine was just emerging from medieval darkness. He strode into the queen's bedchamber, took one look at Elizabeth, and announced, "My liege, thou shalt have the pox."

Angie could feel the shock that ran through Elizabeth's feverish body. Why, the man is a charlatan! There were no spots anywhere on her body! The queen summoned her waning strength to shout, "Have the knave away out of my sight!"

Oh, dear, thought Angie. She really *did* say that.

The next five days were the most miserable Angie had ever experienced. Her illness-free life had provided no preparation for the excruciating suffering that this long-since-vanquished disease could cause. Elizabeth—and Angie—floated in and out of consciousness. During their lucid moments, Angie was aware that the Council was holding worried meetings, trying to decide which claimant to the throne to support. For it was clear the queen was going to die without having named a successor. In one stupor-ridden moment, Elizabeth-Angie asked Cecil and the other members of Council to appoint Robert Dudley Protector of the Realm after her death. They agreed. Anxious to soothe their dying monarch, they would have promised her anything.

Angie knew at that moment Dr. Burcot was being brought back to Elizabeth's sickroom—forcibly. The irascible doctor had been highly incensed at being called "knave," and had flatly refused to come. But a quick-thinking servant had persuaded him to come. By threatening to kill him if he didn't.

Oh, hurry! Angie pleaded mentally. Please hurry! She probed around for Elizabeth's thought, but couldn't find any. She must be unconscious, thought Angie.

No. That couldn't be. If Elizabeth the host were unconscious, then Angie the guest would be unconscious too. And Angie was conscious.

Something was wrong.

Angie cautiously probed again for signs of awareness, and then more desperately. She found nothing.

Keep calm, she told herself. There's some kind of explanation. *Don't panic.* She allowed herself a moment to calm down, and then once again she searched for Elizabeth.

Elizabeth wasn't there.

One thing that had been discovered in the early days of time travel was that the guest had absolutely no control over the host body. No matter how exhausted the host body might be, for example, the guest could not rest until the host did. The guest had no power to influence thought, behavior, or even simple body movement.

Angie looked at the thin hand lying on the coverlet. I will raise her hand, she thought.

Slowly, because the body was weak, Elizabeth's hand raised itself.

Angie stared at the trembling hand, and then allowed it to drop back.

Don't panic! Don't panic! Don't panic!

After a long moment, Angie licked her—Elizabeth's—lips and whispered, "Kat Ashley."

Immediately her serving-woman was at her side. Angie looked at the grief-stricken woman and, taking a deep breath, used Elizabeth's voice to ask, "Who am I, Kat?"

Kat Ashley burst into tears and fell to her knees at the side of the bed. Angie concentrated on fighting off a wave of dizziness. There was no way to avoid admitting the obvious.

Elizabeth Tudor had died.

Dr. Burcot came bursting into the room, furious and raging. But one look at his patient and his entire manner changed. His anger vanished, and he began issuing orders quickly and efficiently. Angie-Elizabeth felt herself being lifted from her bed, wrapped in red flannel, and placed on a mattress in front of the fire. Dr. Burcot held a bottle to her mouth, and urged her to drink as much as she could.

Angie didn't know how many hours had passed before she saw she had pulled one hand free from her flannel wrapping. She didn't know how long she had been staring at the hand before she realized it was covered with red spots. She cried out at the sight. "I don't want to be marked! I don't want to be scarred for the rest of my life!"

"God's pestilence!" exploded Dr. Burcot. "Which is better? To have the pox in the hands, in the face—or in the heart and kill the whole body?"

He's right, thought Angie, just as she lost consciousness.

In less than two weeks, Angie-Elizabeth was out of bed. The marks on her face weren't completely healed yet, but Angie knew it was only a matter of time. Dr. Burcot's bringing out of the skin eruptions had saved her life.

Her life?

Dr. Burcot must be rewarded, and generously so. A grant of land, of course. Good land, which will yield him a rich return. But I should like to offer a personal token too, thought Angie: something more than just payment for services rendered. I'll give him one of the pairs of golden spurs that belonged to my father.

Good lord. She was beginning to *think* like Elizabeth.

Angie was frightened—terribly frightened. For she was completely alone in Elizabeth's resurrected body. That brilliant mind that had ruled the English people during its most glorious period—was gone. Elizabeth was dead, and in her body was one very frightened graduate student, who was very much out of her time.

The time was eight-thirty.

"Well?" said the technician as he began disconnecting the chrono-porter leads. "What's it like to have smallpox?"

Angie didn't answer right away. "You wouldn't believe me if I told you," she finally said.

The technician saw she was disturbed and didn't ask any more questions; for that she was grateful. All she wanted now was to get home, take a tranquilizer, and fall asleep—with the hope, perchance, *not* to dream.

Dr. Genoni, Angie's psychiatrist, had been staring intently at a spot over her head for two minutes.

"You don't believe a word I've said," she complained.

Dr. Genoni came out of his brown study and focused on his patient. "On the contrary," he said. "I believe every word of it."

"You do?" Angie made no attempt to hide her surprise.

"Yes," said the psychiatrist. "I believe you because this has happened before."

Angie was stunned.

"Three times before, in fact," Dr. Genoni went on. "Visitors to Daniel Defoe, Abraham Lincoln, and Julius Caesar have reported the deaths of their hosts long before history says they died. In all three cases, the visitors claimed that they continued to occupy the bodies after death. They did more than occupy them, they *controlled* them. Just as you controlled Elizabeth."

Angie finally found her tongue. "Look, this just doesn't make sense. If Elizabeth really died in 1562, why do we have tons of primary sources that document her career—*until her* death in *1603?* Surely there couldn't have been a conspiracy to . . . fake evidence, to make the world think she was still alive after she'd died? There were too many people who saw her every day—ambassadors, spies, enemies as well as friends. . . ."

"No, I don't think that's what happened," Dr. Genoni said slowly.

"Well, then. What?"

"Angie, what did you do when you realized Elizabeth was dead?"

"I panicked."

"After that."

"Well, I . . . I didn't really do anything." Angie stood up and began to move restlessly about the room. "I was feeling pretty rotten, you know, and kept to my rooms most of the time. No one bothered me about state matters, fortunately. Elizabeth did confine herself to her rooms until her skin was clear again. At least that's what history has told us she did."

"And that's exactly what you did," said Dr. Genoni. "You kept her alive, and you acted out the next two weeks of her life for her. Aside from being frightened, which is natural enough, how did you feel? In complete control?"

"Yes. Well . . . perhaps not in *complete* control." Angie stopped her pacing. "Dr. Genoni, I know this sounds ridiculous, but I was beginning to think like Elizabeth. I had this terrible fear that if I wasn't brought back to the present soon, I'd lose my own personality. That the Elizabeth personality would reassert itself even though the Elizabeth body had died. And that's impossible."

"Perhaps not," said the psychiatrist. "We really know very little about this yet."

"'We'?"

"The directors of the Time-Experience Program and the Psychiatric Advisory Panel, of which I am a member. We've studied the other three Experiences quite carefully, as you can imagine. They came upon us rather suddenly; all three occurred within the last six months."

"Why is that? Is there something wrong with the program? A malfunction in the chronoporters—"

"No, no, nothing like that. Everything is functioning normally. What's happened is that the Time-Experience Program has been in operation long enough that all the 'safe' times in the past have been thoroughly covered. So thoroughly covered, in fact, that visitors are now looking for new areas to explore. As you did. Former time-travelers saw no reason to visit Elizabeth while she had smallpox when there were more glorious moments of her life available."

"Yes, I can see that. But I kept Elizabeth alive only two weeks. She lived another forty years. How could she keep going for that long when I stayed only two weeks? There would have to be people visiting her constantly for forty years if . . ." Angie's voice trailed off. She stared at Dr. Genoni. "Is that what happened? That it was visitors from the future who kept Elizabeth alive and reigning for forty years after she actually died? Oh, I can't believe that! That's incredible!"

"It *is* hard to believe," agreed Dr. Genoni. "But I think that's exactly what has happened."

Angie was thinking. "No, wait a minute. I am the first one to visit Elizabeth when she had smallpox. How could all of her later life have taken place *before* I kept her alive?"

"Perhaps you're only the first one to visit her *so far*," suggested Dr. Genoni.

"What do you mean?"

"Well, what about visitors from *our* future? People who haven't even been born yet, in our sense of time. Couldn't Elizabeth's life already have been preserved—by someone traveling back from a thousand years in *our* future?"

Angie took a moment to absorb this. "Does that mean what I think it means? That all our past has been arranged—or at least controlled—by the people living in the future? That everything has happened the *way* it has happened, because future time-travelers have decided it should happen that way?"

"If that's the way it works, yes. And not only the past, but our present time as well. Angie," said Dr. Genoni gently, "couldn't someone from the future be visiting *you*—right now?"

It was getting to be too much for Angie. She walked over to a mirror, looked at her reflection, and said, "Go home, you snoop. I don't want you here."

Dr. Genoni laughed dryly. "I guess we're all snoops, in a way. And I rather imagine we have some more snooping to do. Take Van Gogh, for instance." His eyes traveled to the reproduction of "Starry Night" on his wall. "It was nothing short of miraculous that Van Gogh didn't bleed to death when he cut off his earlobe. He was suffering from malnutrition at the time. Lately I've been wondering if he didn't *really* die then."

Angie stared at the swirls in Van Gogh's sky and murmured, "But why, Dr. Genoni? Why does it happen like this?"

"Well, there's a kind of logic behind it. Elizabeth had to be kept alive to lead the most civilized nation in Europe into becoming the most powerful nation in Europe. Defoe was needed to 'invent' the novel. Only a Lincoln could have freed the slaves. And Julius Caesar hadn't even *heard* of the Rubicon when he 'died.'"

"But what about Mozart? And Keats? Why were they allowed to die young?"

"I don't know. Unless no one has ever been willing to experience their particular deaths."

Angie walked over and settled herself determinedly in the chair facing Dr. Genoni. "Something must be done."

The psychiatrist looked amused. "I had a feeling we were coming to this."

"Surely it must have occurred to you and the rest of the Advisory

Panel that someone right now might be able to go back and keep Mozart alive."

"It has occurred to us."

"Yet no one has tried?"

"No one has tried."

"Why not?"

"A certain paucity of volunteers, you might say."

"I'M VOLUNTEERING!"

"No need to shout, Angie. I got the message some time ago."

"Let me visit Mozart's death. You can arrange it."

"Do you fully understand what you're suggesting? Even the vicarious experience of death—"

"I've done it before. It didn't kill me. Please!"

"Angie, I can't make a decision like this on my own. I'd have to consult with the other members of the Advisory Panel."

"Consult!" she pleaded.

He looked at her for a moment, and then made up his mind.

"How's your German?" he asked as he reached toward the telecommunicator.

Wolfgang Amadeus Mozart dipped his quill into the inkpot and then hesitated. The sound of footsteps on the stairs had reached his ears. An image of a tall, thin, grave-looking man dressed entirely in gray flashed through his mind. Then came the remembered three slow knocks on the door.

"Herein," said the composer uneasily.

The door opened and the gray man walked in. Bowing slightly from the waist, he said, "I have been sent to inquire as to the progress of the 'Requiem.'"

Mozart stood up uncertainly. The quill he gripped tightly betrayed the trembling of his hand. "I . . . I am working on it now."

"And when may I say it will be finished?"

Mozart fought off the beginnings of one of the fainting spells that had appeared to plague him lately. "I . . . it will take me slightly longer than I had originally anticipated."

The gray man frowned. "May I remind you, *Herr Kapellmeister,* that you accepted the commission for the 'Requiem'—and the fee—a month ago. My employer was willing to trust that you would finish the work within a reasonable length of time."

"And I shall make every effort to do so." Mozart noticed a quaver in his voice and cleared his throat. "My opera, *Die Zauberflöte,* is being produced at the Theater auf der Wieden, and I have been asked to conduct the opening performance. After that I will be free to give my entire attention to the 'Requiem.' "

The gray man mused silently a moment. "I believe my employer will find that satisfactory." He turned to leave, but in the doorway stopped. "And I must caution you again concerning the other condition of our agreement. You are to make no attempt to determine the identity of the gentleman who has commissioned this work."

Mozart nodded assent, and the gray man left.

"I already know who he is," Mozart said quietly to the closed door. "He is Death, and you are the Messenger of Death."

He is not! shouted Angie silently, futilely.

Mozart stood motionless a moment, and then vomited violently and fell insensible to the floor.

Weeks later the composer lay in his sickbed chatting with the group of musicians who gathered daily to comfort the shrunken figure of their friend. Years of overwork and undernourishment were taking their toll. The bones in his face protruded against the waxy skin, and the feverish excitement of his talk was partly an attempt to keep submerged the picture of the gray man that was now with him day and night. Sometimes Mozart would attempt to lay the ghost by singing. *"Der Vogelfänger bin ich ja,"* he would gasp.

After a slow start, *Die Zauberflöte* had begun to catch on. The fickle Viennese audience was taken with the novelty of the work, but the sick man was unable to enjoy his success. He was driven by one idea: he must finish the "Requiem." His requiem.

In a quiet moment Mozart communicated his fears to his wife. Constanze already knew about the mysterious stranger who had appeared silently out of nowhere to commission a mass for the dead, but she was in no way prepared for the interpretation her husband had put on this. She watched him staring intently at nothing and asked what he was thinking.

"I am thinking of death," he answered. "Now I am always thinking of death. So I must finish my 'Requiem,' you see. I am writing it for myself."

Constanze was horrified. "Please . . . don't say such dreadful things!"

"They are not dreadful things, my dear. They are beautiful. Death itself is very beautiful. Is it not the true goal of life?"

Angie ached for the man. Terrible as his physical pain was, it was less than the mental anguish he was enduring. Angie was alarmed to discover there was an infectious quality about Mozart's obsession with the gray man. Even though she knew who he really was, she had to fight hard against being engulfed by the morbid dimension the stranger had assumed in the composer's mind.

In reality the gray man was no more than a flunkey. His name was Leitgeb, and he was the estate stewart for Count Franz von Walsegg, an amateur cellist who wanted to be known as a composer. Von Walsegg had the rather nasty habit of keeping his eye on impoverished composers and anonymously commissioning works by them. These works would then be performed as having been written by von Walsegg himself. Mozart's "Requiem," in fact, was to have its first public performance as von Walsegg's composition—a fact that Mozart, perhaps fortunately, was never to know.

For it was becoming increasingly clear to the composer that he would not live to finish the work. His hands and feet were swollen, his head was pounding, and his kidneys caused him constant pain. Angie screamed and screamed and screamed; and in between her unheard screams, she marveled at the dying man's uncomplaining acceptance of what was happening to him.

The bed was covered with sheet music. Mozart's pupil, Franz Xaver Süssmayr, sat listening to his master's instructions as to how the "Requiem" was to be finished. Mozart had completed the first two parts and had sketched out most of the rest; much technical work still needed to be done.

"Use the fugue from the first movement as recapitulation and climax and ending," Mozart whispered. Then he rolled over to face the wall.

This was it.

Angie probed for signs of awareness, for any sign of life. As she expected, she found none. She was in total darkness; unlike Elizabeth, Mozart had died with his eyes closed. So the first thing to do was open them. She concentrated intensely on the simple act of lifting two eyelids.

Nothing.

Again she tried. Nothing. And again. Nothing. And then she became aware of the total absence of pain. No fever, no burning in the kidneys, not even a headache. In fact, no feeling of *any* kind. She counted to a hundred and then tried to move—an arm, a leg, a shoulder. Still nothing, still no feeling. Surely Süssmayr and Constanze were aware by now that Mozart had died. Surely by now they had straightened the body on the bed, perhaps crossed the hands on the chest. But Angie had felt no pressure of hands, no movement. She felt nothing but the leaden weight of darkness and confinement. This emaciated body she occupied was beyond reclamation.

Without tear ducts and without eyes, Angie began to cry.

The technician glanced nervously at the multiple chronometer panel controlling the chronoporter. "It's a quarter past one, their time," he said to Dr. Genoni. "He's been dead twenty minutes."

Dr. Genoni said nothing.

The technician looked at Angie's body in stasis on the chronoporter. He didn't like this. There was something unnatural about experiencing another person's death.

"Perhaps we should bring her back now?" he suggested.

"No," said Dr. Genoni. "I promised her she could have an hour to try to revive him. We'll wait."

So they waited.

At last the chronometer indicated five minutes until two. The preset chronoporter controls did their job, and the girl's chest began to move in the effort of respiration.

"Angie?" said Dr. Genoni. No answer.

He lifted her eyelid. "Get the oxygen tank," he said quickly as he prepared an injection of Adrenalin. "She's in shock."

"Do you feel up to talking now?"

"Certainly." Angie smiled. "Fit as a fiddle, whatever that means."

Dr. Genoni pressed a button on the control panel, and the head of Angie's hospital bed raised her to a sitting position.

"It didn't work," she said simply. "It was entirely different from the last time. Once he had died, I had no control over his body whatsoever. I couldn't move, I couldn't see, I couldn't feel. I simply lay there trapped until I was brought back. And I think I know why." She hesitated.

"Well? For heaven's sake, Angie . . ."

"I know, I know. I'm just trying to think how to put it. So you won't dismiss my reason as romantic foolishness."

Dr. Genoni waited.

"Mozart wanted to die," she said finally. "Whether the fever had made him irrational or this obsession with Leitgeb as a death figure weakened his resistance, I don't know. But the will to death was there—*all* the time, every waking moment. And in his night dreams as well, which might indicate the death wish had penetrated his unconscious."

"Or sprang from it, more likely."

"Perhaps. I rather think not—his music is too life-affirming. It was an acquired obsession; the gray man turned out to be a convenient symbol to a man so exhausted that death had become a form of beauty to him."

"And Elizabeth?"

"Elizabeth was fighting every inch of the way. To her, death was ugly and unthinkable. She wasn't ready to die. Mozart was."

There was a long silence. Finally Dr. Genoni spoke. "Angie, do you realize what you're saying? That the reason some figures can be—have been—kept alive is that they possess some . . . will to life? Why, that's . . ."

"The stuff of poetry?" Angie suggested. "I know. I told you it would sound like romantic foolishness."

Dr. Genoni pulled a chair up to the side of her bed. "It's been known for centuries, of course," he said, "that a strong will to live often means the difference between success and failure in the medical treatment of critical cases. But I wonder if a medical analogy is really valid. Time-visiting isn't *treatment*."

"But it obviously *can* be life-sustaining. Elizabeth. Defoe. Lincoln. Caesar. The fact that it failed for Mozart doesn't erase the success of the other cases."

"Granted."

"And Elizabeth did die, Doctor. I know. I have died twice. Have you thought what *that* must be like?"

"Yes," he answered shortly.

Angie felt a quick stab of guilt. Of course he had thought about it. "Well, there's no doubt in my mind that it was worth it," she said with a cheerfulness that wasn't entirely forced. "It seems to me the next step is a systematic investigation of all those 'close calls' we know about. Van Gogh would probably be a good place to start."

Dr. Genoni laughed. "And I wonder who thinks she's going to volunteer for that! No," he said quickly as Angie started to protest, "habitual dying could become a rather morbid habit, don't you think? All sorts of impulses destructive to the psyche could develop that we just don't know about yet. We have to tread carefully now. No more death visits for you, Angie. Not for a while, at least."

"Hummph," said Angie.

"On the other hand," he mused, "this might turn out to be a good way to prepare us for our own deaths. It's a possibility. Anyway," he said briskly as he stood up, "somebody else will have to visit Van Gogh." He paused for a moment. "I might even go myself."

"You wouldn't!" Angie exclaimed.

"Oh, wouldn't I?" He winked, and left.

Angie grinned. Of course he would.

Introduction to Nightfire

Sydney Joyce Van Scyoc "began writing and not selling fiction in the late fifties and continued not selling" until she began writing science fiction. Her first published story appeared in *Galaxy* in 1962 and was followed by other stories and four novels including *Starmother* (1976) and *Cloudcry* (1977).

She lives in Hayward, California, with her husband, son, and daughter, seventy-two houseplants and "animals too numerous to mention."

Nightfire

by SYDNEY J. VAN SCYOC

When Corneil Rothler had walked the pod checking duty units and rec areas, it was 8:20 P.M. By midmorning tomorrow the transport would arrive to fly her to Neutral for the Fleet Command Conference. And Zimms' medic shuttle was five days overdue. She frowned, a tall woman with silvering hair and light eyes. Fleet Central's comm-staff could only tell her that the medic shuttle would reach *Pod Nestor* when it could and that Pod Commander Rothler could speak directly with Fleet Commander Hazlet if she wished.

Pod Commander Rothler did not wish. There was no medical emergency aboard *Pod Nestor*. And Corneil had never in the past demonstrated undue concern about minor med schedule deviation. But if the shuttle did not arrive before midnight, only two courses lay open. Fabricate an emergency—or abandon her plan. Corneil stepped into the forward observatory to consider her alternatives.

Her son Herron stood at the view window. Fourteen, Herron hovered on the verge of the growth spurt that would soon bring manhood to features and frame. In November his fifteenth birthday would bestow legal manhood. The last three feet of floor were transparent, an extension of the ovoid window. Corneil stepped across the darkness of night to stand beside her son.

Tonight cloud cover was scattered. Nightfire, the flash of weaponry, the glow of death, was visible sixty thousand feet below. On clear nights the siege of Pittsburgh, in its nineteenth month, provided a show of strange beauty for the occupants of *Pod Nestor*.

It was a show few of them bothered to attend.

Frowning, Corneil raised her head and scanned the starfield until she caught the glint of *Earthhold*. Originally an orbiting observatory and research station, the big satellite plodded wearily across the sky now bearing the displaced, the demoralized, and the maimed from the War of the Americas. But the gleam of its shell was still silverbright. Shunted aboard a hastily constructed hoverpod in the early years of the war, Corneil had often stood at this window as a child, as an adolescent, and yearned for the higher existence aboard one of the five satellites.

Now she accepted her lower station. Not because of the crushing population load the orbiting vessels carried. Conditions were almost as crowded aboard *Pod Nestor*. Not because of the violent disorders that exploded in high orbit. *Pod Nestor* too was periodically convulsed, though on a lesser scale. Her reconciliation stemmed instead from appreciation of the strategic advantage of operating from a bare sixty thousand feet.

It was an advantage that would be lost if Zimms didn't arrive soon. Troubled, she became aware of her son's gaze.

"My father is down there."

Startled, she glanced down. "He is?"

He nodded. "I queried War Authority. He's Field Commander of the 4th Unipatrist Regiment now. It joined the siege force seven months ago."

So Tanner Helm, Unipatrist Infantry, participated in the light show below. Corneil had never met him, although she had studied his lineage carefully before acceding to his selection as father of her child.

"I have his picture now. I requested it from War Authority last week."

"I see," she said slowly. Evidently the age of silent disinterest was past. "Well, do you find much resemblance?"

The boy's eyes flickered away. "Between us? How can I tell? It's just a picture." Then his gaze was back, challenging. "We made a pact last week—all of us. When we reach age, we're going to go down together and join my father's regiment."

She looked at him sharply. "Your friends haven't been talking partisan in public sections?"

"It was a private discussion, in Taggard's bunkroom. And you can't object to me enlisting. You served two years with the 9th Division when you were young. You fought in—"

"I know where I fought. I recommend infantry service to anyone who likes to see other humans die. That's what's happening down there."

"I know what's happening," he said angrily. "And it's going to go on happening until someone wins. Well, now the Patrists have the edge in the Appalachians and the Rockies. Now—"

"The Nationalists hold both seacoasts and large blocks of the South."

"But the Patrists have the Midwest, most of it. The Patrists—"

She shook her head. "No one is going to win the war, Herron. The balance of power shifts—but never far enough. I've had most of my lifetime to observe that. Neither force has ever held clear-cut dominance."

"And no one ever will unless people fight! If everyone who has Patrist sympathies went down there at the same time, even the amps and the psychs, *everyone,* if there was a giant airdrop from the pods—"

Her eyes froze him. "You're speaking in a public section, Herron."

His mouth snapped shut. His eyes darkened. "It would work."

"I think you'd better report to your bunk."

His eyes flared. "And that's another reason we're all going down! There's no freedom aboard this vessel."

"There isn't," she agreed evenly. "Not when it comes to expressing political sympathies. That's why there are no longer major disturbances aboard this vessel either." It had never proven feasible to segregate loftees according to political sympathies. Their daily intermingling, however, necessitated certain limitations upon the basic freedoms.

His eyes locked hers. Then he was gone.

Before she turned back to the window, the podcomm spoke. "Commander Rothler, a disturbance in Film-Three."

"I'm on it."

Filmlounge-Three was stale with massed bodies. Halfway down Section C, a pair of amputees were squared off, bellowing like crippled bulls. Corneil pushed through the clogged aisle. "Tomas! Finnet!"

Heads swung. Tomas was a heavy torso mounted on a Nationalist Army issue wheeled platform. A single half-useless arm hung from his right shoulder. Finnet was a Unipatrist veteran. He retained a single intact leg as well as most of an arm.

"Report to bunks immediately."

Tomas did not accept the curt dismissal. "That patty—"

"Report." Corneil found a reliable face in the audience. "Marlaine, give Tom a push to quarters. You're both confined for twenty-four hours, food allowance halved for that period, all film privileges revoked for two weeks."

Revolt burned bright in two sets of eyes. Corneil met it. "Marlaine," she repeated.

Muttering, Tomas was wheeled away. Finnet hobbled after, anger strangled in his throat.

Film-Three became still. Corneil studied the audience that lounged in the ruined seats. The faces of her people were dull tonight, their eyes shadowed. On the screen a pre-1980 drama crept to its dubious climax.

In the corridor, her brief depression was banished. "Commander, the medic shuttle is entering pattern."

She hurried to the embarkation lock.

But when the silver shuttle had docked, it was not stocky Hal Zimmerman who stepped through the lock door. It was a youth, face gray, eyes nervous, anticipating challenge. "Dr. Kostel reporting."

Challenge he got. "Where is Dr. Zimmerman?"

"He—he won't be around anymore, Commander."

Corneil's face froze. Panic touched her. But there was no way Fleet Command could have guessed Zimms was slated to aid Corneil in a very special way this trip. Zimms himself had not known. "What happened?"

"I guess you would call it apoplexy. It happened on *Pod Aeolus*. Last Friday."

"He's been listed?"

The youth's eyes fell. "Not yet. But I think we'll have to. He's—gone."

Good-bye another old friend, she said silently. Now she would have to extract by artifice from this youth what Zimms would have given her on trust. "What are your own medical qualifications, Kostel?"

"Well, I've been apprenticing under Dr. Mendez. I—"

"Dr. Mendez was licensed under the apprentice system himself. How many years apprenticeship have you served?"

"Almost one—one full year."

She frowned. "It was my understanding that an apprentice could not be released for solo rounds with less than two years service, Kostel."

Kostel pushed a hank of tired hair from his forehead. His hand quivered. "Well, that's what I thought too. But—well, you've probably heard about the new medical guidelines by now."

"I've heard nothing."

"You haven't?" The hand quivered more noticeably. "Well, they just came out. I haven't seen them in print, but—"

"I suppose we'll be briefed at the Fleet Command Conference," Corneil interrupted, not graciously.

He nodded. "Yes, they probably plan to—to—well, anyway, here I am."

She smiled bleakly. "So you are. And I have people who have been waiting four weeks for attention. I'll call a clinic immediately. While we're waiting, you may examine the bed patients."

While the youth made bed rounds, Corneil formulated her new plan. She knew he would find no list prospects on the ward tonight. But she had a handful of defective children to draw from.

"Bring me the file on Tilla Franks," Corneil instructed the duty nurse.

She had the file lying before her when Kostel returned to the desk. "Any new problems?"

"No, everyone seems pretty well stabilized."

"Good. However, I do have a child I want listed this trip."

His expression was startled.

"A defective," she amplified. "Chronological age, four years three months. Mental age about two thirds that. Dr. Zimmerman was acquainted with the case." She touched the Franks file but did not offer it.

"There's a physical problem too?" Kostel wondered uncertainly.

"No, the child is quite robust physically. But there are behavior problems, tantrums, outbursts. The mother is one of my most valuable food techs. I can't have her productivity eroded any further by the off-duty situation."

"But all these pods have special-care sections."

"Filled to capacity."

Kostel fidgeted, shoved at his hair. "But a child—"

"Occasionally it's necessary, Doctor."

His hand shook, then clenched into a fist. "Have you—"

"I haven't had opportunity to prepare the mother yet. I doubt that I will be able to get to it until next week."

The youth relaxed slightly. "Oh. Then it will have to wait until my next call. We have to counsel with the mother before we do anything."

"Of course. However, I thought it might be acceptable to sign the euth-kit over to me now for safekeeping. I'll talk with the mother when I return from Fleet Command and then have someone here administer the injection. If you feel you can delegate that responsibility. Have you performed euthanasia yet, Doctor?"

"I've—never on a child."

"I'm sure it's not a task you relish. Since I've taken the initiative in the situation, I'll be glad to see that the task is carried out by a reliable member of the *Pod Nestor* med staff."

Such an arrangement was strictly proscribed, for a number of reasons. Nevertheless, a quarter hour later all applicable forms had been completed and filed, the death certificate signed, and Corneil had the euth-kit in her desk. She was committed.

She worked until after midnight at her desk. Then she stopped by the bridge. The night nav sprawled lax in his seat, the chore of holding position and altitude delegated to autoequip. Corneil's eyes flickered over the infra-monitor screens. Her forehead creased. "What's happening below?"

Oyama jerked upright, startled. "Huh?"

"Has the war been called?"

"Oh! No! *Pod Galatea* low over the Cleveland area. Pressure trouble. They're holding fire in Pitt, just in case."

Corneil smiled grimly, studying the screens. "Touching."

"Huh?"

"A pod lowers to deal with an emergency, and both armies call fire to a radius of hundreds of miles. Any man who shoots so much as a heat dart will be summarily executed. Then the emergency is dealt with and it's back to sixty thousand for the noncombatants."

"No one can take a chance on injuring noncombatants," Oyama said indignantly.

She shook her head. "You don't call it injurious to confine growing children to a hoverpod? To let their fathers and brothers—and sisters— go below to kill each other at will?"

Oyama wasn't prepared for debate. "No one wants to hurt noncombatants," he reiterated. He turned to his panel, earnestly checking screens and dials. "Holding," he announced hopefully.

"Holding," Corneil murmured, leaving him.

Holding. Forty-one years holding over the confluence of the Allegheny and the Monongahela. Forty-one years of stale air and pressing bodies. Forty-one years of deadly communal ennui, punctuated by brief flares of violence.

Forty-one years. Most of Corneil's lifetime.

She found herself in the observatory, at the big ovoid window. The most civilized war in the history of mankind they called the War of the Americas. When the continent exploded, Europe, Asia, and Africa were called upon immediately to absorb millions of refugees. When their own turbulent internal climates, or their simple unwillingness, precluded the further admittance of noncombatants, the satellite stations were requisitioned and converted for use. Millions went aloft to orbit.

Then the satellites were filled to capacity. With the country, indeed the entire hemisphere by that time, at war, it was not feasible to construct more satellites in orbit. That undertaking required the fully co-operative co-ordination of men and resources. Hoverpods represented a hasty solution. A temporary solution. Both sides agreed to that. The war could not last long.

(a) Because the Unipatrists would push to early victory and see the United States, Mexico, Canada, and the South and Central American republics merge their separate national identities into the projected all-sovereign Pan-world Union.

(b) Because the Nationalists would thrust to swift victory and see the United States, Mexico, Canada, and the South and Central American republics remain independent nations, separate and unequal.

Over a period of five years a fleet of seventy-six hoverpods was lofted over North America. Each vessel was equipped to accommodate 150,000 noncombatants. All remaining North American noncombatants were exiled to the states of Maine, New Brunswick, and

Nova Scotia, which combined were designated Neutral America.

By agreement, neither army had ever brought nuclear weapons into use. And after forty-one years, gains continued to balance losses. In the United States, the Nationalists held the steel centers of Pittsburgh and Birmingham, but the Unipatrists controlled Chicago, Gary, and Detroit. The Unipatrists held much of the broad area between the Rockies and the Appalachians, but the Nationalists held the coastal plains and most of the South.

The pods and satellites, to a greater extent than Neutral America, furnished both armies with a continuing source of fresh man- and womanpower. War seen from altitude provided a cause, a mystique, ultimately an escape. The battlefield became the only place for youth to test and prove itself, for the passions and powers of young adulthood to express themselves, even for vigorous young male to join healthy young female in casual alliance. After the confinement and regimentation podboard, the relative freedom of the battleground was compelling. Even multiple amputees schemed to get aground again. War had become the American way of life.

So had protection of noncombatants. Although in the upper atmosphere and in orbit they breathed air that stank, ate scum, and drank their own recycled sewage, they were reverenced. While there was neither medicine nor food nor clothing to be lavished upon them, there was obeisance. The military would grant anything to the cherished family above, anything it possessed—except peace.

Corneil moved slowly down the corridors to her bunkroom. Herron slept, rebellion smoothed from his features for a few hours. She stood at his side. Did he ever sense, she wondered, that he was more than a son? That he was a device for bringing her goal into ever-sharper focus, for keeping the sense of urgency alive in herself?

Fourteen and a half. Fifteen, a man, in November.

She went to bed. It was her last night aboard pod.

She hoped.

The transport arrived next morning at 9:50. She passed her luggage into the hold. Her conference case she hand-carried.

The passenger bay was dim. Corneil glanced briefly over the shadowed faces of its occupants. Half a dozen of them rose hastily to salute. She returned the formality with reserve.

"Are you ready, Commander Rothler?" the ship's comm inquired politely when she had strapped down.

Corneil smiled wryly. Last year she had been one of the herd. This year, with the death of Fleet Commander Knudsen, with the suicide of Blancard of *Pod Hector,* and the assassination of Natchez aboard

Pod Danae, Corneil found herself second in the chain of command of the quasi-military Pod Service. "I assume you have already picked up all other officers scheduled for this flight."

"As you requested, Commander. All aboard. The first transport is already inbound with the other complement of pod commanders."

"Good. Proceed." She was aware of the assessing gaze of her co-passengers.

"You've made the trip to Neutral a number of times in the last six months, Commander," Chen of *Pod Diomedes* commented cautiously.

"I've been back and forth like a shuttlecock since Hazlet took Fleet Command."

"I suppose you're versed on the new clothing cutbacks then?"

"I drew them up myself."

"Ah." The issue was tactfully dropped. Respect for rank ran high in Pod Service.

Larch of *Pod Typhon* was bolder than Chen. "Did you have a hand in the medical cutbacks too?"

"No, I believe Hazlet drew those himself, with the help of Neutral Authority. I first heard about them last night."

A safe subject broached, they buzzed their way toward Neutral America. Corneil turned to watch the green mountains of eastern Pennsylvania and New York unroll below. The Earth bore her scars well. Many of them were healing.

Many more were being inflicted every day. Their passage at low altitude granted large areas of Pennsylvania and New York and all of Vermont and New Hampshire respite for the morning. But afternoon would come.

Maine: their transport swung low over miles of crumbling gray refugee warrens. A brief runway received them and they stepped out into moist air that should have smelled of salt ocean. Instead it smelled of human sewage.

Fleet Commander Hazlet met them, a nervous man who had failed at soldiering. He still apologized for it with every motion. He came down the line pumping hands, bobbing his head desperately. Then they drove into the morning mist in large green buses that rattled.

SCHEDULED EVENT
Conference Luncheon
Menu: garden salad
           baked potato, boiled beets

                    fresh-caught ocean mackerel
                    vanilla ice cream
                    dessert wafers
                    wine
Price: indigestion for stomachs
                    long conditioned to standard
                    fare of algae and recycled
                    water
SCHEDULED EVENT
Annual Status Report
Presented by:
                    Fleet Commander August Hazlet
                    Pod Commander Corneil Rothler
                    Orbital Representative Cordova
                    Officers of Neutral Authority
Content: depressing
Major personnel losses:
                    3 pod commanders, natural causes
                    2 pod commanders, suicide
                    1 pod commander, assassination
                    1 pod commander, accident
                    2 pod commanders, resignation
                    1 prewar surgeon, natural causes
                    2 prewar physicians, natural causes
                    1 prewar physician, suicide
                    1 prewar psychologist, mental collapse
                    etc.
Minor personnel losses: numerous
Breakdown:
                    32% natural causes
                    22% resigned to join fighting forces
                    15% mental collapse
                    12% accident
                    11% suicide
                     7% violence
                     1% undeterminable
Areas of major cutbacks:
                    issue clothing
                    3 major classes of drugs
                    issue vitamin supplements
                    sanitary chemicals and supplies

New categories of patients to be listed
for euth-dispatch:
>   Discussion postponed for session
>   concerning new medical guidelines

SCHEDULED EVENT
Open workshop on podboard violence,
prevention and control
UNSCHEDULED EVENT
Informal after-hours gathering
Featuring:
>   several large containers
>   of informal liquor

Object: forgetfulness

On the second day of the conference, Abzig of *Pod Dictys* was found in a lane in the refugee warrens. He had been clubbed.

On the third day, Corneil presented a peace initiative she wished endorsed by the conference and forwarded to the commanding officers of both armies. The initiative was discussed at length, then rejected. The assembled pod commanders did not believe it would be productive to present demands.

Or requests.

Or even pointed suggestions.

Pod Commander Rothler accepted the rejection without comment, as she had in previous years.

The final day of the conference arrived, the final night. Neutral Authority officers and personnel joined the pod commanders in a social event that featured large crocks of raw alcohol and stomach-wrenching prewar delicacies.

Corneil walked the railed exterior corridors of Fleet Command Central alone. The stars were veiled in damp clouds and the ocean lay beyond a dank curtain of darkness. But tonight, standing with her hands on the rail, making herself totally still, she caught the scent of salt.

It was midnight when she returned to the party and approached Fleet Commander Hazlet. "There is one matter we still need to discuss. I'll have to stop by your quarters before I leave tomorrow."

Fleet Commander Hazlet was glazed with fatigue and alcohol. "Tomorrow?"

"Yes. Before eight."

Hazlet nodded dimly. "Quarters," he affirmed.

The next morning, Corneil spoke to the transport section early. "If I'm delayed for the flight, hold both transports until I arrive. As I explained some days ago, I will be the first passenger delivered by the first transport."

"Understood, Commander." Transport was accustomed to imperious rankers.

Hazlet's quarters were adjacent to Fleet Central. He opened his door half-asleep. "Rothler." Blearily.

"Yes. A problem we must discuss before my transport leaves. I spoke to you last night."

"Ah." Hazlet groped, licked his lips, admitted her. "Yes, of course."

Briskly, Corneil set her conference case on a small table and opened it. Hazlet was too groggy to recognize the euth-kit until it was already in use. Then it was too late.

Corneil reached the hangar with minutes to spare.

The transport had already taxied when she went forward to the pilot's cabin. "Officer, there are papers I intended to leave with Fleet Commander. I find they're still in my case. I want them delivered directly to him. Immediately."

An aide was dispatched to the runway. He accepted the papers and sped away.

The transport became airborne.

Ten minutes later the comset spoke. "Commander Rothler, report forward to pilot's cabin, please."

Corneil frowned, looking up from the papers in her lap. "The air is rather turbulent at this point, Officer."

"I'm taking her up. Fleet Central wants you on emergency."

A brief interval later Fleet Commander Corneil Rothler emerged from the cabin. Gravely she waited until three dozen shadowy faces rose to meet hers. "Gentlemen, I have a tragic announcement. August Hazlet died in quarters this morning of apparent heart failure."

Her three dozen juniors stared at her in stunned silence.

"As Acting Fleet Commander, it is necessary for me to return to Fleet Central immediately. First, however, I must proceed to *Pod Nestor* to pick up several items I will need. After I have disembarked at Fleet Command, this transport will deliver the rest of you to your respective ships. I'm sorry to inconvenience you, but it's essential."

When she had reclaimed her seat and strapped herself, Chen wondered tactfully, "There was a history of heart disease?"

"In the male line of the family, I believe there was," Corneil said untruthfully. "Even so, August was very young to be stricken."

All around her other men equally young shriveled in silent vulnerability, their faces putty-gray with more than hangover now.

Soon the transport pulled smoothly into the hold at *Pod Nestor* and grappled. "I'll return within a quarter hour," Corneil assured her co-passengers, unstrapping, gripping her conference case.

Disembarking.

Her own second in command met her on the other side of the lock, his face stark. "Commander—"

"I talked with Fleet Command in flight. I assume the news has gone to all pods."

"It has. We've already talked with *Aeolus, Atalanta, Phaedra—*"

"Good. Edwards, I want the exterior door of the landing hold closed now and secured. Also the lock door."

Edwards stared at the door from which she had just emerged. "This one?"

"That's the one. Station several men here. I want none of the individuals on the transport to leave the hold until I've given the order. Remember, please, that I'm ranking officer of this organization."

Edwards, it was evident, remembered.

"Good. Come to the bridge when it's attended to. I'll need you."

She passed down corridors crowded with gaping noncombatants. The day nav popped to her feet when Corneil entered the bridge area.

Corneil smiled. "Hold, Epps. And keep your ears open." She settled in the command seat and keyed the farcomm to life. "Fleet Central, this is Rothler. Have all pods been notified of the change of command?"

"It's been done," the voice from Maine assured her.

"Good. How many individual pod commanders has the second transport returned to pods?"

"Pod Commander Nishiura is now aboard *Pod Jocasta*. The second transport is holding there. The pilot requests clarification whether he is to continue delivering commanders or return to Neutral."

"Tell him I want all pod commanders returned to Neutral. Nishiura is to reboard the transport and accompany the others. Please call me when they're in the air."

Signing off, she relaxed in the seat, permitting herself a brief taste of the moments she had directed her years toward. Her head turned to survey the nav screens. Out there in the North American sky seventy-five pods in addition to this one hung. Their occupants totalled more than twelve million.

Twelve million individuals shocked at the news of Fleet Commander Hazlet's sudden death. Twelve million individuals separated from their own pod commanders for the duration.

And below, Battlefield America.

Edwards entered the cabin. "Guard posted with instructions."

Corneil nodded. "Good. Prepare to take the pod down."

Edwards' face went slack. "Down?"

"Down. I want it to settle at the point of the Golden Triangle, near the juncture of the Allegheny and Monongahela."

"But that's—the siege."

"The siege is about to be lifted. There is a parade ground down there, behind the battlements. We're going to decorate it with noncombatants." Her pale eyes were almost warm. Edwards was disconcerted, caught off balance. In that she hoped he was typical of all seventy-six junior officers who held pod bridges this morning in the absence of their superiors.

Fleet Central was on the line again. "The transport is in the air, Commander."

"Good." She kept repeating that word today. Good. "Now I want you to put me on the general line. I want to make an announcement directly to all pod occupants."

Fleet Central complied. Corneil's voice crossed the skies to seventy-five hoverpods, to their more than twelve million occupants.

"Despite the saddening death of Commander August Hazlet, I have good news for you this morning. Last night at Fleet Command Conference, a general truce was signed between the Unipatrist High Command and the Nationalist Army-Air Force. I'm not free to disclose full details at this point, but one condition is that all hoverpods are to land immediately and be dismantled by their occupants.

"Therefore, in accordance with this condition, acting as Fleet Commander, I am now instructing the acting commanders of all hoverpods to take their craft down. Each pod is to be navigated to the nearest confrontation zone between the two armies, landed with due care, and immediately dismantled.

"Proceed. "

For a moment, she thought the laws of the universe had been altered and the phenomenon of sound edited out. Silence on the bridge was total. Corneil swung, met the wide eyes of Epps and Edwards. "Edwards, have you initiated lowering procedure?"

"I—"

"Do so immediately."

Then she turned back to deal with the sudden burst of sound from the farcomm.

"Fleet Commander, Neutral Authority requests—"

"Central, please relay new instructions to the second transport. I want it to put down at the Nationalist air field north of Boston. To all pods calling in, please relay the assurance that my orders are just that —orders. All pods are to lower immediately and dismantle. Any officer who maintains his pod aloft is subject to disciplinary action."

"Fleet Commander, Neutral—"

"Central, next I would like you to relay messages to Unipatrist High Command and Nationalist Headquarters. Messages to read—call fire on all fronts; noncombatants lowering onto all contested areas immediately. End message."

"Fleet Commander—"

"Get on it, Central."

Central got on it.

Ten minutes later Corneil was on the farcomm again. "Fleet Central, is there any pod which refuses to lower?"

"*Pod Proetus* is the only one."

Corneil called direct to *Proetus*. Within minutes, that pod too prepared to comply.

She called Central again. "Central, it is time to publicly announce the truce to Neutral America. Please arrange the announcement immediately. All ground personnel at your disposal are then instructed to begin the evacuation of Neutral America noncombatants. All ground vehicles and aircraft are to be put to service. Noncombatants are to be distributed along the Atlantic Coast and are instructed to request food and supplies from Nationalist and Unipatrist forces."

"Commander, Neutral Authority—" Central pleaded desperately.

"Neutral Authority will not be able to reach me, Central. My final instructions are that after you have instituted the evacuation of noncombatants from Neutral America, you are to dismantle all communication equipment at Fleet Central and leave the area yourself."

Half an hour later, under the capable guidance of Epps and Edwards, *Pod Nestor* touched ground. Corneil emerged amid her shaken and stunned charges. Many had never stepped foot to earth before. Many had never felt a midday breeze or seen the sun without an interposing layer of glass.

Today they did.

Today the soldiers of the Nationalist Army, just as stunned, laid down their weapons and closed around the downed pod.

Today *Pod Nestor* was dismantled. Not gently. When the first metal plate had been ripped from her side, the first bunk thrown through her cargo port, a new bloodlust gripped noncombatant and soldier alike. Together they slew *Pod Nestor*. They beat her and clubbed her and dismembered her with the savage fury of years. They torched her.

At midday she lay dead and smoking. Gathered around her, Unipatrists, Nationalists, and noncombatants shouted obscene obsequies on her passing.

Herron Rothler-Helm stood at his mother's side. "All the others too?" His voice was hoarse, his face still dazed.

"Every one," Corneil said with satisfaction. The pods were down. Most of them, she felt confident, were destroyed. Neutral America, a seething chaos, had been set aflame by its fleeing inhabitants. Twelve million noncombatants littered the battlefields of the continent, and more were streaming on their way. Both armies were neutralized—and savage with joy.

Unipatrist High Command and Nationalist Army-Air Force Headquarters both denied that there was a truce.

But on the land truce existed. And it was good.

Introduction to Selena

Without knowing very much about it, I have always been drawn to the dance. I have been known to go to incredible lengths—not to mention neighborhoods—to see some dancer work. Through writing a theatrical column in a trade magazine, I've gotten to know some dancers and I find them almost as fascinating in a chair as on the stage.

On alternate Tuesdays in months without "r's" in them, when I manage to believe in reincarnation, I remember some peculiar dreams I've had about dancing and I become convinced that I was a dancer in another life.

When "Selena" arrived in the mail one day, it was love at first sight!

Selena

by BEVERLY GOLDBERG

tick . . . tick . . . tick . . . The doll in the box. I cannot think; I cannot do more. The doll in the box. Shoes—my dancing shoes. tick . . . tick . . . tick . . . I will win; Earth shall know pride and the vehicle will be Selena. Selena will dance as she has never danced before. Leave-taking will be hard and soon. Never again to see my dancemates—it is not fair. Why be best? It is the cause of pain. For the glory of the State: World of Earth Supreme in the Universe: I dance. I, Selena, dance and Earth is proud. tick . . . tick . . . Why do not the clocks of Earth tock . . . tick?—the old books say they do; but here it is only tick . . . tick. . . .

"Selena, are you ready to leave? Have you taken the pills as indicated? Have you said your good-byes?"

"I cannot say good-bye to those I love so dearly. I cry and thus earn great displeasure. I will not risk it. Let us go, farewells unsaid."

"But, Selena, your dancemates . . . I have said my farewells to those I grew together with."

"Yes, you too are going forever. But this hurts you little and the reward for you is to be so small."

"Small? When I will be serving the World of Earth?"

"Let us go, then, to the ship. The voyage will be long and I must practice much. But to dance without joy? That may cost us victory."

"Selena, I have seen you dance. You will bring us victory, and it will be worth the cost."

"And you, Trynde, will your cost bring Earth something of equal value?"

"I will have helped you. We could not send a dancemate alone."

Trynde moved her solid body around the room, gathering the belongings Selena had not packed. She did not comment on the packing already done. She covered the doll protectively. There would be no chance for one such as Selena to win without the doll—the toy that was her personal tie to her past life, her early days; the days before her dancemates.

The packing was done; Trynde led the silent, swaying Selena to the door for departure. Selena was the only one of those present who did not know the joy. She had her peace; she had taken it at three o'clock.

Her leaving gave pleasure. The walk of beauty that was the walk of Selena was part of the joy. Her dancemates had come to see her leave but, being one with her, they were careful not to let her see them. For sorrow was not good on a day such as this. She was their perfection, and in her going was victory for them. The pursuit of victory, the aim of all mates of whatever order, was strong in them and they would not peril it. Selena would go; she would be of them no more. It would be a sorrow, but a sorrow shared.

Trynde guided Selena with gentle force and soon they were on the ship for the long journey. Trynde would have to care for Selena in the body. She must not allow it to fall from the height of perfection her dancemate years had brought. Carefully, Trynde stored the dancemate tapes to use in the training. For Selena was a true mate, and, alone, the dance was not hers. Trynde was of the lone mates; those who could act without the complete sharing of those with whom they were raised, without the unity that gave strength.

For the men of Earth had not developed talents for large groupings, but for small. It was only thus that war was ended. The young were put in the homes of the mates to be raised with others of their own age; mates of gene-likeness-kinship of true talent. None had but joy in what he did; thus all were happy. And the past, the past was the love-toy; the gift of one's own creators given by them with the love of the Creator of all. And happiness was all; all mates together; the mates a part of an order. Selena was a mate of five—five, and Selena. And they were dancemates to all the other groups of five or six or seven in the order of the dance. Selena was a child of a mate of the order of music and a mate of the order of art. And when Selena danced, the dance was music and art and all knew how perfect the choosing had been.

And now Selena was to be the symbol of the good of life on Earth; she was the perfection of generations. And she was to be victorious, for Earth needed this victory. Pride had endured with beauty as the only offering left, and thus Earth must be the possessor of the greatest beauty.

Selena, the greatest beauty of Earth when in motion, was settled on the ship by Trynde. With cool competence Trynde made all the arrangements for the practice; and then she let Selena sleep; and while she slept, Trynde slipped the continuing medication under the skin; and Selena slept on and on. When Trynde wakened Selena for practice and necessity, she gave her the medication of the dancemates. Dancing needed strength and endurance and the means for these were available: the State provided them. Dancemates were young always—the medication kept them in their youth, but kept them from leaving their youth. For their hearts were not as strong as the State wished. But Selena was a dancemate and she knew not pain and she had a long youth and she had the joy of the dance. The dance with her mates was a joy—the dance without mates a terror not to be contemplated. The group danced and joyed together, and sorrowed apart. But the other worlds would not agree and so the Earth had decided to relinquish Selena for victory. She would dance alone. She would dance with joy untrue; she would have to give more than did any other, for she would be dancing with a heart that could not rightly dance alone.

The practice began. The music began. The mates appeared. Trynde had brought them to Selena by the miracle of the medication and in the miracle of tri-v-tapes.

tick . . . tick . . . I, Selena, dance. I dance with you, my loves. I joy with the oneness of us. And I leap and I dance. Oh, yes, I, Selena, feel the wind and the trees and the love of the god in my breast and my body. I, Selena, dance. And I dance . . . tick . . .

*tick . . . Again I hear no tock—but therefore I am home: for the tick
. . . tick of Earth is with me: World of Earth Supreme in the Universe. And I, Selena, dance. tick . . . tick . . .*

Trynde shut the metronome away and the tapes and the screens
and then she picked up the limp body and, watching the rapid rise
and fall of the hard breasts, she murmured, "Sleep, Selena, till the
time of the dance. We will practice and Earth shall win. I will help
Earth win and the victory will be good. But you must know you are
oneness, a oneness I cannot make true." And Trynde slipped the
medication under the skin of Selena and when Selena's sleep was deep
enough she was spoken to by the voice tapes and told her of the tick
. . . tick . . . tick that was Earth and joy and the dancemates together, sharing.

And there was practice . . . and there was sleep . . . and there
was Trynde and Selena . . . and time passed and then there was the
world of the contests. Selena was hurried to the Earth station on 5
Orion and placed in the room for waiting. Trynde worked with her
there. But Trynde saw that Selena, the dancemate, had much to do;
for Trynde learned of all the entrants, and she feared. The need for
victory was strong in her; it was a need that grew as the separation
from mates began to burden her. But she saw that Selena danced and
that Selena danced with the spirits of her dancemates, thinking she
was dancing with the flesh. And Selena grew tired and Trynde gave
her more of the State's medication, so that she was again strong. The
weeks passed. The time was near.

Trynde began to give Selena the new medication so that Selena
danced always with her mates. She talked to her mates and knew
them to be a part of her again and she was happy. Selena shared her
doll with her mates, and the toy of the past brought comfort it had
never brought before and Selena was happy.

The time had come. All was readiness. Trynde watched, as did all
the members of the contest worlds, and Trynde feared. Selena—en-
trant of the oldest of the worlds—was to be the last. Selena had to be
the best, as Trynde knew. Trynde had mates whose voices were echo-
ing in her ears and she answered that she would provide the best.
And as Trynde slipped the gossamer veils over the lengths of Selena's
hard slenderness, and as she slipped the shoes on Selena's feet, she
slipped the medication under Selena's skin. And Selena began to feel
the joy. Then Trynde slipped the disk that was on the pin into

Selena's twisted locks and Selena heard the tick . . . tick . . . tick and knew she was with her mates. And Trynde watched her and heard her name called and heard the Earth proclaimed.

As the music began to sound, Trynde slipped still more of the medication under Selena's skin. And she moved Selena toward the stage, the great stage illuminated with myriad lights and shadows as requested by Earth. She whispered fiercely, "Your mates," and Selena heard the tick . . . tick, and she rushed onto the stage to join her mates.

Victory.

For Selena danced. Her body moved the shadows and those who saw (and who did not see?) knew beauty and knew the god. Selena moved and the air danced. Selena danced and the sounds of the worlds vibrated in motionless accord with sighs for the beauty and the grace. And Selena danced. And the hall was silent; the music stilled. And Selena danced. The dance was all. Selena was all. And Selena danced. And Selena danced.

Trynde slowly walked up the steps and onto the stage. She stood over the body and intoned:

"Selena—for the glory of the State: World of Earth Supreme in the Universe."

And Selena danced no more.

Introduction to Uraguyen and I

One of the first writers to submit a story to *Cassandra Rising* was Miriam Allen deFord. I loved the story she sent, but had certain reservations, so I wrote and explained my feelings. She readily agreed to revise the story, but it was decided that the revision would wait because she was deeply involved in other projects. Ms. deFord died before that revision was done. Miriam Allen deFord was a great and gracious lady and she is profoundly missed.

I asked Juanita Coulson if she would undertake the revision along the lines Ms. deFord had agreed to, and she kindly acquiesced. Ms. Coulson is the author of a number of science fiction novels (*Crisis on Cheiron, Singing Stones, War of Wizards*) and is as well known for her excellent gothics and historical romances. She and her husband, Robert, edit and publish the Hugo Award-winning fanzine *Yandro*.

Uraguyen and I

by MIRIAM ALLEN deFORD
and
JUANITA COULSON

Only two things are certain about every human being you meet: he was born and he is going to die.

But not Uraguyen.

He was born, but he never had to die—not as long as he remained dictator of Veladion.

At first, when he had been the bright young hope of the Lower Depths Revolt, there was a long list of volunteers. When the news of his illness leaked out, he was almost embarrassed—or said he was; maybe at that period he really was—by the flood of offered kidneys. (They said it was nephritis, but pretty soon everybody knew or guessed that it was the beginning of his long struggle with cancer.) I should know: I was one of the earliest of his old-time followers to offer myself. I'm glad now that somebody else was chosen. But we were sure that Uraguyen was indispensable. He had to be kept alive and well.

Kidneys: everybody has two of them. Everybody has two lungs, too, and can live with one if he has to; as time went on and the doctors reluctantly announced (they were still talking at that period) that Uraguyen was suffering from a tumor in the left lung, which was malignant but had not yet metastasized, the volunteers thronged again. This time I was not one of them; I was beginning to have melancholy doubts about the way the LDR was going.

You know what usually happens: first the nearly hopeless rebellion against oppression, the riots, the guerrilla warfare, the imprisonment and torture and executions; then the long hard battle, the growing upsurge; and at last—victory. The condemned and excoriated leader of the rebels becomes the hero and finally the king or emperor or president or whatever name is given to the head of that particular nation.

Perhaps he does lead his nation into a better life, at least for a time, or stays what he was, the spokesman and inspiration of a new free regime. There have been such men and women: Morgos of Pythaire was one such in our own era, and so was Gaethera of Kon. Today I hope . . . but let me go on.

But all too often, now as in the remote past, once the new leader is settled in his dominance, little by little he hardens, and his rule hardens with him, until once more we find ourselves crushed beneath a despotism as unbearable as the one against which we had revolted. They say even "Good, Kind Sethir," as he liked to be called, whom we of the LDR overthrew and liquidated, came to the throne as the young commander of a dissident movement.

We who marched with Uraguyen in the bright early days shut our eyes and ears as long as we could deceive ourselves. One by one our new freedoms vanished, one by one the old tyrannies against which we had fought and which we thought we had conquered returned, always in the name of plausible necessity—the secret arrests, the concentration camps, the torture chambers, the hidden murders, the appeals to security as a brake on liberty, and "peace" as a substitute for justice. The day came when to be heard quoting passages from Uraguyen's own early speeches was a sure way to disappear suddenly and forever.

Nevertheless, the old image remained. Uraguyen was no petty upstart who had attained power as if by accident and could be defeated when he abused it. Of his kind, the man was a genius. To the great mass he remained not only the head of state, but the leader, superhuman and almost divine. From his own experience he could sense the merest beginnings of rebellion and suppress them ruthlessly. He was guarded as few men have ever been; the slightest suspicion of less than fanatical devotion among his closest associates meant instantaneous exile from the palace which he—who once had been mobbed in the streets by worshipers fighting to touch his garments—now seldom left, and never except surrounded by soldiers with laser guns. No such mass movement as the LDR originally was could hope to survive or even to be born; he could not be assassinated; the one deep secret dream of the disillusioned was that, like all living creatures, he must age and must die.

But, thanks to the miracles of science, that dream too was dissipated.

They say that even an Old Terra, in its last years before the Holocaust, organ transplantation had been tried with mixed success. How astonished and envious those pioneers would be if they could see our surgeons here on Veladion at work. There is literally no part of the human body which they cannot replace safely.

That hard early experience in the guerrilla days of the LDR had taken its toll. At the time Uraguyen had seemed as healthy and strong as any of us, but perhaps even then the seeds of the cancer lay within him, waiting a chance to strike. The stresses of that period gave the disease an opening wedge. He aged rapidly, before his time. One organ after another became affected. However, with our marvelous surgical techniques, he could simply spend a few days (closely guarded) in a hospital wing of the palace especially built for his needs, and then be back again as good as new.

As I have said, in the earlier stages of the cancer, and of his dictatorship, there were many willing volunteers. But it is one thing to donate a paired organ, an eye, or a limb; it is another to lose one's heart or liver or both lungs, and with that one's life. That grim fact—and Uraguyen's ever-increasing tyrannies—choked off the stream of donors. He was alienating all those who had once loved him enough to die for him, and there was not even a wife who might forgive, and sacrifice herself, that he might live. "Why marry?" he said to me once. "There isn't a woman I would want who wouldn't be overcome with joy if I would take her." (That ought to have warned me, but we were all blinded then.)

So when, about five years after his first series of transplants, it was found that the lung cancer had returned and now affected both lungs, the new as well as the old one, there was no response to the subtle feelers encouraging volunteers.

In view of his past actions, we anticipated some grasping excess, some obvious seizure of a victim—a thing so inhuman and outrageous that it might, at last, produce the explosion of revolt we hoped for.

But Uraguyen was too clever to move openly. He had other solutions to his problem.

There was purchase—generally the vital organs of those who had already chosen suicide. But few of those people were in the perfect physical condition required for transplantation purposes, and those few demanded astronomical prices for the bodies they were so soon to discard. It was their last chance to leave a legacy to their families or to some worthy cause; and in a society such as ours where suicide, like abortion, was a matter of private judgment these people were looked on more often with admiration than odium. But then the abuses of the system gradually altered public opinion. Once those who had called such dealings "cannibalism" were regarded as cranks or reactionaries. Now they were listened to and applauded, and another source of vital organs disappeared.

But a very nasty rumor began to circulate among the growing-though-hidden and much imperiled anti-Uraguyen faction.

We had long suspected that those within Uraguyen's inmost circle sometimes were taking advantage of death sentences passed upon criminals who happened to possess healthy organs. The condemned received no pay, of course; but most of them preferred death under anesthetic to our rather severe means of execution. It was an utterly corrupt practice, though few protested the callous exploitation of those they assumed were guilty of murder or other heinous crimes.

But now it was whispered: What happens to the political dissidents who are arrested and then disappear? And how many of those supposed "murderers" were truly guilty of any wrong-doing? Could it be that people are seized and convicted not for crimes or because they are suspected of opposition to the dictatorship—but merely because some privileged man or woman needs, say, a new heart?

And for "privileged man or woman" substitute above all only one name—Uraguyen's.

That realization was a catalyst, and there was an immediate result —a firm resolve among the rebels to find some way to kill the tyrant and stop his regime once and for all.

To do that, however, we had to convert, subvert, or swindle Noble Doctor Levingorm. Levingorm—the only being on Veladion whom

Uraguyen trusted. Levingorm—the scientist who had received three Gastikos Awards for his astonishing medical discoveries. Levingorm —who alone with his specially trained nurse-assistant was allowed to anesthetize the dictator and give him another kidney, heart, or pancreas, as Uraguyen's organs yielded to the onslaught of the cancer.

Levingorm had not been one of us when Uraguyen had been the young and idealistic leader of the LDR. The doctor had entered the scene later, after the disease struck Uraguyen. Levingorm's skills had proved invaluable, and it was Levingorm who first proposed using criminals and then political prisoners as donors when the offers to purchase organs no longer met response. And the Noble Doctor had been well rewarded for his services; next to Uraguyen himself, he was now the only really powerful man in our country, and he enjoyed that power.

This was the man we must somehow win over to our cause, or buy over, or compel over. It seemed impossible, but there was no other chance. Uraguyen's security forces blocked all other avenues to the throne.

By now the LDR had a successor, the New Revolutionary Movement. It was triple hush-hush, naturally. If any of our names, mine most of all, had been known to Uraguyen, it would have meant a horrible and not very quick death. Of all the former rebels once close to him, few were left, and fewer still retained that all-consuming passion to end the rotten system which was crushing Veladion. But *I* did, and they looked to me for leadership. I must spearhead this campaign.

I could not, for good reasons connected with our common past, approach Uraguyen personally. I must not remind him of my existence or give him any hint of the underground supporting me. But those same reasons out of our past determined that I alone of the NRM would be the one to bell this terrifying cat.

To do that, I must work through Levingorm, who I did not even know.

But I must, because if the rumors were true, fate had now taken a hand, and if what we suspected were true, it was the one opportunity we would have to succeed.

We have a gifted surgeon in our organization—no Levingorm, but one of the very best. He was the one person in whom I could, and can, confide totally, the one I could rely on no matter what would happen. He warned me, repeatedly, of the risks involved in the project I was contemplating. But I convinced him it had to be done.

Like the rest of us in the NRM, our surgeon's revolutionary affiliations were a profound secret, and his professional standing remained unblemished. As a colleague and former classmate he was able to socialize with Doctor Levingorm, and to subtly and indirectly discuss a "hypothetical case." Of course, Levingorm did not chatter idly about his most important patient—his *only* patient. Yet he must have felt his own crisis approaching, a growing threat to the power and position he enjoyed, because he let drop several clues that gave our surgeon the information we needed.

As the transplantations had multiplied, the progress of Uraguyen's malady—even its continued existence—had ceased to be public property. All mention of it was crushed. But any intelligent person, even those among Uraguyen's scarce remaining faithful devotees, could see how tyranny was spreading: the ferocious "security," the obsessive secrecy, the sadistic cruelties—and inevitably the whispers started. We began to ascribe Uraguyen's increasing inhumanity to a physical cause. I was far from the only one to guess that this time it was the one absolutely crucial organ in his body that was affected, and our surgeon's delicately probing conversation with Levingorm confirmed my suspicions.

A tumor had been discovered in Uraguyen's brain, and it was found to be malignant. It was in the cerebral cortex, it was metastasizing, and it was inoperable even for a genius like Levingorm. To operate would literally destroy that which he was trying to save.

Not only did Levingorm—and we—know this awful truth, but so did Uraguyen. And the dilemma tortured him far more than it could have any ordinary man.

Above all, he wanted to live and continue to reign. But though brains could be transplanted, and had been, and though helpless victims—too many of them!—were at his mercy, this operation involved problems unlike any other.

A total brain transplant meant not only a transfer of living tissue; it meant that all that made Uraguyen himself would be exchanged for all that made some other human being *him*self.

So far, Uraguyen was still functioning normally mentally, that is to say, normally for him. He was still in control, still making decisions. And he could fully comprehend the bitter reality of his situation; he must either die altogether, or he could live on with his body possessed by another mind.

He was in the position of a king who had to abdicate but who could pick his successor. Any other man on Veladion, I am positive, would have simply let it go, would have asked for euthanasia and left the future to chance. But not this man. His colossal ego and lust for power continued even as he faced certain death. If he, as himself, must die, then he, as himself, must be resurrected, in the same body and with the same appearance, by somebody as like himself as possible.

Such was his incredible demand—and if it was possible that he *could* find a brain and personality very similar to his own to take his place, Veladion would lose its last hope for freedom.

We could not allow that to happen. From now on, *we* must control events, not Uraguyen.

Time was on our side. The disease was progressing rapidly, and with each day chances lessened that a transplant candidate could be found in time. Uraguyen's insistence on receiving precisely the "right" brain threatened not only his life but Levingorm's, for if the dictator died, his surgical power-behind-the-throne would also fall with him.

Levingorm was the key. His frantic search for a brain donor gave the NRM the entry it needed. Thanks to my all-important surgeon contact, I was able to plant the necessary "suggestion." As one fellow professional to another, he broached to Levingorm the possibility of providing a donor for the proposed transplantation.

And Levingorm instantly snapped at the bait. That in itself was an indication of the stage of Uraguyen's disease. If we did not act quickly, Levingorm might be driven to find his *own* donor. That could not be allowed.

From that point on my surgeon friend was the only person to be in my complete confidence. He wanted what I wanted, would dare anything for my sake. And he could be counted on to replace Levingorm at the crucial stage, if that became necessary. He had connections no one else in our underground had. He could concoct the countless counterfeit records we must have if the scheme were to succeed.

Oh, I was frightened, of course. Never believe in the cool and intrepid hero or the calm, collected martyr. So many things could go wrong in half a dozen ways I couldn't foresee, and once the project was under way, I could never stop it. But I had to go on, for the sake of Veladion and her lost freedom.

Scrupulously, carefully, running against time, I built up a case history, embodying point by point every detail I knew would appeal most strongly to Uraguyen. Without the help of my surgeon conspirator it would have been impossible. It is because of this and because I assume my obligations to him that you have noticed I have not mentioned and will not mention his name. I will protect him always, and give him every recompense within my power.

Levingorm was becoming frantic, sensing time slipping through his grasp. Either a donor must be found soon or even the rest of Uraguyen's body was doomed. He would not take a healthy brain from among the many at his mercy; he clung to his power-mad demand for a donor built, so to speak, to his order.

And that was what I did to myself—built a physical and psychological façade of data to convince Uraguyen, and to hide the real personality beneath.

There were two major hurdles to jump. A plausible reason must be found for the person to be willing to sacrifice himself. And there would inevitably be some sort of face-to-face confrontation. Uraguyen would insist on seeing his victim—his replacement. It was physically impossible for me to disguise myself so that he would not recognize me at once. And he would never for a minute, thanks to our intimate past acquaintance, believe that I could meet his high specifications, or that I would offer to die that he might live. Donate him a kidney, long ago, yes; but not my brain, then or ever.

We surmounted the first hurdle without too much difficulty. We—the surgeon and I—concocted an "applicant" who was very near Uraguyen's own age (true!) and shared in nearly every way Uraguyen's own ambitions and dreams. But this applicant had never had the "breaks" that Uraguyen had enjoyed. He too had once been a rebel in the LDR when he was younger. However, his post had been out on Veladion's frontiers, far from the seats of power. Item by item, he satisfied Uraguyen's requirements. As I had calculated, this was the psychic twin Uraguyen demanded.

The "applicant's" data went on: now, with no financial means for transplantation, he was suffering an incurable cardiac disorder, the one flaw in an otherwise healthy body. Nothing awaited him but imminent painful death. Therefore, having always been a dedicated follower of our ruler, as his last loyal gesture he would offer his brain to Uraguyen—proud that he so much resembled the leader, and asking only the honor of being of service to him.

All this was thoroughly investigated by the Security Force, and the falsely documented history stood up against their inquiries, as it had been designed to do. But Levingorm was no fool. The uncanny perfection of the "applicant's" profile made him question matters privately. And that, too, was as I had planned, for without Levingorm's co-operation, willing or otherwise, the project would fail. Now, without either side ever fully revealing itself, we approached each other, and I felt sure Levingorm would work with us—for his own reasons.

He did not care for the future good of Veladion, but for the survival of Noble Doctor Levingorm. So be it, so long as he was our tool.

The more difficult hurdle remained to be crossed, the necessary confrontation with Uraguyen. To be sure, only one such interview need take place. When the actual operation was performed, I would not be brought in before Uraguyen was already unconscious.

The solution was amazingly simple. I was given a stand-in. An obscure (and hungry) professional actor, from the distant part of Veladion where I—the "applicant"—too was supposed to reside, was hired for enough money to quiet his doubts. He was persuaded that this was a test of sorts, and that a successful outcome would bring him not only great wealth but status far above his fellow performers. He was thoroughly coached, presented to Levingorm, and by him to Uraguyen as the candidate—and accepted.

(It is regrettable that on his way back to his home the actor's one-man plane crashed, and he was killed. My surgeon-conspirator objected strenuously to the sabotage, but I patiently told him that it was impossible to trust any outsider. The same consideration applies to the fatal explosion, soon after the operation, in Noble Doctor Levingorm's laboratory, where he and his nurse were working. My surgeon protested that execution as well, arguing that despite his perverted medical practices during Uraguyen's reign Levingorm's death was a great loss to science. Quite true. But Levingorm knew far too much, and his loyalty, as he had proved during the operation, was in question. It was too bad, but his death was therefore unavoidable.)

It may sound frivolous, but as a matter of fact the one thing I most lamented in becoming (or "inhabiting") Uraguyen was the inevitable death of my own body—which in truth was in excellent health and was much more attractive than Uraguyen's own! I had given up so many things precious to me, no longer mine to have. For the rest of my life I would be trapped in Uraguyen's flesh, and that grieved me for some time after the operation was successfully completed.

But that was a childish reaction, and I was later ashamed of it. What I had done was to sacrifice everything for the most noble of goals: to create a "new" Uraguyen, who would lift from Veladion the terrible burden of those years since he had taken over as our evil tyrant. The loss of my own body was, after all, a small price to pay for such a great victory in the name of freedom.

It was done. I who write this am now to all intents and purposes Uraguyen. Since once I occupied his body I became Veladion's absolute dictator, I was able to arrange immediate liquidation of those

officials who had abetted him and install in their places my own loyal
staff and begin to mold them to my wishes.

But five years after the transplantation, I sometimes wonder if it
was worth my terrible martyrdom. Why does it become increasingly
necessary to forbid my natural impulses of compassion in the interests of security? Why am I forced to stamp out firmly the plots of
those who stupidly question my enlightened policies? Why, I ask myself, have these subversive dissidents sprung up, within the very organization to which I belonged and in whose name I sacrificed my
own body? Is it fair that I should be so beset by these misguided
fools? I have suffered and struggled for Veladion's sake. Surely I
know what is best for her.

My surgeon friend, one of the few from the old days who still
stands staunchly by me, keeps arguing tactics. I am afraid he is blind.
He does not understand the ramifications as I do. Only the other evening he said, "Have you never considered simply letting go? Allow
freedom to grow of its own accord. It must be nourished, not forced."

I tried to make him see reason, but it was futile. Imagine! He even
had the audacity to remark that perhaps Uraguyen had meant well,
once. Did I not recall how idealistic Uraguyen had been in the early
days, how much we had thought alike? But once Uraguyen had
seized power, matters grew impossible.

I refused to listen, outraged that my loyal friend would dare make
such a comparison. His obstinate attitude presumes on our relationship. He, of all people, should understand why I must do the
things I do to preserve all that is dear in Veladion. How quickly he
has forgotten—he who was willing to risk everything with me in order
to save Veladion from Uraguyen's tyranny.

But I will *not* chastise him, though his prattlings grow ever more ir-
ritating. For his own sake, he must eventually see the truth and comprehend why I must keep a firm guiding hand on Veladion's helm.

I shall and must persevere, in the face of all opposition, even his.
We must have security against our foes without and, alas, within. We
must have tranquility. I repudiate vehemently the malicious accusations, brought me by my trusted investigators, that Veladion under—
shall we say this incarnation of its leader?—is no better off than it was
before. I know I am right, and therefore I have to yield to the political realities, even though it breaks my heart to suppress those who
were my comrades.

You may wonder why I am recording all this—let us call it a
confession—at all. I suppose it is simple vanity, though I may disguise
it to myself as a desire for historical accuracy. I am making provision

that it shall be concealed and remain unopened until fifty years after my death. Time will be the judge of my work.

And those fifty years must be far in the future—*must!* I have so much yet to do for Veladion, and death waits upon me all too eagerly. It was a risk inherent in my original sacrifice, and the bill comes due often. The cancer recurs, again and again, for the disease lurked within Uraguyen's body, too deep to be detected in all its hiding places. And I must pay the consequences, because when I assumed Uraguyen's power, I inherited his sickly shell of flesh as well.

I have already had a few minor transplants. But I am determined never to have a major one—unless of course it becomes vitally necessary. My surgeon is not the genius Levingorm was. I am not sure he could successfully perform a brain operation of the delicacy required if . . . but that will not happen. I know better than anyone alive the dangers of such a procedure, the possibilities for deception within one's own ranks.

It is only occasionally, in the super-busy life I now lead as ruler of Veladion, that I have time for personal reflection. When I do, most often I remember vividly the last time Uraguyen and I met face-to-face. It was when he was just beginning to display the signs of the brutality he later inflicted on all of us. I, as his chief lieutenant in the old LDR, was delegated to remonstrate with him.

He had always been arrogant—we called it heroic self-confidence, once—and he turned on me viciously.

"You!" he sneered. "What do *you* know of the necessities and prerogatives of power? Do you think I ever really shared that soft, sloppy idealism I had to pretend to in order to put myself where I am today? Go back and tell those fools in what's left of the LDR that I will tolerate no more of their nonsense. Tell them to knuckle under or expect the worst."

I remember my helpless rage then, my fervent longing for the strength to answer him on his own terms. And now, in a strange way, I *have* that strength—his *own* strength.

He carried out his threat, then, as I have. But let me acknowledge it, for the historians yet to be born: his last words to me still rankle. It is hard to expunge all the emotional impact of what one has experienced in childhood and youth.

He laughed and said, "As for you, little sister, you lie low and shut up, or you will meet as horrible a death as I can arrange, whether I am your brother or not!"

Jacqueline Lichtenberg calls writing science fiction the "entire definition of my existence," and quotes Karl Wallenda about his return to the high wire after an accident killed some of his troupe: " 'To be on the wire is life, all the rest is waiting.' That's the way I feel about sf writing. Everything else I do is done so that I can be permitted to write sf, and nothing else."

Her first publication was in *If Magazine* in 1968—the first story in her Sime series. Her novel *House of Zeor,* also part of the Sime series, was published by Doubleday in 1974, and a new novel, *Unto Zeor, Forever,* was also published by Doubleday earlier this year.

The Vanillamint Tapestry

by JACQUELINE LICHTENBERG

Raymond Yost didn't like the idea of working on loan to the Intelligence Agency. He was a scholar, not a spy. But his feet carried him relentlessly along the springy floored, brightly utilitarian corridor toward the Vesting Chamber. He turned the last corner, squared his bony shoulders, and paced the final fifty yards with thin-lipped determination.

He didn't like the idea of working so close to a partner's fission-time either, but he'd keep his word, even if it killed him . . . and it probably would.

He'd said that many times in the last nine years, and each time he'd survived. Director Proken kept saying that experience would polish his technique, but, privately, Yost thought experience would polish him off. He'd never had the nerve to try the pun on the bald-headed, blue-skinned Director of Humanoid Correlationists.

At twenty-nine, all Yost had to show for his life's work was an Interplanetary Health Certificate claiming that his six-foot, hundred-fifty-pound, Terran-born body was in excellent, if underweight, health. But, every morning, he searched for the first gray hair among the ashen blond. He'd vowed that when it appeared, he'd quit the Central Correlationists for the sedentary life of a desk scholar.

At the end of the corridor, he paused before the ornate, ten-foot-high doors, took a deep breath, and placed his hand on the sensor plate. Yost gritted his teeth at the grinding whir of heavily taxed servos, badly in need of the attention of the very scarce maintenance crews, but slowly the doors swung inward revealing familiar, red velvet shadows.

The well-upholstered hush, soft, reddish shadows and mixed incenses of the Vesting Chamber created a wholly different world from the angular polished-chrome-and-fluorescent sterility of the rest of the Station. Within that chamber, haunted by the distant moaning of thin, dark winds through jagged rocks, Yost always felt he could believe the stories about the Ballatine race-memory being somehow connected with the spirit world or the Beyond where God sat on His throne and Created. The Ballatine reticence to discuss theology could be due to any number of things. Still, it would be nice to know if there really were a Creator.

As he crossed the threshold, allowing the doors to close behind him, Yost felt his post-hypnotic conditioning taking hold and he yielded. Brushing aside the last wisp of mysticism, he checked his assignment card. It read, G-12, Kolitt.

The door closed and Yost moved to the railing in front of him to survey the huge chamber, which was the off-duty home of CC's resident colony of Ballatine. He was on a circular mezzanine, seven levels above the main floor. All the balconies were partitioned into smaller chambers by heavy hangings richly woven in dark-hued patterns. Only the main floor showed hard, reflecting surfaces, and, Yost knew, those were merely the roofs of compartments which were as thoroughly hung inside as the balconies. He could see some of the small, spidery humanoids that served the Ballatine on Bellet, the Ballatine homeworld. "Friends-of-one-part" the Ballatine called them, soulless host bodies to provide mobility for the symbiots. It was their placid certainty in recognizing "soul" that had given rise to the rumors about the Ballatine.

Yost had never been in a main-floor compartment, and he knew he never would be. That was where the Ballatine conducted their conjugation and fission rites. Investiture and Divestiture always took place in a balcony chamber. He was on level G, now he needed to find number twelve and pick up his senior partner for this assignment.

He stepped back to the door, looked both ways along the narrow aisle, spotted number two, three, and four and followed along until he found a hanging with a number 12 woven into the abstract design. He pushed the soft velour aside, allowing the tactile sensation to trigger another post-hypnotic command, and entered.

The incense Kolitt had chosen for his tiny, wedge-shaped home smelled like sandalwood, fresh air, and eucalyptus. Even without his hypnotic conditioning, the California-born human found it pleasantly relaxing.

And then he saw the Ballatine, ten pounds of amorphous, red- and black-veined, blue-white tissue floating at ease in his nutrient bath of enriched, Bellet seawater.

Yost checked his card against the clipboard hung from the glassite bowl, double-checked the codes, and then clipped the card in place and lay down on the cot. He rolled up his left sleeve and dangled his arm in the water, brushing the Ballatine gently to signal his readiness.

Only the first contact occasioned a twinge of instinctive revulsion . . . the primeval human reaction to soft, warm, slimy creatures. Then Kolitt commanded the nerves locally and Yost relaxed. The Investiture would take a good twenty minutes, and for the most of that he would be blind, deaf, and dumb, so he let his absent hypnotist talk him into a refreshing nap. Kolitt, like all his kind, would be considerate, but the procedure could still drive an unprotected human insane.

Yost woke to an oddly alien environment that gradually converged on normality. Then the Ballatine spoke silently in his mind, ::Friend-of-two-parts, I greet you. Have I matched sensory inputs?::

Yost nodded. ::Perfectly. You are Kolitt.::

::Correct. And you are Raymond Yost, among other things.::

::Correct. Now. We've many grave matters to discuss.::

::True. And meanwhile, you will make haste to consume calories lest I damage your health. Allow me to check my synapse linkages before we leave?::

::Please do. Control is all yours. Take me to the Commissary.::

Still lying on the cot, Yost felt his individual muscle fibers tensing and relaxing as the symbiot checked his control. Gaining co-ordination, his body rose to its feet and then, suddenly, he blacked out.

He didn't loose consciousness, so he had time to feel true panic be-

fore the room swam back into focus. He was seated on the cot.
::What happened?::

::Deepest apologies, Friend-of-two-parts. Slight fibrillation. No
damage. It won't happen again.::

Panic allayed for the moment, Yost asked the question that had
haunted him since Proken had talked him into this madness. ::Kolitt,
do you feel . . . all right?::

The inward silence lengthened until Yost felt as if Kolitt were gone.
::Kolitt, I apologize. I didn't mean to offend . . .::

::Yes, Friend-of-two-parts, our pride is sometimes our worst
enemy. Yet, if you doubt me, we'd best undertake no mission together. A partnership such as ours can survive only on trust.::

::If you tell me you can do it, I won't doubt.:: Yost considered
Ballatine integrity about the only constant in the shifting universe.

After a moment the reply came and Yost was able to read intona-
tion in that silent voice. ::Ray,:: said Kolitt gravely, ::I have at least
six months. I've been thoroughly briefed, and I believe we can perform the task set us.::

::Then let's go. We certainly haven't time to waste.::

Kolitt went through his calisthenic routine and then, with increasing smoothness, piloted their body to the Commissary and even displayed unusual talent in feeding themselves. Yost was surprised at
such immediate proficiency until he remembered he'd never worked
with such a mature Ballatine before.

But Proken had wanted two Seniors for this mission, and he'd
wanted the most experienced Ballatine on the staff . . . namely Kolitt. And Proken usually got exactly what he wanted.

All through the meal they discussed the details of the mission. The
Ballatine's skill at the quasi-telepathic form of communication grew
steadily until Yost could read nuances of meaning even more clearly
than he could human facial expressions.

All during their four-week journey to Harnuit, the technical details
held their attention almost exclusively. They went over everything
from local language, customs, and values to planetary geography, political history, and economic resources. In short, they approached the
field of operations as Correlationists rather than as spies simply because they knew no other method.

They were still discussing their problem as their tiny ship fell toward the Harnuit Spaceport . . . the one and only spaceport on the
planet.

Yost relaxed and let the Ballatine cope with the antiquated, non-
human-built landing grid. He watched his fingers flying over the com-

plex board and reflected that, next to women, symbiots were the handiest kind of people to have around. Too bad the two were incompatible. A Ballatine supplied absolute total recall, an enormous encyclopedic knowledge, assorted manual skills, freedom from parasitic invasions, swift repair of injuries, and, most important to travelers, companionship. All at the cost of two or three thousand calories a day . . . and Ballatines weren't even fussy about the original form of those calories.

Yost had become close friends with every partner he'd ever had and now found himself warming to Kolitt in the same way. It was becoming more and more difficult for him to accept the idea of Kolitt's approaching death. Though no further mention had been made of it, it was never far from Yost's thoughts.

When their ship was safely grounded, Yost said silently, ::O.K., where to?::

::It's your turn, I'm going to sleep.::

From Kolitt's heavy tone, Yost guessed that the landing had tired his partner so he locked the ship and went to do battle with the local customs authorities. Despite their reputation, spies spent as much time on dreary routine as scholars or anybody else.

Harnuit's largest and capital city, Tobuin, sprawled in rural splendor, practically untouched by galactic civilization. The natives liked it that way, and they didn't welcome tourists.

The terms of Harnuit's Confluence Membership placed an absolute embargo on all Rotsuctronic devices. And practically all modern equipment depended on the ubiquitous Room Temperature Superconductor. What tourist could live even half a day on a strange planet without his personal translator, telepathic shield, and deodorizer? What scholar could operate without his computers and recorders? Unless he was a partner of a Ballatine.

The Harnuiti were spindly-legged, green-skinned humanoids with large, saucer eyes and tiny mouths equipped with double rows of needle-sharp teeth that their thin lips could scarcely cover. Yost knew that, despite appearances, they were not related to anything resembling a Terran frog. Their dental structure indicated a carnivorous ancestry, but they were omnivores. And, like most other humanoids of NCO worlds, they could interbreed with almost any other NCO world's humanoid species . . . though the results weren't always viable.

Unraveling the hows and whys of the strange, seemingly unnatural phenomenon of interbreeding had been Yost's life work until he took up spying, and a surge of new energy lifted his feet as he moved out of the spaceport area and into the city. Every assignment started with the elements of tackling a new planet, learning its languages and cultures, and, finally, moving out among its people to see at firsthand. He always got a thrill out of that first foray into the strange, and it didn't fail him now even though his objectives were different.

With his jump bag balanced on one bony shoulder, Yost bought a couple of the fist-sized, high-caloric Hardnuts from a street vendor who fished them out of glowing coals and presented them wrapped in fleshy, purple leaves while holding out one knobby, green hand for Yost's wooden coins. Bowing his gratitude, Yost continued down the street, nimbly avoiding piles of dung.

The light held a strange, charcoal-smoke quality that lent colors a glare-free softness very like the first lowering of ominous, black storm clouds. It had a vaguely disturbing effect that hadn't been apparent from the tapes Yost had studied. To allay his nervousness, Yost had to keep reminding himself it was the nearly perpetual half-solar eclipse of this latitude that created the effect.

Vaulting the open sewer trough, he crossed the boulevard and entered a likely looking inn whose sign was a faded half circle under which was printed, in native script only, "The Inn of the Half Sun."

The interior was dark and deserted. A lone native drowsed on a high stool in a corner beside a patch of much-bescribbled wall. The untailored length of dingy, gray cloth wound around his emaciated, obviously male frame emphasized his unhuman proportions. But the cloth's relatively clean, new look made it obvious this was the proprietor, desk clerk, and bellboy.

Yost took up a stand at a respectful distance, swung his bag to the straw-strewn floor, and cleared his throat. The sound startled the frail old man and he managed to pry his eyes open. The sight of Yost startled him into a puckered gape that revealed the brown-stained, irregular teeth set loosely in shrunken gums.

The old man said, "Yes? You want something? In the middle of siesta? At high noon, you want something?"

Yost knew the natives slept through the grueling seventy-degree Fahrenheit heat. He said in the local dialect, "I apologize for disturbing you, but I need a room."

The old man peered at the human silently, estimating his worth. He eyed the stuffed bag, then turned to the wall to find a vacancy in his register. "Top floor, west end. Twenty zuit a day."

Yost knew he'd been offered the worst room in the house for twice the price of the best. He had the money, but he dickered the old man down to five a day and breakfast nuts, never letting on that he preferred top-floor corner rooms.

When they'd concluded the deal, Yost hunted about the large empty room that served as a tavern, found the local excuse for a broom, shouldered his bag, and climbed the stairs with a nonchalance that left the old man gaping at the human's enormous strength. That also was calculated. Now, they wouldn't try to roll him.

He found his room, with the lockless door swinging gently in the breeze from the unglazed windows. As he'd expected, it was a long, rectangular room with two inches of reeking, soggy straw on the floor. He swept the straw out into a neat pile in the corridor, propped the broom beside it, and set up camp. It took him twenty minutes to arrange the tent, air mattress, cookstove, and security alarms to his satisfaction. Then he took his nuts to the window and surveyed the city, absorbing the sinister atmosphere created by the weird lighting.

Presently, his partner joined him. He made no overt sign, but Yost knew another being now shared his eyes. It was a comfortable, secure feeling. As he gnawed the warm, blue nutflesh and savored the smoky taste, Yost said, ::I call a strategy conference.::

::Convened,:: came the silent agreement.

Yost felt the wry smile that went with that. It raised his spirits a bit as he said, ::That caravansary over there::—he focused his eyes on the tallest structure in sight, a dun-colored adobe tower—::looks promising. Hire a native guide, some transport, and set out for Rogahm's studio?::

::Why don't we try the Art Gallery first? That's where the tapestry disappeared from and they're the ones that have been complaining loudest. We're here to find out why, so why not ask? Could save a lot of trouble.::

::That's what I like. A subtle Ballatine. Walk right into a public building and start asking questions that are bound to alert the entire Harnuit underground. The Curiosity Corps could use a couple more like you.:: He gave their agency one of his favorite nicknames in hopes of maintaining his good spirits.

Too late, the stony silence within alerted him to his mistake. Fission inevitably produced two Ballatines. He hadn't meant to imply that Kolitt's children would be unwelcome.

::I'm sorry, Kolitt. I just meant that we think too much like CC data collectors and not enough like spies for this mission.::

Kolitt came back, ::Misunderstanding nullified, Friend-of-two-parts.:: He used the Ballatine idiom for mutual apology. Yost knew it was a formula that erased the whole incident. But, it seemed far more powerful than necessary. And he'd never known a Ballatine to toss that phrase off lightly.

Kolitt continued, ::I don't think the frontal approach is out of order. Asking questions is our profession, so why not ask some?::

::O.K. That's what we'll do, first thing after sundown.:: He fell silent, nibbling at the second nut and at his latest pet worry.

Finally, Kolitt said, ::All right; what's eating you?::

Yost started a flip reply, then swallowed and said seriously, ::Listen, Kolitt, we've chewed this assignment over a hundred times. We've discussed every aspect of it, except one.::

::Go on.::

::The first time you took control, you loused it up. That's never happened to me before.::

::It's never happened to me before either. I thought I explained.::

::No you didn't, not really. It's not that I don't trust you . . . but if you run out of time, I'm in bad trouble . . . right?::

::You have a point, Friend-of-two-parts. But, you can count on at least twenty more weeks.::

::What caused that first fumble?::

Silence.

::All right. Here's a worse one. Conjugation?::

The silence clicked off into abandonment.

::Kolitt?::

A few moments later, he replied, ::Here, Friend-of-two-parts.::

::I don't want to embarrass you, Kolitt, but I feel I have a right to know. There practically isn't a race in the whole Confluence that doesn't have strong emotions on such functions. Humans are no exceptions.::

::Ray, I . . . was on the verge of accepting a . . . relationship when Proken called me for this assignment. I thought about it very hard, for a long time, and decided it would be best to wait. Do you understand now?::

::Not exactly. I've never had a post-conjugal partner, but I understand there is a difference.::

Kolitt was amused. ::Yes . . . indeed.::

::What caused that fumble?::

::I was thinking too hard about . . . someone else. That preoccupation is gone now, so there will be no further difficulty.::

::Except that you're maybe a bit more nervous and sensitive than you used to be?::

The symbiot conceded, ::Maybe.::

::Aren't you afraid?::

::Of what?::

::Dying.::

::No. Dissolution of personality at the proper time and in the proper way is not frightening.::

::It frightens me,:: Yost admitted. Since he'd probed so deeply into Kolitt's privacy, at least he could share his own most private fears. He asked, ::Where does a 'dissolved' personality go? Is death the end? And if it is, does that mean that the whole, frantic churning of life is meaningless? Is there a God to receive our souls? Or does the concept of soul have any reality? Does life have any meaning? Does death have any significance? It won't matter how long I live. Death will always frighten me.::

::I *am* sorry.::

Yost read true sympathy in that, but also the ever-present refusal of the Ballatine to discuss any aspect of theology. They wouldn't even go so far as to assert that humans, or any other species, need not be frightened. The closest thing to a statement on theology that anyone had ever gotten out of a Ballatine was that friend-of-two-parts appellation. And that was never really explained or discussed either. Yost was not surprised when Kolitt retired for the rest of the afternoon, refusing to engage in any conversation.

As dusk fell and the town lit up with torches, hearthfires, and candles, Yost went in search of the local Art Gallery.

Harnuit's art was not connected with the religions and the Harnuiti didn't decorate everything in sight. They reserved their efforts for items called Tapestries displayed only in public art galleries.

Yost found the capital city's Gallery down a narrow, dingy alley lined with tiny shops that overflowed onto the dung-paved ground. Across the end of the alley, two crude wooden doors opened in an unadorned wall spilling a soft, yellow radiance on the jumbled merchandise.

Entering the flickering shadows, Yost dropped a coin in the metal box chained to a post, and clasped his hands behind his back in the local gesture of concentrated reverence.

The Gallery was a single, large, low-ceilinged room divided into compartments by opaque draperies suspended from the insect-infested rafters. The first compartment opened directly before the door and Yost nodded appreciatively at the way the clean, black draperies focused the attention on the display piece hung across the end of the compartment.

The Tapestry was a rectangle, Yost estimated about six by seven feet, and it consisted of thousands of brightly colored, translucent beads strung on a transparent fiber and woven into a richly detailed, abstract design. By the dancing light that filtered through the Tapestry, Yost distinguished several complementary shapes among the tightly packed beads. At first, he thought he was on the wrong side of the hanging, but then he noticed that the light came from lanterns set in a very narrow space behind the Tapestry and backed by a shiny material.

Stepping back to admire the effect, Yost said silently, ::This looks like something *you* could appreciate, Kolitt?::

::I shall reserve judgment, Friend-of-two-parts. The form seems to have possibilities.::

Surprised, the human said, ::Are you an artist?::

::Not really. A connoisseur, perhaps.::

Yost sniffed. ::What's that?::

::What?::

::I smell something. Spice? Incense?::

::There are no new olfactory signals of that description originating in your nasal passages.::

::No? Well. That must be what Proken meant when he said Harnuit's art is quasi-olfactory.::

::I suggest we speak to the proprietor of this establishment.::

::Certainly. How do we find him?::

::Walk about. He'll find us.::

Yost did as he was told, pausing occasionally to examine one or another piece. All of the designs seemed to be abstract and each had its own scent. The proprietor found him as he was enjoying spiced peaches and brandy.

The green-skinned, white-robed figure emerged from the shadowy maze to stand half bathed in the eerie, flickering light. He seemed to be of a heavier build than the other natives. In a low-pitched, cultured voice he said, "Welcome. May I be of service?"

Yost sorted himself into the native language and answered, "Perhaps you can answer a few questions for me?"

"Of course. I know every piece in my Gallery."

"There is one in particular I've heard about. The Newsnet Interstellar reviewer called it the 'Vanillamint Tapestry.' Do you know it?"

"Of course. However, you will not be able to view it. It has been stolen."

"No!"

"We have taken the matter to the Interstellar Authorities; however, we despair of ever getting it back."

"Was it *that* significant? You have so many excellent ones here. What could make any single one that important?"

"Each one is unique. Until its theft, the 'Vanillamint' gave much joy to many of my clients."

"Was it an item of great value?"

"How does one measure the value of the unique?"

"Perhaps the artist could be persuaded to sell me another one like the 'Vanillamint'? Could you tell me where to find him?"

"Tapestries are not *sold,* sir. However, the creator of the 'Vanillamint' is a novice so I doubt if he has anything else as significant."

"Then how do the artists make a living . . . if they don't sell their work?"

"Their Hermit Colonies are supported from the public treasury."

"Oh. Then the creator of the 'Vanillamint' . . . what did you say his name was?"

"Rogahm."

"He lives in a Hermit Colony?"

"Yes, of course."

"And you are the sole agent displaying his work?"

"Yes."

"What else of his is here?"

"Why nothing. I told you, he is a novice. The 'Vanillamint' is the first of his works worthy of display. That is one reason he is so anxious to get it back."

"I thought *you* owned it?"

"Oh, no. How could it be possible for a work of art not to be owned by its creator? I'm merely his legal representative."

"I see. I'm still curious about the creation of these Tapestries. Would it be possible for me to visit Rogahm's studio?"

"I don't think so. Even I go there very seldom. It was on my last visit that I discovered the 'Vanillamint' just being finished. He's certainly not had time to do anything significant since . . . and I assure you his previous work is quite worthless."

"If it's that worthless, perhaps he could be persuaded to part with one or two examples. I should like to visit him."

"It would be a difficult trek through perilous and unpleasant desert and, I assure you, quite fruitless."

"I've already come a long way. And it's my time, my discomfort, and my curiosity, sir. If you could give me some clue how to find him, I would be most . . . generously . . . grateful." Yost allowed his hand to drift toward a pocket suggestively.

"Well, since you put it that way . . . I can do even more. I'll arrange for a guide. My own personal servant, Groumain. He's very reliable and a willing worker who can make your journey less unpleasant."

"That kindness will be unnecessary. I'm sure I can find someone. . ."

"Oh, no trouble. In fact, I insist."

"I couldn't take your servant from you, even for a short time." And, he thought, I could do without your spy.

"It's no hardship. I have others. Truly, I insist."

They dickered over the price for several minutes and finally agreed that Groumain would assemble transport and camping equipment and meet Yost at the Inn of the Half Sun in two days.

As they walked back to the inn through the teeming, dark streets, Kolitt said, ::I believe Groumain may be an error.::

::What! Subtlety at last? I know he is. But how could I have refused?::

::A good question, but utterly academic. We shall have to keep an eye on this Groumain.::

::You know, we shouldn't get too melodramatic. Central Intelligence is out chasing thousands of clues on an important theft of a something-or-other which we aren't cleared to know about . . .::

::Which *you* aren't cleared to know about.::

::Oh? Well. I guess one of us had to know. Anyway, they wouldn't have sent two amateurs on a really hot trail. They're not looking for the Tapestry. It's just that it disappeared coincidentally. So I think we ought to stop seeing spies everywhere and just enjoy ourselves. I don't know about you, but I could use a vacation from chasing will-o'-the-wisp theories about the evolution of intelligent life. A ride through picturesque desert country sounds inviting.::

::Friend-of-two-parts::—Yost recognized the grave tone he'd come to associate with Kolitt's approaching demise—::I'm incapable of enjoying this waste of time. The only reason I'm here at all is that Proken is an unusually persuasive administrator and my ancestors owed him a favor.::

::I know what you mean.:: Yost couldn't count the times he'd been talked into tackling distasteful or dangerous jobs by the "highly persuasive" director. ::And I do hate having to sit here doing nothing for a whole day.::

::So, we'll look up our guide and watch the preparations.::

::Fine idea.::

::But first, another meal and a night's rest.::

::You're determined to put some weight on me, aren't you?::

::Not particularly. I'm more interested in putting some weight on me. But you could certainly use some reserve.::

The next morning found them waiting for Groumain at the caravansary as the smoky light of the half-sun grew slowly into full dawn. Yost stood beside the stone watering trough that occupied the center of the yard and watched the caravansary come to life under the crisp dew of a chill dawn. Discreet questioning of the handlers obtained excellent character references for Groumain, and when the native guide arrived, Yost was reassured by his appearance as well.

Groumain was taller than most of the locals, well fed, and of a healthy green hue. The length of cloth wound about his torso was a clean black and he had a spring in his step that spelled self-sufficiency. As they watched him organizing transport and supplies, Yost and Kolitt both agreed he was more intelligent, efficient, and dominant than one expected in a slave. He was scrupulously honest in his dealings and the fairness and firmness of his prices were unquestioned.

When he'd rented a corner stall and hired a boy to clean it and care for the rented animals, Groumain came over to Yost, obviously appreciative that the human had not interfered with his work since introducing himself. "Sir, perhaps you could give me some idea of how many maisu will be needed for your baggage?"

Yost eyed the huge, pad-footed, green-haired beasts with broad, flat rumps, bulging sides, and four spindly legs. They were something of a cross between a water buffalo and a camel but with the vile disposition of a llama. "I believe one will be sufficient for my kit."

"My master has informed me you require three times the food of an ordinary man. This is accurate?"

"Yes."

"Then we'll need two maisu for supplies. It's a long way into the desert. With luck, two talu."

Yost translated. About three weeks. Three weeks out, three weeks back, and four weeks home. Ten weeks and they had only twenty . . . nineteen and a half. He said, "Yes, I realize that. I have my own camping equipment, but I'll leave the food and water supplies to your judgment."

Groumain looked around the rapidly emptying caravansary. The watering trough was deserted as the sun now shown weakly on it and the walls surrounding the square stood on their own shadows. The maisu huddled in their ground-floor stables with their attendants, and the caravan travelers, the few who were laying over for the day, had taken to their second-floor rooms, above the thickest of the animal stench. Groumain said, "I'll complete our arrangements this evening and we'll leave in the morning."

Yost nodded. "That will do." Of course, he'd check the "arrangements." He was no stranger to deserts.

The next morning, Yost appeared with his bag on his shoulder, dressed in a crisp, blue traveling coverall, almost before the nut vendors had fired up their coal basins for the day. He insisted on helping the stableboy load the maisu and unobtrusively took inventory. The only problem would be water and everyone he'd spoken to had said there was plenty in the northern desert if you knew where to look.

Yost checked his folding dousing rod, slung it on a chain around his neck, and pocketed his purification kit. They were both legal on Harnuit since they employed nothing more sophisticated than solid-state, integrated circuits and basic chemistry. But some things were best not left to baggage.

When Groumain arrived, they shared a quick meal, mounted their maisu, and departed with the largest caravan Yost had yet seen assembled at the caravansary.

The lead maisu was carrying a boy and two huge ceramic jars of water with skins stretched across their mouths on which he beat out a rhythm. The sound had a musical boiiioing reverberation that soon had the maisu marching in step, one TWO THREE four . . . one TWO THREE four . . . over and over to a chanted tune that seemed the quintessence of movement.

Yost breathed deeply, head high, thoroughly enjoying himself in spite of the dust, ripe dung, chafing crotch, assorted vermin, and depressing lighting. He thrived on strange and colorful experiences, primitive or sophisticated, and he'd certainly been in more miserable circumstances on many occasions, so he was prepared to enjoy an interlude of relative comfort.

They followed the caravan for all of the first week while segments of it split off almost daily to seek their own destinations. Each day the sun became dimmer and they marched longer into the noon hour. Then one day, as the caravan settled down for siesta around an oasis that consisted of an adobe-walled well with hand-drawn bucket, Groumain peeled off to the north.

Now that it was gone, Yost noticed they'd actually been on a trail of sorts. But here the ground was almost virgin. And it wasn't long before Yost felt the lack of a drummer. The four maisu ahead of him now marched in random rhythm and their loads swayed sickeningly.

They marched through the whole day as the gloom increased to-ward full eclipse. The sparse desert vegetation became even more scraggly and finally disappeared, leaving the sharp stones with only the wind to grind them to sand. The footing became so bad, the maisu often refused to put weight on one foot or another in a random pattern of jarring limps.

The days passed, and Yost found himself relying more and more on Kolitt to keep his spirits up. Toward the end of the second week, as the watery gloom deepened toward dusk and the lighting seemed particularly oppressive, he said, ::This artist's colony is supposed to be under the exact center of the fully eclipsed part of the continent. How do they stand it?::

::You find the lighting has an emotional impact?::

::Well, doesn't it?::

::Not on me.::

::Why?::

::Because human nerve impulse codes aren't my natural aesthetic referents. Now, if I were using a friend-of-one-part I might be able to judge the effect. But I doubt if their eyes could take this light inten-sity. So, I'll never see it other than as a partner to a friend-of-two-parts.::

::Do you regret that?::

::No. Working for CC, I go places and see things that I'd never be able to experience otherwise. The price is high. Sharing the body of an intelligent creature, a friend-of-two-parts, rather than being master of a domesticated nonentity that never talks back or vetoes . . . or fails to eat enough . . .::

::Was that a gentle hint?:: said Yost, unwrapping a nut as his maisu plodded jerkily behind the others.

::Not so gentle, Ray.:: Yost read burbling laughter of embar-rassment. ::I'm starving!::

::So I'm eating. Just be sure this beast doesn't make me motion sick.::

::Have I ever let it do that?::

::No. But there's always a first time.:: Yost would never forget one particular first time . . . at least, he wouldn't until he'd delivered his partner safely home. ::How are *you* feeling?::

::As well as can be expected for my age. You have nothing to worry about.::

::Nevertheless, I do worry. What do you mean 'as well as can be expected'?::

::I require more sleep and I'm always hungry. That's all. It shouldn't bother you. Your kidneys are sufficient for the task.::

::You're growing?::

::Spontaneously. An unavoidable necessity.::

Yost remembered the course in Ballatine physiology he'd taken nine years ago. He should have reread the text before this mission, but he'd been so rushed . . . and it would hardly have been polite after Investiture. ::As I recall, the growth curve is unaffected by conjugation?::

Silence. Total withdrawal. Yost felt a panic of abandonment and was instantly contrite. ::Kolitt?::

::Here, Friend-of-two-parts. Another point . . . a friend-of-one-part doesn't ask questions.::

::I'm sorry.::

::Partly my fault. Yes. It is unaffected.::

::Then you'll be about double your size by the time we get home.::

::Three quarters.::

::And if we don't make it?::

Silence. Then Kolitt seemed to choke on his negation. ::Please . . .::

Yost prompted, ::It happens anyway, doesn't it?::

Anguish. ::God help me, no, not like that!:: It was the first time Yost had ever known of a Ballatine invoking a deity. The overwash of emotion almost knocked him off the maisu.

::Kolitt, I'm sorry, but it helps to face facts.::

::Friend-of-two-parts, believe me, I'd die first. If necessary, I'll simply leave you. But it won't be necessary. There's plenty of time.::

Yost couldn't help wondering if the Ballatine would be able to commit suicide at such a point in the life cycle. As he recalled, the texts had been vague on the subject. At any rate, he wasn't eager to try Divestiture outside of Chambers and without the protection of hypnotic conditioning.

Yost said thoughtfully, ::*Can* God help us?::

Silence.

Yost let the subject drop. A slip? Or a figure of speech picked up from a lifetime association with humans? He knew he'd draw no further comment from the Ballatine, so he applied himself to eating the smoky nut and kept a careful eye on his compass. With Kolitt's memory, they should have no trouble finding their way back alone, but he was uncomfortably aware that he might be making the trip in true solitude.

Through the long, dry, but not uncomfortably hot days Groumain was the perfect servant. He was quiet, efficient, thoughtful, and industrious. He even made it his business to learn how to set up Yost's tent, and from then on refined his technique until he could make or break camp faster than Yost thought possible. Between a Ballatine and such a servant, Yost often reflected, traveling in primitive fashion was a real pleasure.

Nevertheless, when Groumain announced that the next day would see them at Rogahm's, Yost knew a lightening of spirit that only served to underscore the sense of doom from the watery, charcoal-smoke lighting. He found himself eager to get the job over with and get out of this forsaken land.

They made camp for the night beside one of the typical adobe wells that dotted the trail at two-day intervals and, about midnight, Yost woke to sharp hunger pangs. ::Kolitt? Hungry again?::

::Apologies, Friend-of-two-parts. I'm consuming energy at an increasing rate. I'll calm your stomach. You need your rest.::

::I'm awake now. You must really be starving. I'll just take a walk, eat a nut, and look at the stars. At least the night sky isn't smoky!::

::All right.:: Yost felt Kolitt's embarrassment at allowing his host to feel even slight discomfort. ::But, Friend-of-two-parts, make it two nuts.::

Yost rolled out, thrust two nuts into the glowing remains of Groumain's fire, and scooted back to the tent for a warm coat against the desert night's chill. Dressed, he skewered his nuts on the slender metal rods Groumain had set out for their breakfast and moved quietly out of camp, lighting his way with a lantern.

::Keep watch, Kolitt, so we don't get lost.::

Presently, he found a nice boulder with a seatlike depression and settled down to munch the warm nutflesh while admiring the night sky. That was another good thing about traveling with a Ballatine. No matter what you ate, or how much of it, it always tasted magnificent.

::Ray! Let me!:: Kolitt commanded sharply as he took control of Yost's head and eyes.

Yost relaxed and let the Ballatine focus his gaze, knowing that the symbiot had no peripheral blindness. The streak of light across the northern sky was just fading when he found it. Kolitt said, ::I couldn't tell if it was a meteor or . . .::

::Or a ship landing?:: supplied Yost. ::There's no spaceport over there . . . only the Hermit Colony . . .::

::And Rogahm.::

::Ohhh . . . bah! This is ridiculous. Send a couple of overly imaginative amateurs to chase . . . what? What in the universe are we after, anyway?::

Silent chuckle. Then, ::Let's go back to sleep.::

::I'm not sleepy anymore. I'll dream sinister spaceships!::

::You're exhausted. I guarantee you'll be asleep the minute you zip yourself in.::

::All I do all day is sit on that damn maisu. Groumain is the one who fights with the contrary beasts. How come I get so tired?::

::Because *I'm* working hard! Now *move* before I do it for you.:: Kolitt's tone reminded Yost of a soft-hearted parent trying to scold a lovable three-year-old. The Ballatine wasn't that much his senior!

Smiling, Yost replied, climbing to his feet, ::Don't get tough with me, little partner. I'll starve you.::

Kolitt laughed, ::You already are!::

Chuckling, Yost made his way back to his sleeping bag.

The next day, about noon, they topped a final ridge and drew up to survey the Hermit Colony. The watery gloom threw the desert into a tricky, shadowless perspective and Yost found it difficult to estimate the size of the crater that cupped the fifty or so huts of the Colony. The glare-free lighting emphasized the brilliant colors of the stones that lay strewn about the floor of the crater, but somehow the harlequin patchwork of color lacked any trace of high-spirited gaiety. It wouldn't take much to make it sinister as mysterious spaceships.

The garishly bright purples, greens, blues, blacks, and reds were mixed with whites and oranges that seemed to glow in the weird light. There were a dozen shades of scintillating browns and too vivid yellows and hundreds of hues he couldn't name. The effect was so grotesque, he searched for a harmless, commonplace simile. Yes. It looked like a paint laboratory's testing site! He could hardly believe it was natural . . . and yet, he'd read the reports and knew, intellectually, that it was a work of nature . . . though it looked more like the work of the devil.

There were no paths between the rectangular, pastel-colored huts that lay widely spaced among the rocks and around the sides of the crater. A single, clean trail led from the rim near them straight across the floor and disappeared halfway up the other side. Yost moved his maisu closer to Groumain's and said, "Which house is Rogahm's?"

The guide pointed a long, green finger. "On the far rim, the pink one."

Kolitt said to Yost, ::If I'm not mistaken, that's on a direct line

between our camp last night and the point where the ship landed.::
::Or meteor.:: To Groumain, he said, "Well, let's go."

Silently, the native led off down the sloping side of the crater and struck a brisk pace along the cleared pathway. Soon they were climbing again and before long they'd run out of path and dismounted to lead the maisu the rest of the way up to the rim.

From the top of the ridge, Rogahm's hut commanded a view of the northern desert plane and all its boulder-strewn barrenness. Yost counted a dozen steep ravines within the first mile. If a ship had landed in that . . . well, it'd probably crashed. And if it had crashed, they'd have heard the explosion. So, it must have been a meteor.

They circled the pink building and found that the northern wall was composed of nearly a hundred small panes of glass, revealing an interior as colorful as the plane it faced. The hut was filled with Tapestries hung on movable wands suspended from tangled rigging that concealed the rafters.

A native emerged from the depths of translucent veils and approached the door warily. He had a lighter green complexion than Yost had yet seen and walked with a pronounced limp, favoring his right leg. His garment was a swirl of grays and whites, and when he got closer, Yost could make out what looked like a solid mass of burn-scar on his torso and upper arms.

When he opened the door, the native ignored Yost and growled tonelessly, "I'm not ready to show. Go home." And he slammed the door.

Groumain said, "Wait here. I'll see what I can do."

He wrestled the door open and disappeared into the sparkling dimness, leaving the flimsy frame to slam lopsidedly shut behind him.

Yost turned to inspect the rocky northern view. The impression of an impending storm was stronger here even though the sky remained clear blue.

Presently, Groumain called Yost in. They found Rogahm covering a large table with an enormous sheet to conceal his unfinished work. Beside the table were large basins filled with the unstrung beads jumbled together without apparent regard for size or color. He grunted, "Well!"

Groumain said, "This is the human I was telling you about."

Rogahm measured Yost's length, mumbling under his foul breath, "The answer's no. Now go away and leave me alone."

Yost took a deep breath. He thought, that's why they call it a Hermit Colony. "I'm really very interested in your work. Can't I just look around? I might find something over which we could come to some kind of agreement."

Yost watched the fire of avarice kindle in those purple eyes and then cool. Rogahm said, "I don't *sell* my work." He made it sound obscene.

"But you do *lend* it for hanging where it might be viewed by more people. Your contract with the Gallery is only for Harnuit. And what is worthless to Harnuit eyes may not be worthless offworld. That might be"—he patted his pocket suggestively—"mutually satisfactory."

Rogahm hesitated, then grunted and turned away. "Look! But be quick about it!"

Yost went to the end hanging and began working his way through the close-packed aisles. It was hard to get the total impression of any one piece and he rarely found any quasi-aroma. But, on the whole, he couldn't see any difference between these and the ones in the Gallery.

Kolitt said, ::This one!::

::What about it?::

::I like it. I think. At any rate, I'd like the chance to judge it in more familiar surroundings. If we are to bargain for any of these, let it be this one.::

Yost stood back to scrutinize the piece. As all the others, the colors were combined by no rules he knew. But, yes, it did seem to have something of the sandalwood and eucalyptus air that Kolitt favored. ::O.K. It's all the same to me.:: He went in search of Rogahm and found him seated on the floor staring out at the eternal desert.

"I've found something." As Rogahm unfolded his crippled frame and struggled to his feet, Yost looked around. "Where's Groumain?"

"Prospecting."

Yost shrugged. The Gallery certainly had other artists in the colony. He led the way to Kolitt's choice and began the bargaining. He set his offer high enough to spark greed but low enough not to seem too eager and let himself be jacked up 20 per cent. Then he held firm, refusing to be put off. He'd learned a thing or two from watching Groumain.

Finally, Rogahm grabbed one of the ropes hanging from the overhead pulleys and yanked. The Eucalyptus Tapestry rolled up as it fell to the floor. "So take it and get out of here. And don't come back!"

Rogahm stalked off into the obscuring layers of Tapestries, leaving Yost to gather up his prize.

The Tapestry proved surprisingly light to his offworld muscles, and it took him only about fifteen minutes to lash the roll securely and carry it out to the maisu. Groumain still hadn't appeared, so he tied it to one of the beasts and then stood gazing out at the weird landscape, breathing deeply of the faint breeze. ::Well, partner, you've got your Tapestry. But what else have we got?::

::I'm not sure. Let's take a walk around the building.::

::What for?::

::Come on! I'm in no mood to argue.::

::All right.:: Yost suppressed a little thrill of alarm at his symbiot's shortness. Yost knew no Ballatine would ever force a partner to do his bidding. But, by the same token, Yost was morally obligated not to deny a partner freedom of movement since the Ballatine had no other alternative. But, considering Kolitt's condition, Yost wasn't sure just how far he could trust him if it came to a real clash of wills.

He mooched all around the pink building and then leaned on the side wall again, gloomily examining the northern desert. ::Well?::

::The building is about twenty per cent larger outside than inside.::

::It is?::

::The studio had all the necessary living accommodations. And there were no obvious doors on the back wall. Yet, there *is* an additional room.::

::Probably storage.::

::Probably. But storage of what, do you think?::

::All I can think about is the sense of doom radiating from that devil's rock garden out there. You know it's stronger here than anywhere farther south?::

::Truthfully, I hadn't noticed. It doesn't affect me. Let's go ask Rogahm about his back room.::

::Do we have to? He's already thrown us out.::

::Friend-of-two-parts. This will undoubtedly be my last mission . . and my last report. I don't want that report to be any less perfect than my previous ones, and an uninvestigated observation leads to an imperfect report. Let's go.::

::All right. But the sooner we get out of this gloomy atmosphere, the happier I'll be.::

He pushed his shoulder away from the wall, dusted the chalky pink dust off his coverall, and picked his way around to the door. There was nobody in sight, so he went in, checked the work area, and then looked among the hangings. He nosed along the back wall of the studio and, near the center, behind several thicknesses of Tapestry and a clutter of dusty art supplies, he found an ordinary-looking door.

::You see, Kolitt, just a storage room . . .:: He pushed open the door and called, "Rogahm?" before he noticed the strange quality of the light.

It was a steady, white light . . . a fluorescent. And the room was no Harnuit storage chamber. It was a gleaming, Confluence-style, lock-and-key installation. One end was an efficiency apartment. Down the center was a neat, Rotsuctronics workbench and along the walls were rows of storage cabinets and lockers. Near the workbench, the door of a floor safe stood up on its hinges. Bent over some apparatus on the workbench were Rogahm and . . . an offworlder!

For twelve heartbeats, Yost stood there staring at the pair while they stared at him. The offworlder appeared to be some mixed breed from the Sirius Cluster. He had blue skin and a bald head, but his eyes were golden, pupil-less orbs set behind two nictitating membranes. His arms looked strong, but his tunic revealed a contoured back as if vestigial wings had grown there. No telling what other odd combinations were hidden under his gray jumpsuit.

Yost found one corner of his mind bemusedly returning to his lifelong professional problem. How could it be that so many different planets throughout the galaxy could develop such similar chemistry that such misogynous interbreeding could occur? The man existed . . . but it didn't take a scholar to guess that he was the many times illegitimate offspring of a long line of careless prostitutes. Anyone with such a build was automatically tagged a criminal in modern society . . . and very often became criminal because of it.

The mere sight of the Mixie sent chills of horror through Yost. He felt Kolitt's impatience as the Ballatine attempted to take control and retreat. But it was too late.

The offworlder's hand came up, leveling a gun at Yost. The gun, like the man, was a bastard, but he had no doubt of its effectiveness.

One of the Mixie's huge, blue fists jerked an order toward Yost's left, the end of the room he hadn't examined. The cage he saw there left no doubt of the Mixie's status. It was a plain, unfurnished cube about seven feet on a side and closed in front by a transparent energy barricade generated by a unit housed in a bulge on one of the side walls. Sanitary facilities consisted of a hole in the back corner. This type of animal-display cage had been outlawed five years ago. Now, only outlaws had them.

::Kolitt. What do we do?::

::Follow orders, Friend-of-two-parts. This type of hybrid tends to be very strong and proud of it. They love to use their strength against the society that hates them . . . and you appear to represent that society.::

Yost took a deep breath and glided carefully into the cage. His buttocks had barely cleared the sill when the field snapped on with an ear-tingling sizzle. He turned to watch his captors.

Rogahm was still bent over the Rotsuctronics bench, expertly adjusting some apparatus. He looked up to say to the Mixie, "What are you going to do with him?"

"I told *you* to get rid of him. Now you'll have to take care of him until the boss decides if he can be of any use. Let's finish this up so I can get out of here quick."

While Yost watched, they bent to their work as if nothing had happened. ::Kolitt, what do you suppose they're up to?::

::Quiet. I want to listen.::

The Mixie straightened up, dexterously twirling a long filament onto a spool with thick, blunt fingers. Then Yost saw they'd been duplicating a record fiber.

The Mixie spoke the native language flawlessly. "Now," he said to Rogahm, "if you hadn't let that fat leech talk you out of the Tapestry in the first place, we wouldn't have to go to all this trouble!"

"It wasn't my fault. How was I to know he'd like it? And how was I to know they'd go and steal it right out of a *Gallery?* If I hadn't let him take it, he'd have known something was phony about this studio."

"Well, somebody sure as hell does. From now on, no more cute tricks with the Tapestries. You take good care of that snoopy character till the boss says what to do with him." He snapped a cover on the filament reel and picked up the duplicate from the bench. "I've got to get moving. Check the . . ."

Just then there was a clatter as the front door opened and Groumain's voice called, "Rogahm! Have you seen my offworlder?"

Rogahm limped out into the studio calling, "No! Probably wandered off into the desert to get lost. Had three of those up here last twenty-day. Attracts 'em."

Groumain said, "Yeah. Didn't strike me as the type, though."

"Never can tell with these weirdies."

"Won't take long for this guy to starve. Eats three times the rations of an ordinary man and never puts on a bit of padding. Maybe he was sick or something? That doesn't make sense . . . why would he spend so much time bargaining over a Tapestry and then just wander off?"

"Sick in the head?"

"Could be. Well, I'm not going to lug that worthless thing back with me. Help me bring it in. Maybe you can make something useful out of it. How much did he give you? Our cut . . ."

The door clattered again. The Mixie stood rock-steady near the bench with his weapon leveled at Yost, as if it could penetrate the energy barrier. It probably could. He didn't feel like experimenting so he stood silently as the outer door clattered again and Groumain called, "See you in twelve twenty-days."

Rogahm came back, letting the door swing to behind him.

The Mixie said, "Well done for a change." He approached the cage, inspecting Yost skeptically. Maintaining the Harnuit dialect, he asked, "Who are you?"

"Raymond Yost."

"Why'd you come here?"

"To get a Tapestry."

"Why?"

"I heard they were interesting. And they are."

"You're a human." It was an accusation and condemnation.

Yost didn't answer. The Mixie made a threatening gesture. "Well!"

"You might say so." He didn't dare admit to being a pure-blooded, Terran-born human.

"Who do you work for?"

"Myself."

"And who else?"

"Just me."

The Mixie chewed his overly prominent lips as he glared at every stitch of Yost's trail-worn blue coverall. "You're no art collector."

"Desert travel does that to one."

"How come you eat so much?"

"The metabolism I was born with demands fuel . . . just like yours." Yost switched to Confluential Standard for that, but the Mixie didn't even blink one pair of eyelids. Instead he asked, "You got a Ballatine?"

Levelly, Yost replied, "No." But he owed his steadiness to Kolitt.

The Mixie was silent for several minutes, then he said, "We'll see about that." He turned back to the bench, took one of the two spools, and tossed it into a floor safe. His back muscles bulged impressively as he heaved the plug into place and set the lock. Yost noted bemusedly that it was the same ordinary-type safe he had in his office. If it was good enough for a criminal, it was certainly good enough for CC.

Yost leaned his back against the wall and slid down to sit on the floor. ::What do you think he meant? There's no way he can detect you, is there?::

Yost was shaking so badly, he didn't see the Mixie drawing Rogahm into the studio saying, "Check out front. I've got to get moving. See you in a twenty-day."

After they'd left, the Ballatine answered his partner, ::No, there's no way *he* can detect me. But . . . well, Friend-of-two-parts, all the races of the galaxy have those who are for society-as-it-is and those who are against it.::

::You mean there are outlaw Ballatine?::

::I wouldn't put it that way . . . but that is the effect. The fine points of the Ethic hardly seem pertinent.::

::Kolitt, you're Senior Agent on this mission. How do we get out of this?:: Yost was paralyzed by the thought of an outlaw Ballatine entering his body to do battle with Kolitt. He'd always dismissed such tales as the nightmares of the ignorant. All Ballatine were so damned *Ethical*. But now, an Ethic of the outlaw?

His partner interrupted his chill thoughts. ::Now that we have what we came for, we are free to return and make our report.::

::Have you cracked up?::

Yost felt Kolitt's laughter before he realized his unfortunate choice of idiom. Fairly bubbling with mirth, the symbiot said, ::Not yet, Friend-of-two-parts, not yet. The successful completion of a mission always has a euphoric effect on me.:: He sobered. ::There is much danger ahead, but we are headed home.::

::You keep saying that, but I don't see it.::

::It's in the Tapestry, Ray. The filament he used to make the Tapestry . . . it's a recorder fiber. Confluential Intelligence was chasing some information that was on a recorder fiber . . . the kind of information that can be sold. So we've completed our assignment.::

:: But what good's it going to do us, or anybody?::

::It will take time and luck to get out of here . . . and more, it will take good timing. But I think we can do it. You still have your dousing rod and water kit.::

::You have a plan?::

::A few ideas. It all depends on how well he feeds us, and on what.::

::I don't follow you . . . but you think we'll have enough time?::

::We'll have enough time if we have enough food.::

They heard the muffled clatter of the front door and presumed the Mixie had just left. ::Call Rogahm and get him to feed us.::

"Rogahm! Rogahm!"

Presently, the artist limped in. "What!"

"Did he leave orders to starve me to death?"

Rogahm looked disgusted and turned back to the studio. "I've got work to do. I'll feed you when I get around to it."

"A corpse doesn't eat very well . . . or answer questions."

The native turned back to his prisoner skeptically and then shuffled to one of the cabinets to wrestle out a case of Service field rations. Cracking it open, he extracted four of the packets and a tube of water. He set them on the sill of the cage and disappeared around the side to push the button. The field extended over the rations and they were sucked into the cage.

Yost said glumly, "Thank you." As the old man shuffled out of the room, Yost picked up his meal. ::T.Y.U.'s,:: he read the labels. ::Will this do you?::

::Yes, Friend-of-two-parts, I believe it will, in sufficient quantity. But only if you eat it.::

Yost bit off the corner of the flexipack, chewed it, and then sucked on the pasty substance that was supposed to be a complete nutrient to his species. It tasted just marvelous, though he knew without the induced appetite it would be hard to choke down. He'd polished off all four of the packets before Kolitt was satisfied.

::Friend-of-two-parts, I'm going to sleep.::

Yost didn't argue. The Ballatine needed his sleep for sorting the memories that he would pass on. So Yost settled down to being bored and lonely . . . and scared.

The days passed slowly. There were no outside windows, so Yost lost contact with the ebb and flow of the wan sunlight. He didn't regret the loss particularly. He was accustomed to living under lights. And the blue-white fluoros didn't cast billows of doom clouds through his thoughts. But Kolitt became increasingly withdrawn, leaving Yost with nothing to do but feed the fires of his imagination with twigs from the tree of speculation.

If the Mixie came back before he escaped, he might bring another Ballatine. The uncertainty of what that would mean was more chilling than the thought of dying.

But, then again, he might foil their plans by dying in his cage. The quantity of food was not proving adequate to Kolitt's appetite. And, when Rogahm failed to supply the rations, Yost could feel Kolitt's creeping starvation as a drain on every tissue of his body. In spite of the Ballatine's selfless efforts to limit his consumption and ease Yost's discomfort, the hunger became a kind of feverish nightmare heightened by the fetid closeness of the cage's air.

It was during one such bout that Yost sat propped against one featureless wall of his prison, drowning in physical misery. He kept telling himself it was only a matter of lasting out a temporary sentence in hell until Rogahm would feed them.

But then he discovered he'd been panting until his throat was raw and his limbs were twitching spasmodically. This would never do! He projected urgency into his silent call, ::Kolitt! Kolitt!::

But there was only the silence of abandonment. Almost sobbing, he tried again, ::Kolitt! Please!::

::Yes, Friend-of-two-parts.:: The symbiot's tone was quiet and assured.

::Kolitt, can't you *do* something? You can control my nerves. Why don't you damp my sensitivity to this hunger?::

There was a long silence and then a projection of infinite sadness. ::I'm doing all I can, Friend-of-two-parts. Remember that I, too, suffer in desperation. I share with you only the most minor portion of that. I dare not do more to alleviate your misery for fear I might injure you permanently. The only thing more that I could do would be to leave you.::

That sobered Yost. ::It's not that bad yet, Kolitt . . . is it?::

::I had not judged it to be that serious, Ray. But if you find my presence intolerable despite my best efforts, I have no other recourse.::

::It's not intolerable.:: To himself he thought, damn Ballatine Ethic . . . to them death was always preferable to risking damage to a host . . . and you couldn't argue with them. ::I guess I just forgot that it's even worse for you. I'm sorry I mentioned it.::

::You need not be sorry. Partnership implies a claim on attention . . . even if only to . . . how do you put it? Oh, yes, to *gripe*. I understand that this is an activity essential to human mental health.::

::You needn't be so damn snide about it! Ballatine are pretty queer people, too, you know.::

::Now it's my turn to be sorry, Friend-of-two-parts. I didn't intend to be derogatory, only to make conversation. I thought it might help break some of the positive feedback of the misery cycle.::

::What? Oh, you mean, take my mind off my problems?::

::I believe I said that.::

::Well, then maybe you'd care to speculate about what the immediate future holds for us?::

::I hope that Rogahm will come to feed us very soon.::

::I hope so, too, but that's not what I meant.::

::I know, Friend-of-two-parts, but I'm curiously reluctant to discuss the grimmer possibilities.::

::Then let's not discuss it. Let's drive right to the heart of the matter. Kolitt, how much time do you have before you must . . . well, leave me?::

The silence lasted so long Yost was again becoming acutely aware of the throbbing ache of hunger. But finally Kolitt said, ::It's very difficult to say. There are many factors to be considered. Starvation has affected me severely. I estimate roughly six, perhaps seven, weeks.::

::What! That's less than half . . . !::

::I'm well aware of *that,* Friend-of-two-parts. And it may not be time enough to complete our mission. Therefore, I elect to exercise the prerogative of the Senior Field Agent and tell you all I know of our mission before I reach the point where I might . . . misplace . . . such memories. It's not a great amount of information, but it will have to go into our report.::

::But, Kolitt, if Intelligence didn't clear me . . .::

The impatience in the symbiot's reply was Yost's first hint of the nerve-wracking battle the Ballatine must be fighting. ::They *should* have cleared you, Ray. I'm not responsible for the idiocies of deskbound spy chasers! Since our lead has turned out to be a hot one, you're entitled to know.::

::What I don't know, they can't extract from me.::

::You won't know anything they don't know already, and it won't make any difference if they know that you know. If we don't get away from here before the Mixie comes back . . . well, that crowd can be counted on to interrogate to destruction.::

Yost had contemplated just such a fate so often that he couldn't work up a new horror. ::O.K. what's the big secret?::

::In a word . . . Rotsuc deposits. Precise co-ordinates of nineteen deposits on ten planets in the Empty Wedge. All with assay values greater than the richest Confluential deposit.::

Yost whistled. Nineteen deposits of the rarest mineral known to civilization! And all on uninhabited planets, unclaimed by any member of the Confluence. And all rich! It could destroy the economy overnight! Rotsuc would be so cheap that devices based on Room Temperature Superconductions could be made disposable. Without even trying, he could think of three expensively impractical applications that could become common. And . . . currency values were based on Rotsuc!

Yost asked, ::And that's the information that was on that fiber?::

::Apparently. Unless, of course, they're only involved in some ordinary deal.::

::No wonder Intelligence went chasing off in all directions and even borrowing manpower! Do they know the locations?::

::No. It was the most closely kept secret of a private development company. The theft can't even be announced without pulling the props out of the market.::

::I can see that!::

::Then you can also see that it is essential that one of us get home to file the report.::

::Of course. But I don't see how we're going to make it inside of six weeks. There are no maisu here in the Colony and we'd never make it back on foot.::

::That is true, Friend-of-two-parts. Therefore, we shall have to commandeer transportation.::

::What transportation? Jet-assisted maisu?::

::Our Mixie friend should return next week. Whatever he uses should be suitable.::

::Very nice. And how are we going to talk him out of his own, personal ship?::

::Friend-of-two-parts::—Kolitt was contrite—::I hadn't intended to ask his permission.::

::You mean just . . . steal . . .:: Yost realized how ridiculous his reluctance sounded. But then it hit him. ::But, I thought Ballatine didn't steal . . . ?::

::That was your choice of word, Ray. I had intended to commandeer his ship on an official priority and leave Director Proken to straighten out the legalities. That's his specialty and I think he owes us something for our trouble . . . don't you? We're not leaving the Mixie stranded. He can counter-commandeer our ship and call for his at the pound.::

::Give a philosopher enough paper . . . ! I still call it stealing, but it doesn't bother my conscience. There's only one little problem. The Mixie may object to us leaving his cage.::

::I hadn't intended to ask permission to leave. We're both free citizens and he has no right to detain us.::

::Agreed. I'm all for it. But how are we going to get out?::

::*That,* Friend-of-two-parts, was the problem I was working on when you called me. I'm certain I have the information that will unlock this cage, but I seem to have misplaced it in my recent . . . housecleaning . . . LISTEN! Isn't that Rogahm coming now?::

Yost perked up . . . yes! Now he could hear the scuffling limp of the native's distorted gait. With starvation postponed, Yost hoped time might pass a little faster. He layed himself out and pretended to faint when Rogahm came in. Perhaps that would improve the food service.

And it did. It hardly seemed like a whole week later when Kolitt roused Yost from his reveries. ::Friend-of-two-parts, I think it is time for us to leave.::

::You still haven't told me how you intend to pull off this miracle.::

Silence. Followed by that grave tone that had come to make Yost so nervous lately. ::My apologies, Ray. But I have only just located the memory of the final steps.::

::Well then, let's go! What do we do first?::

::The power pack of your dousing rod will make a fine detonator for our bomb. Get it out and extract the power capsule.::

Yost fished the little cylinder out of his coverall, unfolded it into a Y, and unscrewed the stem. ::I don't get it, what bomb?::

::It was an obscure item one of my ancestors read in a chemical safety journal. Now, get out your purification kit.::

Yost dug the palm-sized sack of gelatin out of his shoulder pocket. ::Before we set off on any escape attempt, I think I'd better . . .::

::I know. But don't put it down that hole. The T.Y.U. rations have provided us with a unique catalyst which we'll need for our bomb. But first, squeeze half the gelatin out of the packet and drop the dowsing power pack into the space. Then you can use the stem of the dowsing rod to fill the packet with catalyst.::

Yost did as he was told, surprised that the semisolid his bowels produced was nearly odorless and an ashen gray color. The Ballatine must have been up to some subtle tricks. ::Now what?::

::You can locate the cage's generator by tapping along the wall with the dousing rod's V portion. The rod's circuitry will react to the generator's rotating field.::

Yost followed directions and, sure enough, the half-dismantled dousing rod reacted to the generator's fields, giving him a beautiful electric shock that sent him sprawling halfway across the cage. He picked himself up saying, ::And why didn't you warn me?::

::Friend-of-two-parts, even Ballatine make mistakes. Fortunately, this wasn't a serious one. And may I remind you that electric shock is more uncomfortable for me than for you?::

::Yeah. Well. Let's be more careful. Did you mark the spot?:: It would take a Ballatine to tell one point from another on that featureless, gray wall.

::Of course. Now we'll use the remaining gelatin to attach the bomb to the wall.::

::That gelatin isn't a glue! It won't hold the weight.::

::Mixed with a little dilute uric acid, it makes a fair plaster.::

Working with mounting skepticism, Yost said, ::What's going to set this thing off?::

::When you poke the V portion of the rod into the force-field barrier, the generator will hit the resonating frequency of the power pack.::

::Are you sure it won't hit *my* resonating frequency first? And, remember, humans aren't explosion-proof. Are you sure this won't kill us?::

::Sure enough to stake *all* our lives on it.::

Yost thought . . . all our lives . . . by Kolitt's count that was three . . . one human and two Ballatine infants. He shut up and worked grimly. The ship would probably ground any minute and they'd have to be gone before Rogahm and that Mixie got back or they'd surely be finished. It should be easy enough to get lost in the night desert, but then how would they find the Mixie's ship in all those rocks . . . ?

The explosion deafened Yost and stunned him almost senseless. But his body was up and moving before the reverberations had died.

Making a supreme effort to collect his wits, Yost wrested control from the Ballatine and dug in his heels. ::Kolitt, wait! What do you know about safecracking?::

::Nothing, Friend-of-two-parts. Let's go! We don't have much time.::

::How much time?::

::Perhaps fifteen minutes. But I can't guarantee that. I'm only guessing he'll cut through the Customs Satellites' midnight blind spot.::

Yost knelt by the floor safe and examined it. Even at close range, it looked just like the one he had in his office . . . and they had a reputation for being temperamental. Especially when installed horizontally.

::Friend-of-two-parts, the Mixie might have a surveillance-neutralizer on his ship. He could come down at any time.::

::I don't think so. He was in an awful hurry to get out of here. I think he was trying to make rendezvous with a hole in the customs net.:: Now that he was out of the cage, the heady aroma of cool, fresh air was going to his head. He was a man and he was going to act like one. He spun the dials on the safe door and began thumping on the mechanism here and there.

::Ray! If they find us here, they'll surely kill us. The mission . . .::

::Exactly,:: Yost grunted as he pounded his way around the circular rim of the plug. ::The mission comes first. If that tape contained Rotsuc locations that Intelligence doesn't have, we've got to bring it back. If it doesn't, we've got to know because we don't want to send Intelligence on a wild-goose chase that could divert enough manpower to let the real thieves get away.::

::But::—the Ballatine adopted a reasoning tone—::Friend-of-two-parts, you'll never open a safe with your bare hands. What do *you* know about safecracking?::

::Very little. But I know something about cracking *this* safe. I do it all the time.:: He continued pounding the safe in a spiral toward the center. Sweat beaded his brow and he felt faint from the exertion after his long confinement. ::You know how it is around Central. You can never get a repairman when you need one. So, one night, I took the safe repairman out and got him drunk and he taught me how to open these safes without the combination. It works on mine, maybe it'll work here. Give me a few more minutes.::

::I can't give you what I don't have! Ray, let's get out of here while we still can.::

::I thought you weren't afraid of death?::

::This is not the proper time for me to relinquish personality. I thought *you* were afraid of death under any circumstances.::

::Well, I am.:: He spun the four dials in reverse and began pounding them in sequence.

::Then let's go. To stay here is suicidal!::

::Kolitt, remember it was you who wanted to come poking our nose into Rogahm's back room. You said you didn't want to file a faulty report. If we don't get this tape, it'll not only be a faulty report, it'll be an inconclusive one. At the moment, I'm more afraid of Proken than I am of the Devil!::

After a short silence, Kolitt said, ::I guess I don't understand humans as well as I thought I did.::

::Nor do I understand Ballatines. Is your own personal survival more important than this tape?::

::No. Not really.::

::Then kindly stop my hands from shaking! I've got to adjust these dials.::

Kolitt said nothing, but Yost's fingers steadied and his breathing eased. He turned each of the four gently clockwise, past the zero, and back to zero. When the fourth dial registered zero, Yost stood and twisted the handle set flush with the plug's surface. Then he heaved, feeling the Ballatine add to his strength. He'd pay for that drain on vital resources later, but it would be worth it. He got the plug up on its hinges and knelt to rummage in the hole. It held only three fiber reels. He stuffed all three into his pockets and said, ::Let's go. You guide. My night vision is lousy.::

Crouched low, the Ballatine guided them through the dark studio; he snatched up the rolled Tapestry lying near the door and was out into the night heading into the northern wilderness.

Black boulders hulked on all sides and tiny pebbles rolled and crunched underfoot. The stars decorated the moonless sky but shed no light to see by. Yost knew that the Ballatine had placed his own, light-sensitive tissues between the rods and cones of the human retina and could see perfectly now that the yellow sun was gone. Of course, the boulders wouldn't be surrealistic color splashes in the infrared.

Finally, chest heaving, they crouched between two large boulders to watch the clear sky. ::O.K.,:: said Yost, ::now what?::

::If my time sense isn't too badly warped, our friend is due to ground any second. Watch carefully, we must get the bearing exactly right if we are to pick up our ship before he discovers we've left.::

::We'd make better time without lugging this Tapestry along.::

::Correct. But we may need it. Hang on to it.::

::All right. But I can't imagine what we might need it *for!*::

::Perhaps that is for the best, Friend-of . . . THERE!::

Yost's head whipped around to follow the fire-streak to ground and almost before the afterimage had faded from his retina they were moving toward it, weaving through the black shadow of the moonless night but always progressing toward that invisible landing field in spite of countless detours.

Eventually, they crept to the edge of a ravine and looked down the rock-strewn slope to a cleared floor just large enough for the one-man scout that stood silently on its struts. It was an aerodynamically veined, missile-shaped, surface-to-surface scout. The flat expanse of the vest-pocket landing field was illuminated by a circle of glowing panels that cast a soft, green luminescence on the underside of the ship, and provided landing-grid services of a sort. It appeared to be deserted.

::Friend-of-two-parts, I recognize the model and I have the skill to pilot it, but I must retire now to locate all the memories. Do you think you can get us inside?::

::Leave it to me.::

Yost hefted the Tapestry and made his way down the slope, bracing himself against the loneliness that struck as Kolitt withdrew. He watched the ship for a while, circling outside the perimeter, among the boulders, trying to decide if the Mixie were still inside. Finally, he dashed under the ship's landing gear and attacked the hatch. Much to his surprise, it opened to the third standard combination he tried.

He guessed that a professional thief wouldn't rely on fancy locks because he knew how simple they were to open. Suspiciously, Yost climbed into the brightly lit interior, pulled the Tapestry up behind him, and dogged the hatch so it couldn't be opened from outside. Then he prowled the empty compartments with a heart-racing caution until he completed a thorough inspection from drive to pilot's couch.

He seated himself at the controls, secured the webbing, and surveyed the instruments. Very similar to what he knew, but a much older model. Not as many autocircuits.

::Friend-of-two-parts, allow me.::

Yost yielded to the Ballatine and in a neat twelve minutes they were spaceborne, hyperlight, and headed home. Yost had to admit he couldn't have done as clean a job. Race memory had some advantages. He said, ::That was almost too easy.::

::Ray,:: Kolitt reproached, ::there was nothing at all easy about it. I'm living on nervous energy and if I don't get some nourishment very soon, you are going to have real trouble.::

Yost freed himself and rummaged about the tiny galley. While he prepared a meal, he munched on a few packets of rations and tasted everything that was open. The Mixie wasn't a very imaginative chef, but a hungry Ballatine will make anything taste delicious.

When he'd seated himself before a hot meal, Yost said, ::There's enough here for the four weeks it'll take to get home. Are we going to make it?::

The gravity was back as the Ballatine replied, ::I honestly don't know, Friend-of-two-parts. If I don't make it, you'll deliver our report.::

::There must be something I can *do* to help!::

::Nothing. Except eat well.::

::If I somehow improvise a nutrient bath . . .::

::Friend-of-two-parts, I will not allow . . . that . . . to happen. Death is preferable. Before I left, I saw my conjugal brother safely through fission, so my duty to my line is discharged. Only my personal survival is at stake, and I do not wish to survive in *that* manner. Do you understand?::

::Not really. Or maybe I do, I don't know.:: Yost thought about it for a few minutes. For a Ballatine to fission, prematurely and without conjugation, would mean that the children would be the social equivalent of bastards . . . and they would probably have some sort of handicap . . . possibly be too weak to survive. . . . Yost remembered that overwash of violent emotion he'd gotten from Kolitt in the desert. If the Ballatine felt so strongly about it, it must be worth a life. . . . ::Yes, Kolitt, I think I do understand.::

::Then there is something you can do, Friend-of-two-parts.::

::Yes?::

::Hang the Tapestry in the sleeping quarters and then go to sleep. You're going to be very tired soon.::

This time, Yost wasn't inclined to argue. If his partner could derive some comfort from the Tapestry, the least he could do was to hang the thing.

The minutes mounted to days and the days to weeks. Yost spent a lot of time drowsing or exercising. Kolitt came less and less often to talk and seemed lethargic and mentally disorganized. Cooking was a hobby of Yost's and, with six meals a day to prepare, he kept busy enough. When he wasn't busy, he found himself worrying fruitlessly. There was absolutely nothing he could do.

In an effort to dispell the gloom, Yost took out the fiber reels he'd stolen and played them through the ship's main viewscreen.

The first one was a cryptic list of names and numbers. Possibly a payroll, but to whom? The names were some sort of code.

The second proved to be even less interesting. It contained nothing but binary digits. The computer identified it as a standard routetape to a local pleasure planet.

But the third! It also was mostly numbers, but even Yost could see that it was a list of co-ordinates for ten planets and longitude and latitude listings for nineteen different sites!

Using the excitement that discovery generated, he composed their report. He made it completely detailed and scrupulously accurate and, when he'd finished, he took several days to polish it.

Finally, he affixed his signature to the completed document and then called Kolitt.

It took several tries, and when Kolitt finally answered, he was groggy.

::Friend-of-two-parts, you want me to read and sign the report?::

::Yes. At least that gets the formalities out of our hair.::

There was a long pause as if the symbiot were laboring to think clearly, then he said, ::I'm afraid my signature would be quite meaningless at this point. I trust you. . . .::

::Meaningless? Why?::

::I'm . . .::—another long, labored pause, then sharply—::Ray, go lie down on the bed.::

::What? I just got up! It's almost time to eat.::

The Ballatine's reply was faint and, Yost thought, a bit ragged. ::Don't argue! Go! I haven't got . . . !:: Yost felt Kolitt's mental gasp. Something was very wrong!

Yost climbed to his feet and moved gingerly to the sleeping compartment as if afraid that a sudden jar would dislodge a delicately poised disaster.

He lay down on his back and said, ::There. Is that better, Kolitt?::

::Look at the Tapestry.::

Turning his head, Yost examined the hanging. At Kolitt's request, he'd hung it in front of a glow panel so that something of the Gallery's backlighting effect helped bring out the sandalwood and eucalyptus aura. The glistening beadwork was all swirling color and sparkling fire. The shades were dark, mostly reds and browns but with black and gray patches worked into an optical illusion of three dimensions.

Almost, Yost could see why Kolitt liked it. It *did* remind one strongly of Kolitt's Vesting Chamber. Then, Yost felt the familiar soothing relaxation taking hold. He shook himself and blinked hard at the ceiling.

::No! Friend-of-two-parts, look at the Tapestry!::

::I can't. It's too good. It can even trigger my hypnotic conditioning.::

::I know. That's why we brought it along. Ray, *please* don't make this any harder than it has to be.::

Suddenly suspicious, Yost said, ::Make *what* harder?::

Kolitt said in throbbing sadness overlayed with determination, ::I must . . . leave you, Ray. You've been a good partner, and I dare not risk staying with you longer.::

::No! Kolitt, what's the matter? I thought you had another two weeks, at least?::

::I'm not sure, Friend-of-two-parts. My judgment is slipping badly. I almost caused an injury to your brain just now. It was only luck that saved you. I'm becoming clumsy, awkward, and dangerous. I sense, already, the beginnings of disintegration. I can't tell if there are hours or days yet remaining, but I can't risk damaging you. Now, will you look at the Tapestry and try to let yourself relax? It will all be over very quickly.::

::No! Kolitt, look. You estimated four weeks ago that you had six maybe seven weeks. We've been eating pretty well lately. Maybe you don't feel well, but you said yourself you can't trust your judgment. Why not trust your original estimate? We'll be home in a few days with a whole week to spare. Hang on a little longer. Take it one day at a time. I'm sure you can make it.::

Kolitt lectured tightly, ::Now that food is plentiful, the starvation-stimulated growth is accelerating. I cannot tell by exactly how much, nor can I predict the exact moment when I must leave you before I lose the power to do so. Divestiture is not simple, Friend-of-two-parts. My purpose would not be served if you were to die as a result of my clumsiness.::

::Kolitt, we've beaten the odds fantastically so far. We're riding a streak of luck. I *know* it won't run out on us now. How terribly tragic to throw your life away for nothing! How horribly final and irrevocable is death.::

Very quietly, the Ballatine said, ::That is also true for you, Ray. You've told me how much you fear that ultimate end. I can't ask you to face that . . . or worse, life imprisoned in a useless body.::

::It won't come to that.::

::Which of us is in the better position to judge?::

::You just admitted that your judgment is faulty right now. But mine is the same as ever. And I say, don't panic. Wait. Life is a treasure that cannot be replaced. Fight for it!::

::Your fear of death renders your judgment faulty, Friend-of-two-parts. You fear it so much you're unable to believe that it can happen to you. That is a typical human trait, I understand. It allows you to take illogical risks in the face of danger. You demonstrated that you have that blindness in full measure when you stayed to open the Mixie's safe.::

Yost suppressed a thrill of triumph. He'd succeeded in drawing the Ballatine into conversation. Argument was the *Ballatine* racial weakness! ::I was right, wasn't I? I *did* get the thing open, and the tape was of the Rotsuc deposits and we did get away.::

::That, Friend-of-two-parts, is utterly irrelevant. The probability of success was unacceptably low.::

::I can see you're no gambler!::

::Very true. And I do not propose to gamble with your life.::

Damn! Yost thought hard, then he said, ::But it's my life, and my right to gamble with it. What have you got to lose? Maybe you don't fear death, but some ways of dying are preferable to others.::

::Also true. But you *do* fear death. . . .::

::But death is the inevitable destiny of all life. I must face it one day. Haven't I the right to choose my own way of dying? Would you rob me of the right to find the circumstances which would give my death meaning and give me the courage to face that ultimate fear?::

::You surprise me, Friend-of-two-parts. I had no idea the average human could plumb such depths of the Ethic.::

Yost didn't object to being called "average." He knew the Ballatine was comparing him to the great human philosophers from the Sirian Totarch clear back to Aristotle. He said, ::But that doesn't answer my question. Do you have the right to rob me of choice?::

Very slowly, as if deliberating each word, Kolitt said, ::It is not ↓ who robs you of right. In this case, you are assuming a right which the Ethic does not grant you.::

::But I'm human. I don't live by the Ethic.::

::You have labeled yourself an agnostic and you speak like a philosopher yet you claim not to subscribe to the Ethic. Then, from what do you derive your morals? Have you considered what would happen if it were known that a Ballatine had caused the death or injury of a friend-of-two-parts? On what grounds do you claim the right to take that risk?::

Yost had to admit that Kolitt had him there. If the ship parked itself in orbit over Central and his body were discovered, a thorough autopsy would be mandatory. They'd certainly discover the cause of death. The Ballatine's relationship with every other intelligent species was based on absolute trust. One incident, no matter how voluntary, would destroy their usefulness as partners and put a serious dent in Central's resources. It might even destroy the stability of the Confluence. Being so huge and diverse, the Confluence was a rickety political structure at best. Deprived of partners, could Central's Agents hold it together at all? Yost didn't know.

But somehow, deep inside, he knew that if something were right for society but wrong for the individual, it could not possibly be the correct course. And wasn't that a moral judgment?

He started talking, not quite sure what he was going to say. ::You subscribe to a system called the Ethic which focuses on relating the individual to society. The good of society is the ultimate goal, and all actions and beliefs of the individual must be structured to that goal. Ballatine society bases its morals on the Ethic.

::Such systems were not unknown to human philosophers. I think most humans consider such ideas as lofty goals full of praiseworthy idealism. They consider the Ethic a standard of excellence. But I don't know any humans who actually live by such principles. And I don't know anyone who loses any sleep over their failings.

::The people I've grown up with gave me my morals. You see, Ballatines derive their morals from the Ethic. But humans seem to do it, at least in practice, the other way around. We derive our ethics from our morals.

::But where did our morals come from? The segment of human society from which I come has a moral system based on an ancient, monotheistic religion.

::I've never considered myself a member of any religion. But I've accepted the morals of the religions most prevalent in my environment. All those religions are basically designed to help man deal with the racial fear of death. We all have a great emotional need to know what lies on the other side of the black curtain. You're right, Kolitt, we can't really conceive of personal . . . dissolution. I suppose that looks pathologically egotistical to you. And maybe it is. But so is our morals system. Our religion is focused on the relation of a man to himself and to God . . . not to society. We're more interested in guiding the individual to 'right' action so that, ultimately, he can stand in front of his maker with pride.

::I think, Kolitt, that I'm intellectually an agnostic but emotionally, where it really counts, when it comes to actually making a moral judgment, I do believe in a Creator. And I can't believe that the Creator would want a man to do wrong just to continue a social order. I don't know where that belief comes from. It may be irrational, illogical, and un-Ethical, but nevertheless it is my firm conviction and I can't go against it.

::I suppose, if there is no Creator . . . no God . . . then the whole fabric of morals by which I've lived simply disintegrates. But I don't *know* . . . I have no way of knowing . . . if God exists or is merely the figment of our imagination. I don't have the intellectual faith of a religious person to sustain me, therefore I have the right to face death in whatever way seems meaningful to me. I choose to risk my life to save a life. Such risks are considered morally 'right' among humans. Can you convince me that God does not exist? That our moral system is completely wrong?::

There was a long pause, but Yost didn't sense the total withdrawal he'd expected. Finally, Kolitt said, ::Does your morals system give you the right to impose your values on another who does not subscribe to the same system?::

Without hesitating, Yost said, ::Yes, I'm afraid it does, Kolitt. I told you our morals were based on religion . . . and it's a proselytizing religion. Most humans would deny it, these days, but when the chips are down, we really believe we have the one and only 'right.' But in a way, you really do share our values. You don't want to die . . . like this. I'm not trying to 'save' you from the proper death you seek. The only way you could convince me that I'm wrong is to prove to my *emotions* that God doesn't exist.::

The long silence showed that he'd made the Ballatine really think. Eventually Kolitt said, ::You refuse to co-operate with Divestiture unless I can prove God doesn't exist?::

::I believe I said that.::

::If I attempt to leave without co-operation, your sanity would certainly be forfeit. I think that if I insist, you will co-operate.::

::Does the Ethic allow you to take that risk?::

::No. But neither does it allow me to remain with you.::

::So, we're both reduced to a choice between evils. A very sticky moral choice. Shall we adjourn to the galley while you think about it?::

::You've made up your mind?::

::Yes. Apparently, I have.::

::I fear that no Ballatine will ever understand human psychology. You realize, of course, that if I leave without your co-operation, and you are rendered insane, it's the same as if I didn't leave and you die.::

::Yes. I have you over a barrel.::

::A very colorful image but somewhat inaccurate.::

When Kolitt's silence lengthened, Yost got up and went in search of a meal. What he was doing scared him more than all his imagined tortures at the hands of the Mixie. He hadn't planned on it. It had just happened. It was another one of those things a man just *had* to do, scared or not.

Again, the days began to pass, but ever more slowly. Yost spent many hours alternately arguing with and encouraging the Ballatine.

He used every trick of Ballatine psychology he'd ever heard of and even invented a few new ones. He knew that if Kolitt hadn't been suffering from disorganization he'd never have held off even six hours, but six days later, the planetfall alarm went off.

Yost was resting at the time and the Ballatine was in a long period of total withdrawal. Yost clambered up to the control room and threw himself into the pilot's couch. ::Kolitt! Wake up, partner, we're home!::

::What?::

::Home. Where the devil did they hide the radio . . . ? We can't sit up here in orbit and wait for the tugs!::

::Ohhh . . .:: Yost felt that groan as if Kolitt was pulling himself out of a feverish slumber by main force of will. ::Let me.::

::You all right?::

::No!:: the Ballatine snapped, ::I'm not all right, and haven't been for days! I only hope I can still pilot this thing. Let me!::

::All yours.::

Yost watched his hands fly as Kolitt worked the radio, got Ballatine Central, and rattled off a command in his own language, ignoring the painful stretching of Yost's throat. The speaker snapped a crisp reply as Kolitt guided the ship down into the emergency berth near the gleaming, gold Ballatine dome nestled among the towers of the sprawling CC complex.

As soon as they had touched down, Kolitt threw the lock seals to "open" and relinquished control of their body with a sluggishness that scared Yost. ::Friend-of-two-parts, go down to the lock . . . someone will meet you. Do as he says. Hurry.::

Yost moved. As he approached the lock, a friend-of-one-part, undoubtedly guided by a Ballatine, beckoned him urgently to follow. They descended three levels and then hit a large, main corridor lined with plush hangings vague in the dim, red light. The three-foot-tall, anthropoid friend-of-one-part sped along, never looking back. Yost stumbled and nearly fell as a strange sensation twisted his guts. Kolitt said, ::Hurry, Ray. It has begun. There are at most only minutes left before I can no longer accept . . .::

Suddenly, they came to a large, ornate door that flew open at the Ballatine's touch and they were on the main floor of the Vesting Chamber. His guide scampered between the room-sized cubicles and finally opened one of the doors.

Beckoning Yost on, the Ballatine disappeared into the dim interior. Yost entered and stood surveying the fission chamber, wondering what to do. It was well upholstered and richly hung with soft velveteen and was very dim even by Ballatine standards. In the center of the carpeted floor was a pool of crystalline fluid lit from below by a dim, red light. Yost could see the silhouette of a very large, amorphous Ballatine writhing strangely in the fluid nutrient. He'd never seen a Ballatine undulate like that.

"Hurry!" said the guide, "lie down beside the pool . . . here."

Confused, Yost stood dumbly, unable to relate to the scene before him. The friend-of-one-part took his arm and guided him gently into place, draping his arm deep into the warm, syrupy liquid where it was promptly engulfed by the gooey softness of flaccid, Ballatine flesh.

Within him, a crawling, creeping, seeping withdrawal made him choke on a scream. He struggled to rise, but the Ballatine friend-of-one-part was holding him down.

Then he knew what was wrong. The unusual entryway hadn't triggered his conditioning! No velvet mystery, no velour hangings, no incense! He said, "My . . ." He couldn't control his throat.

He tried again, "I . . ." He gagged!

The friend-of-one-part placed a hot, calloused hand on Yost's forehead, fingers gentle but firm. "Easy, Mr. Yost, Kolitt doesn't have much time. Relax. Fix your eyes on the ceiling and relax." The Ballatine's voice droned on, a deep crooning that blended with his hypnotherapist's tones. Gradually, he found himself letting go, falling into the limbo of complete trust. But it was different. He didn't go completely under. He could still feel the weird symphony of sensations, but it no longer sent him into a panic.

The crawling continued for an eternity. He heard himself whimper as he lost visual and auditory contact. And then, gradually, his senses cleared and there was only one thread of contact left. Dizzy, he almost surrendered consciousness before he heard Kolitt say, ::Thank you, Friend-of-two-parts, and good-bye. There is no way to disprove that which is. God does exist.::

Yost succumbed to oblivion. And when he swam up to consciousness again, he wasn't sure if he'd heard that last. Had he imagined it? But, if not, what did it mean?

He propped himself up on one elbow and looked into the pool. Four red- and black-veined Ballatine floated quietly in the crystal fluid. Two were smaller than the other pair, but they seemed alive and well.

Yost said, wiping a tear off the corner of his eye, ::Thank you, Friend-of-two-parts.::

Introduction to Space/Time Arabesque

I swore when I started this book that there would be no "ecology" stories in it. In a philosophic sense, I am deeply troubled by some aspects of the ecology movement; I do not hear in too many of its spokesmen a concern for fundamental human liberty. Too often it seems to me that the solutions being offered are potentially as devastating as the original problem. What shall it profit a man if he gains fresh air and loses the right to breathe?

Sworn oaths aside, there are two "ecology" stories in this collection: Zenna Henderson's "There Was a Garden" and Quinn Yarbro's "Space/Time Arabesque."

Quinn has published a couple of dozen short stories and several novels, including *Tallant & Moon* and *The Time of the Fourth Horseman*. Two more, *Hotel Transylvania* and *False Dawn*, are scheduled for publication in 1978. Quinn is also a serious musician and is at work composing a suite of songs called "Il Magnifico" for tenor and strings with the text taken from the poetry of Lorenzo de' Medici.

One final note on "Space/Time Arabesque": despite appearances, it is the most carefully proofread story in the book.

Space / Time Arabesque

a cautionary tale

by CHELSEA QUINN YARBRO

With ponderous speed the stagecoach lumbered over the dusty plain pursued by the painted, be-feathered hostiles.

"Why the hell couldn't it've been Indians?" complained the shot-gun rider as he poured lead into the howling mob behind them. Bullets had proven ineffective and it wasn't easy melting down his ammunition in a frying pan atop a wildly careening coach. It was not a good day for the shotgunner.

"Giddap!" yelled the driver as he snaked his whip over the ears of the horses. The horde at their back was drawing nearer and looking uglier—and wierder—all the time.

"Crevass ahead," warned the shotgunner, who had pulled up splinters from the roof and was seeing what he could do with improvised flaming arrows. Aside from setting the coach afire, not much.

A creature remarkably like a spoon-billed dinosaur regarded the coach with dim curiosity as it rattled past.

The driver stoically ignored it, tugging heartily on the reins, tettering the wheels precariously over the brink, jarred back to safety. In the stage's gritty wake, unheeding, the savages went down the yawning maw of the canyon wall, and just as unheedingly up the other side.

"Consarn it!" The shotgunner stomped on his hat as he scowled at the bounding backs of their tormentors. "I thought we had 'em for fair that time."

"Not today." The driver knew what he was talking about. Any day that featured fissures like the one that had gaped beneath them as the last one had, bands of whooping tripedal horrors; well, those days you just didn't get ahead. What was more, he was over three hours late and heaven only knew where—and it was certain that Wells Fargo didn't. The last time he'd looked the sun was happily setting into the south.

"We're on again," sighed the shotgunner, and added with a lonesome note, "It ain't Indians, but at least it ain't them things," and he pointed toward the far rim of the canyon where the multicolored aliens undulated to wheetles and tweeps played on their own filagreed snouts.

Wearily the driver urged his horses on to the south-setting sun.

Amid the stiff sighs of brocades and ruff, Sir Walter Raleigh bent his knee to the Queen's Grace and presumed upon their long acquaintance with the invitation, an she cared to blow a joint.

"God's Teeth! Hath stashed some?"

He led her into the galliard, leaning slightly toward her when the movements of the dance allowed. "I'll not reveal what thou'lt not share."

She considered this, missing one step and rapping him with her fan

for her error. "Let us draw aside some little while, my smiling priva-
teer, and have some talk of this."

With a gracious inclining of his head in what might be a bow, Sir
Walter followed the Queen's Grace off the floor. The sweet music of
Thomas Tallis floated after them.

"Now," she declared as they stepped into an alcove as she gave
her farthingale an expert twtich to assure their privacy. "Prithee
vouchsafe me this intelligence. Where be the stuff? I charge thee on
thy honor and for the love you bear my Crown to make this known
to me."

It was dangerous to play with Good Queen Bess when she got
short-tempered, but Sir Walter was ever a bold man. "But say the
word that will take us from this place and the secret is thine, good
Queen." He grew even more audacious. "Sweet lady, heartless lady."

She showed the beginnings of a murderous frown. "Well do I
know the worst of your reputation, else I'll have thought that you do
not love me."

"But listen," he said quickly, changing tactics. "E'en now I have it
hard by me and were you but to slip away with me, we could to the
Hinde whiles Drake is off a-wenching and disport ourselves otherwise."

Her shrewd eyes widened a bit as she struggled with her cravings
and her position. "Stay awhile," she said at last, in a voice full a
cajolery. "On what pretext do I leave me court?" From shrill to
shukiness: "An I leave this room, t'will be a rare uproar. How's to
succeed?"

"Do but command it, and it must be as you wish. Who," he
wheedled gently, "mine radient lady liege Glorianna, be Queen here?
There's pleasure for you waiting if you but give me the word. All of
the weed I brought with me is thine at the asking. And thou know'st
it brings so sweet waking dreams." His eyes grew bright and his idle
gloveless hand made bold to finger her great sleeve.

A beautific smile spread over her rather pointed features. She extended her arm in a sweeping gesture that encompassed the entire
gathering. "Off with their heads," she commanded serenely.

The study was completely draped in pink silk. The walls, the
chairs, the curtains that shut out the bright Vienna afternoon, all was
pink silk. For that matter, the body of Richard Wagner was also
covered in pink silk. Pink silk was his favorite.

Reluctantly he wrenched his mind from the luxurious pageant of
his sumptuous daydreams to his dear hatchet-faced Cosima. There

were grim realities to be dealt with. Ah, the tragedy that genius should have to deal with realities. His friends had had the effrontery to refuse to lend him any more money. So far no one had offered to produce this latest opera and he was becoming more broke than usual. And the other day the mercer had demanded at least partial payment on the silk.

Wagner rose and paced the room, humming furiously off-key to himself, his Remberandt jacket of blue velvet sliding over the pink silk. How unfortunate that this picture must be denied to the world. Finally he sank artistically and unhappily onto the pink ottoman with a towering sigh.

There was nothing for it: he would have to sell his patent on the electric tuba.

The receptionist had the finest nose a plastic surgeon could make— pert, pretty, and almost natural enough to be real. She was the best advertisement her boss had ever had, and she looked at the tattered, bandaged man who smelled of turpentine.

"Your first appointment, sir?" she asked in her best professional voice, knowing it was and doing her best to impress him.

"yes, it is." His speech was mildly accented.

"You'll find the doctor can work wonders," she announced, wondering what wonders the strange man required. "Now, sir . . . may I have your name please?"

"It's Van Gogh. G-o-g-h."

In a laboratory that exists to take care of this sort of thing, a young assistant fumbled with panic-stricken digits. He had meant no harm, he had been careful; and it was such a little, new, unimportant world. He thought that a few things might not upset it. But he was wrong. It was so delicate. He twiddled the knobs again.

The discrepancy might not be noticed and he would be safe. But if it was, he would be out of the program forever, a serious threat to an immortal No one had told him that the balance on the tiny worlds was so blasted precise—why, anything could throw it off.

But he was relieved. Just one or two minor adjustments would put it all to rights and no one the wiser. Everything would be fine as soon as he lined up *that* impulse with *that* graph.

The fatherly man with the shiny head looked unhappily at the dignified Frnechman and quiet Oriental gentleman who stood with him beside the gigantic map. His hand rested on a flagged pin tagged Saigon.

"I really am sorry," he said, and he really was, "but you must see that I can't commit this country to a course that might lead to armed conflict somewhere other than our own continent. Korea proved that."

The Frenchman looked at the Oriental and the Oriental looked at the Frenchman. The Frenchman raised his brows. "It wouldn't have to be a *real* war," he said.

"Oh, don't worry," the fatherly man said reassuringly, showing them his famous fatherly smile. "I'm sure there are countries willing to take you on. Have you considered asking Pakistan?"

The trouble with crime, reflected the man in the alley, was it's facination. There was a pure, dreamlike intoxication to it, a passion that possessed the intellect as well as the baser parts of men. He toyed with the long surgical knife hidden in the folds of his ample cape. Ah, the shine of it was hypnotic. It was so pristine, so neat. It was almost a shame to ruin it. Blood, after all, was a messy business. But there it was. He sighed. He shook his head. Pity about hose poor women. Messy, as well, Always so messy.

There was an element of perfection in his murders. First of all, the women had meant nothing to him; they were the refuse of society, and although the papers might scream headlines of shock and capitalize on the horror, most would secretly agree that they had come to their proper ends. They were nothing more than a demonstration, the necessary testing of a complicated theory, an experiment which required a control.

But what they had been to others was also significant. Their used bodies were the crux of the matter. They had lured men; men who were weaker than he had succumbed to their lusts rather than their passions. And secretly he felt that there was no harm in ridding the world of garbage.

a cab went by in the gray darkness, visible for a moment in the fuzzy glare of the streetlights. A poorly disguised Bobby got out of it. The man in the shadows clucked his disapproval

Drawing nearer to the wall, a precaution against what might be an untimely recognition, the man weighed the alternatives. Weighing alternatives was a speciality of his.

"There is no excuse for doing this thing foolishly or excessively," he said to himself. "Ergo, consider. It is well past midnight. No women have gone by and there are a great many police about." Certainly it was awkward. The circumstances did present a greater challenge, but without any genuine accomplishment in the final analysis. All that excitement wasted on poor, stupid, exhausted trollops.

With a reluctant sigh he put his knife away into the heavy folds of his inverness cape.

Now he would change his tactics, since he fully understood about murder. He could now plan other, more interesting killings.

Of course, next time he would kill someone important. He ran over his mental list with relish. It would be difficult to pick and chose amoung so many.

Remarkable, he thought, all this Ripper nonsense. With a low chuckle he sucked at his curly pipe as he wandered back toward Baker Street. He trusted that Watson would have tea ready.

The red-headed girl in the van of the army adjusted the visor of her helm and pointed across the river to the fortress held by the English. Above her the lily banner of France flapped listlessly in the sultry air.

"We cannot cross," said her second in command. "There is no possible way."

It was as if she had not heard. She did not turn, staring across the river as if sight alone could build bridges. "If we have faith in the Good God we can do anything. We will reach the other side. We will defeat the English. We will free france. God has said so; it is His promise. To think otherwise is blasphemy. We will but fulfill His word. . . ."

Her lieutenants looked at each other and shrugged. Perhaps the Maid was only a crazy farm girl. Convincing the foolish Dauphin was one thing, but crossing a river at flood was another.

"We can't do it," ventured the boldest of her men with a silent plea to the others for support.

"There is always a way with God on our side. God will defend the Right. St. Michael and St. Katherine have promised us the victory this day."

This was met with silence. The knights were too familiar with the whims of the ineffective Dauphin to rely on his support for long, and this girl could lead them into disaster. And the loss of France to the English.

"You are doubters of God's power?" She turned to them, the shime of her armor making then wink. "I say to you that God will help us. I tell you that St. Michael protects us with the Sword of Righteousness. I say that Jesus walks with the men of France and the archangels guide our footsteps. Our weapons cannot fail, we have the victory."

"The river is too deep," they told her.

She farily snorted with indignation. Then, commending her soul to God and St. Michael, she turned a scornfull gaze to her soldiers and with an eloquent twist of her thirteen-year-old head she urged her great warhorse into the river.

The valient animal struggled. He thrashed and strove and despite the heavy armor he and his rider wore he did his best to swim. But the current was swift and the river in deep flood. It was no use. A little beyond midstream, with the French looking on in despair and the English cheering from the walls of Orleans, horse and rider went down for the third time.

They stopped him at the Mexican border, telling him that he was too old for fighting wars.

"Damn it," he said irascibly. "I have my rights. Deny me as you will, I can die any way I like. I want to die for freedom."

Still he was refused.

"I hate the trappings of death. Just let me disappear."

No, they said.

He coughed, trying to hide the asthma that plagued him. "I have nothing left here. Nothing of worth. Nothing is keeping me."

But they sent him back to San Francisco and poor Ambrose Bierce had to be content with the 1917 Nobel Prize for Literature . . . not that he was content, but even he learned to be philosophical.

The assistant had the uneasy feeling that all was not quite back to normal. To be sure, there was only a little unevenness in the matching lines, but that might be almost enough to alter the fragile balance.

He squared his mandibles resolutely, took stock of the display board, and made a few, very few, very minor adjustments, holding his breath as he worked. He must take care . . . slowly . . . slo—ow—ly.

"Which will you have: the Nazarene or Barabas?"

"The Nazarene! The Nazarene!" roared the crowd.

In the hazy August sun the Yorkists rested and gave thanks for victory. In his pavilion Richard Plantagenet rubbed at his polio-twisted shoulder and brooded over the rebellion.

Tudor had fought well at the last, when forced to fight, but had made his campaign by treachery. The accusations of his nephews' murder laid to his door. . . . Even now the memory of his defense before Parliament was fresh in his mind. Richard knew well how little it would have taken to change the course of history. If Tudor had been able to win over his cousin, the Duke of Buckingham, then all might have been lost.

Suddenly Richard the Just of England laughed. What if Tudor's stories of Crook-backed Dick had caught on? What a monster his memory might have become for generations. The fairest King of England would seem a villian and Tudor, instead of a treacherous bastard, an avenging angel.

With resignation he rose to receive the nobles of the last vestiges of the Tudor armies.

On the Yellow River a bargeman poled his boat and the sound of the nightengale rippled through the gentle air. In the Inn of Three Gold Dragons the young poet waited for the concubine to come to him. Now he was a man and within his rights in the Laws of China. And tonight he would celebrate his age and his status with the woman his father had paid for. He would wander in the sweet garden of her thighs and touch the gates of heaven in their loving.

The door behind him opened and the beautiful moon-maiden came toward him, holding out a flask of wine on a tray with delicate porcelain cups. The blue flowers in her gown shown in the lantern light. Her face was round, smooth, and pale, as delightful as the laughter of children, serene as the moon. She looked at him and then sat demurely beneath the ornamental maple tree.

"You are most enchanting," he said to her. "I am honored to be with you this night."

"This is your first time?" she asked him in her shy, silvery voice, hands lingering suggestively on the rim of the tray.

"I blush to admit it."

"Here," she whispered to him as she extended her arm toward him. "This will make it easier the first time. Wine makes all living more beautiful and more pleasant." She handed him the cup.

Already half-drunk from the woman and the night, Li Po took the cup dazedly, lifting it to his lips in the gauze of a dream.

"Drink. It brings much joy," she urged him.

He tasted it. The worst of cold reality thrust in upon him with the acrid stuff as it rolled across his tongue. "Phath!" He spat it out. "That is terrible! I cannot drink that! Never! Keep me from wine always!"

Wilkie won.

The assistant beseeched any Power that might be nearby to keep the Instructor away from the lab just a little while longer. He knew that he almost had the problem solved. There were one or two factors to line up and a couple of simple details to verify, but it was really quite simple now. All he needed was time.

He curled around the console and groped for the gauge to settle the whole thing.

"Aw, goddamn," whined the shotgunner as the procession of flagellants approached them. All carried whips that they flailed over themselves and each other impartially. They were thin, gaunt beings, hardly human, with the deadly Tokens on their chests, armpits, and groins. They chanted as they went, the whips beating out the terrible rhythmn around them. They were possessed not of demons but of disease.

"One Indian!" the shotgunner pleaded. "Just one flaming Indian."

The flagellants paid no heed to the coach but continued on their masochistic way.

The driver didn't even look around.

The tall man, bearded and gray-eyed, looked at the dispatches on his desk. He was grateful for the end of the bloody Civil War, but it had taken a toll of him. Laughter was rarer with him now than it had been, and he knew he needed perspective. So tonight he and Mrs. Lincoln would be going to the theater.

He was looking forward to the play. It was David GArrick as Lucky in *Waiting for Godot*. He had heard it was more fun than congress.

The bells of St. Basil's and the Annunciation boomed as ominously as the sound of guns as Tsar Peter pulled himself up to his near seven feet and icily informed the Boyars that their long patriarchial beards would no longer be tolerated at court. The Boyars gesticulated helplessly, feighing ineptness.

"Here," said the Tsar with an air of great patience. "Use this." And he handed them his personal, portable, battery-powered Norelco shaver. "Europe has much to teach us," he said sardonically.

The battle of Thermopylae was won, as Darius was to remind himself morosely ever after, by a handful of Spartans, three M-1 rifles, two air pistols, a sackful of grenades, and one roving reporter with a walkie-talkie.

> Oh, give me a home where the mastadons roam
> And the trilobites romp through the clay.
> Where a large reindeer herd is attacked by a bird
> That can carry a dozen away!

Tetrazzini sang it and Paris loved it.

The thing was made of a stone not unlike cinnabar, and it shown like metalic spicie in the torchlit room.

"You see," said the strange black man in the peculiar clothing emblazoned fwith the mystic symbols *MIT*, "it will be much easier with this. This will simplify the task considerably, Pharoh." He pressed the hidden button and the weird artifact hummed to the waiting Egyptians.

"What does it do? The sound is remarkable," Pharoh conceded, "but has it any worth? Is it a religious object? To what god?"

"Watch!" the black man commanded, and even as he spoke the platform with Pharoh on it rose into the air.

The Egyptians fell back, awed.

But Pharoh, beyond initial surprise, showed nothing but absorbed interest. "Yes. I see. But does it do more than make a sound and hang things in the air?"

"It does." The black man gestured with it and the platform with Pharoh swung easily about the room, dodging frightened guards.

"I see," repeated Pharoh as the platform settled to the floor careful as a spinster. "But what is this to me?"

"Exhalted One," the black man said, "place as many men on this platform as you like and still it will sing and float for you. With this simple device, mountains will rise as high as you command. Slaves and mules will not be necessary to you any longer. All you need do is have this little gadget and men to load and unload your platforms."

"Uuummmm," Pharoh mused. Then his sharp eyes became eager slits. "My tomb. My tomb," he whispered. Then, raising his voice, "Wizard, for wizard you surely are, I require you to build my tomb with that, so that it may be larger than any other, and more beautiful."

At that the black man smiled, murmuring to himself, "I wonder how Cal Tech is making out with the Mayans?"

The last knob was meticulously eased into place. The dial sounded a decisive click. The assistant held his breath, ran a quick scan over the screens just to be sure. This developing world project was ticklish business, as he was finding out.

He heaved himself the equivalent of a sigh of relief. Then he admitted that for a while he was afraid that he would have had to take the whole thing back to LET THERE BE LIGHT to put all back in order.

But he had been lucky this time. All was secure and no one the wiser.

The door opened. His Instructor strode in, somber and full of lore. He fairly crackled with all the things he knew. Quickly he regarded his assistant, an air of suspicion about him. His hoary wisdom included a knowledge of young assistants and thier overenthusiastic tendencies.

The assistant returned the look with perfect blandness.

The Instructor was puzzled, but turned away.

It had worked! The assistant congratulated himself on his success and blithely led the Instructor to the display board.

And all went well for the first few ranks of screen, and then the Instructor became attentive in his boredom. That was the trouble. The Instructor waved aside the assistant's narration and looked closely for himself.

Even then everything went along splendidly for the assistant until a cry of "Lay to and prepare to board!" came from the display board and the assistant watched helplessly as the three galleons with the arms of Spain on their sails swung wide and prepared to grapple the moon.